The brisk knock on the hotel room door had Phoenix jumping off the bed and rushing to press her eye against the peephole.

She saw Justin standing there. Well, mostly just his chest and chin because he was so tall, but she knew who it was.

Frowning, she had to wonder what had him knocking so urgently. She reached to flip the safety latch and then opened the door.

"Hey, what's—?" She didn't have time to finish her inquiry as he backed her into the room and let the door slam behind him.

He cupped her face in his hands and leaned low until his lips were mere inches from hers. "Phoenix."

In shock, she managed to say, "Yeah?"

His eyes narrowed as he moved closer. "I've been thinking of doing this since last night."

He closed the distance, and then his warm lips were covering hers. Her thoughts focused on his words. He'd wanted to kiss her, just as she'd wanted to kiss him.

The amazing part was that they'd both been thinking the same thing. Thankfully, he'd done something about it when she hadn't had the guts to.

He deepened the kiss, pressing closer until she was up against the wall with him against her. She let out a sound that could only be described as half frustration and half satisfaction as she sank deeper into his kiss.

Justin pulled back just enough to lean his forehead against hers. He let out a breathy laugh. "I guess the front desk clerk saw this coming, huh?"

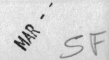

Also by Cat Johnson

One Night with a Cowboy

Two Times as Hot

Three Weeks with a Bull Rider

Midnight Ride

Midnight Wrangler

And read her novellas in

He's the One

In a Cowboy's Bed

MIDNIGHT
Heat

CAT JOHNSON

ZEBRA BOOKS
KENSINGTON PUBLISHING CORP.
http://www.kensingtonbooks.com

ZEBRA BOOKS are published by

Kensington Publishing Corp.
119 West 40th Street
New York, NY 10018

All Kensington titles, imprints, and distributed lines are available at special quantity discounts for bulk purchases for sales promotion, premiums, fund-raising, educational, or institutional use.

Special book excerpts or customized printings can also be created to fit specific needs. For details, write or phone the office of the Kensington Sales Manager: Attn.: Sales Department. Kensington Publishing Corp., 119 West 40th Street, New York, NY 10018. Phone: 1-800-221-2647.

Zebra and the Z logo Reg. U.S. Pat. & TM Off.

First Printing: March 2016
ISBN-13: 978-1-4201-3625-8
ISBN-10: 1-4201-3625-9

eISBN-13: 978-1-4201-3626-5
eISBN-10: 1-4201-3626-7

10 9 8 7 6 5 4 3 2 1

Printed in the United States of America

Chapter One

"Well, look who's here. Justin Skaggs, how the hell are ya?"

Justin paused at the sound of his name, his hand still on the door he'd just pushed open. As he moved into the bar and his eyes adjusted to the dim light, he saw the guy who'd greeted him before he'd even had a chance to clear the doorway.

Accepting that there was no way around it, Justin pulled out the barstool next to the man who'd known his family for decades. "Hey, Ray. How you been?"

"Eh, same old thing. Y'know how it is." The older man, whose clothes reeked of cigarette smoke, hacked out a raspy cough before soothing it with a swallow of his beer.

"Yup." Justin dipped his head, knowing one thing for certain—that Ray should stop smoking. He should probably stop drinking, too, if he wanted to see his grandkids grow up.

As for Ray's statement about everything being the same old thing, Justin could definitely relate. That was exactly the problem in this town—things were always the same. The same people doing the same things in the same places.

In a community that small, there was no avoiding running

into people he'd known for most of his life. Folks who knew him and his family's past. Even when he wanted to get away from everyone for a little bit, *especially* when he needed to get away, it seemed he couldn't.

All he'd wanted to do tonight was to be alone. His goal was to get shit-faced on some beer—or bourbon, if that's what it took—and then sleep it off in the truck in peaceful oblivion for a few hours. He obviously needed to drive farther to find a watering hole where no one knew him. Possibly across state lines, and even that might not be far enough.

Justin raised one hand to get the bartender's attention. "Bottle of light beer, please."

His original plan to consume massive amounts of the hard stuff wasn't going to play out, so he'd have a light one and then leave. One quick beer, a short good-bye, and then he'd get back in the truck and drive until he was so far away no one knew him.

"How's your momma doing?" Ray's tone was imbued with the same undercurrent of sympathy Justin had gotten used to hearing over the past two years.

"Good. Thanks." Justin hated the question he seemed to be asked everywhere he went. What could he say to answer it?

Certainly not the truth—that his mother, a formerly vibrant woman, was now broken. A complete and utter mess.

His mother was as good as a woman who'd lost both her husband and her oldest son in the span of less than a decade could be.

Both men had been taken way too young, his father ten years ago by a massive coronary and his brother more recently by war.

Some days she didn't get out of bed. Justin would come home from a full day of work at the Double L Ranch and find her in the same pajamas she'd been wearing when he'd left that morning. Still sitting in the same spot, either on the sofa in front of the television or, on really bad days, in her bed.

Other days, few and far between, she'd make a small attempt at normalcy. He'd come home and find her cleaning or cooking. But those days had become less and less frequent. More often than not, he'd be the one making dinner when he got home from the ranch at night.

As the man of the house—the only one left—Justin did his best to support his mother. He'd bring her food and coax her to eat when she didn't want to. He'd give her space when she looked like she needed that or an ear to bend when that was what she needed most.

But some days, like today, Justin couldn't deal with his own life, never mind his mother's. Lord help him, because he felt like shit when he did it, but those were the days he'd disappear. Fire up the engine in his brother's old truck and drive.

As the bartender delivered the beer Justin had ordered, the door swung open, letting the light of the afternoon inside the sanctuary-like darkness of the bar.

Justin raised the bottle to his lips and drew in a long swallow of the icy-cold brew. It slid down his throat, washing away at least a little bit of his stress. If Ray remained quiet, and the bartender kept the cold ones coming, maybe he could stay and hang here for a bit.

"Hey, is that Jeremy's truck I saw parked outside?" The newcomer's statement was like nails on a chalkboard, erasing whatever calm Justin had managed to achieve.

"You driving Jeremy's truck?" Ray asked Justin.

Justin glanced from the guy who'd just entered—Rod, the old-timer who owned the lumberyard—to Ray.

"I like to run it once in a while." He downed another two

gulps of beer, bringing the bottle closer to empty and the time nearer the moment he could leave.

Rod pulled out the barstool next to Justin. With him on one side and Ray on the other, Justin was penned in. Trapped in polite conversation when all he wanted was to be an antisocial bastard.

"If you're ever looking to sell it, give me a call. I always did like that truck." Ray's offer was the last thing Justin could take.

Jaw clenched, Justin nodded. "I'll keep that in mind."

Jeremy was dead. His truck was one of the last things left on Earth that had mattered to him. He'd loved that damned truck. Justin couldn't sell it any more than he could bring himself to take it over and drive it as his, full-time.

Didn't they understand that?

He said he drove it to keep the engine in shape, but the truth was, Justin got in it when he wanted to feel close to his brother. And, truth be told, sometimes when he wished he could chuck it all and join his brother, wherever that might be. Even after going to church his entire life, he wasn't so convinced Heaven existed. At least not exactly in the way the preacher said it did.

One more gulp and the beer was empty. Justin stepped off the barstool and dug in his pocket for his wallet.

"You going?" Ray asked.

"Yup."

"Put that beer on my tab." Rod directed the statement to the bartender.

"Thanks, but I got it." Justin threw a bill on the bar. "See y'all later."

He didn't wait for change from the bill he'd tossed down or good-byes from the two men. Instead he yanked the door open and stepped out into the air. Only then—outside and away from the oppressive presence of people—did he feel like he could breathe again.

Shit. He wasn't fit to be around any other living thing today. Maybe he should pick up a six-pack, drive to a field somewhere, sit in the truck, and drink it.

It was coming up on two years since Jeremy had died. Justin knew he'd have to be there for his mother that day. Hell, for the whole month probably. But now, with over a month left to go before that grim anniversary, he'd give himself this time to wallow in his grief.

Justin would let himself get angry, too. At God for letting a good man die too damn young. At the bastards who'd planted that roadside bomb. Even at Jeremy for reenlisting when he could have been home safe instead of in Afghanistan.

He slid into the driver's seat and stared down at the set of keys in his hand. The truck key. The house key. The key to the padlock on the toolshed in the backyard. Some mysterious key he didn't recognize. He was starting to wonder if even Jeremy had known what it opened. . . .

Justin ran his thumb over the smooth metal of the ring. It was the same key ring Jeremy had carried in his pocket since the day he'd bought the truck. He'd carried it until the fake leather tag on it that read *Chevy* had worn and frayed around the edges. He'd carried it until he'd deployed that final time.

Knocking himself out of the daze he'd slipped into, Justin reached for the radio and hit the Power button. The same station that had been playing the last time Jeremy drove the truck before leaving blared to life.

He couldn't bring himself to change the station, just like he couldn't throw out the stack of fast-food napkins stuffed in the glove compartment or the two-year-old, half-empty tin of chew Jeremy had left in the console under the dash.

Justin turned the key in the ignition and the engine fired

to life, rumbling beneath him. It would be better to run it more often than the half dozen or so times a year he did. That would keep the tires from getting flat spots, or worse, dry rot.

He should be pushing it, too. Taking longer trips at highway speeds to get the fluids circulating and blow the carbon out of the engine.

But there were the ghosts of too many memories in this truck. It hurt to drive it. Then again, it hurt when he didn't drive it, so what the hell did it matter?

It would be good for both him and the truck to gun it. Open up the engine and let the mud fly.

Decision made, Justin threw the truck in Reverse, backed out of the space, and shifted into Drive.

He hit the accelerator, peeling out on the gravel of the lot as he turned onto the main road, heading in the direction of the interstate. He would hit the highway for a few miles . . . or fifty. Let the road heal him for a couple of hours.

Escaping, running away from his problems, was no way to deal with them. He knew that. Any psychologist would tell him that. The grief counselor his mother had agreed to go to a couple of times sure as hell would have.

Justin didn't care what the experts said. He had to do what he had to do. If getting out of town or getting drunk— possibly both—was what he needed to do, then that's what he was going to do. The experts be damned.

Getting away for a little while sounded real good. Finding himself a woman wouldn't hurt either. A night of some mindless sex with a stranger would certainly be a distraction.

The problem was, he couldn't stand his own company right now. He couldn't imagine charming a woman into bed for the night in his current mood, so he might as well forget about that.

The old guys at the bar annoyed him. The radio announcer was grating on his nerves. His own thoughts were like salt rubbed in a wound. There wasn't a chance in hell he could stand talking to a woman long enough to woo her. . . .

It was safer for everyone if he behaved as antisocially as he felt and steered clear of all living things, so that's exactly what he intended to do.

Chapter Two

Phoenix Montagno looked at the devastation around her.

The havoc she'd wreaked in the space that was her apartment hadn't produced the results she'd wanted. All she'd made was a big mess.

Papers covered every square inch of the carpet immediately surrounding her, and in spite of the chaos she'd created, the one piece of paper she needed wasn't among any of the others.

She sighed. How could she lose her birth certificate?

When she'd moved out of her parents' house, she'd made sure to take everything important. That had included her high school and college diplomas and her birth certificate.

Her diplomas were there, along with her income tax paperwork going back three years—as if she'd ever need that. She'd never be audited. Not on her minuscule teacher's salary. The IRS had far bigger fish to go after.

She'd found her social security card, but what she'd been looking for—the birth certificate—eluded her. She even remembered holding it in her hand and thinking how she'd better put it in a safe place, but she'd be damned if she could remember where that safe place was.

It should have been right there with everything else. Why wasn't it?

Her parents were going to flip.

They'd offered to keep her important papers for her, locked up in their fireproof document safe. Instead Phoenix had insisted she would be responsible for holding on to her own things. She'd taken it, against their advice, and now she'd lost it.

Her father had always said she should be more organized. How everything important should be in labeled folders inside a locked, preferably fireproof filing cabinet.

That was his way, not hers. They were different people and they operated completely differently. Just as she hadn't picked up even a little bit of her mother's perfect house-keeping skills, her father's organizational skills had also skipped her generation.

Phoenix huffed out a breath in frustration. How could she lose anything in this tiny apartment?

Her place wasn't small in a bad way, just cozy and quaint. She loved the home she'd created and the space she'd chosen to create it in. From the big windows that offered a view of the park across the street to the location, close enough to town so she could walk to school and the coffee shop on nice days.

Most important of all, it was all hers.

Besides, it was what she could comfortably afford right now on her teacher's salary—living in California wasn't cheap—but the point was, her place was too damn small to lose something in it.

It was also too small for the big, not to mention ugly, metal filing cabinet her father would have her get if she'd listened to him—or if she admitted to him that she'd lost her birth certificate.

Phoenix liked her own filing system. She kept her important papers in a big floral hatbox on the floor in the corner of the room. What didn't fit in there went into a few more decorative rectangular boxes. They were sold by stores for photo storage, but she used them for paperwork and was very proud of her decorating savvy in repurposing the items for her own unique use.

The most pressing things that required attention, such as bills that needed to be paid, went into the wicker basket on top of the hatbox. She had a system and it worked fine for her—usually.

She had to find that certificate, and not just because it was an important piece of identification. She needed it or there'd be no passport. Without a passport, there'd be no trip to Aruba during midwinter break with her friend Kim.

That was enough inspiration to find the birth certificate, but on top of her trip and her need for official ID for any number of reasons in the future, if she had to admit to her parents that she'd lost it, she'd never hear the end of it.

Sometimes it was painfully obvious she'd been adopted, and she wasn't talking about her blond hair and blue eyes being the opposite of her father's dark brown hair and eyes and her mother's chestnut hair and green eyes.

When it came to her temperament, her interests, her easygoing nature, she couldn't be more different. She loved her parents to death, but she was nothing like them.

The differences just proved the nature versus nurture debate. She could grow up with parents who had every aspect of their lives planned, organized, and compartmentalized, but somewhere deep in her DNA she carried the genes that made her the opposite of the couple who had raised her.

Usually being a fly-by-the-seat-of-her-pants kind of girl worked for her. Not today.

This was too much to deal with alone. She needed backup.

Crawling toward her phone, on the floor just past the mess, Phoenix stretched and grabbed the cell before flopping back onto her butt amid the explosion of papers.

Phoenix dialed the number and waited for Kim to pick up. "Hello?"

Bracing for her friend's displeasure, Phoenix drew in a breath. "We have a problem."

"What kind of a problem?" The wariness was clear in Kim's tone.

There was no way around it. She had to 'fess up. "I can't find my birth certificate."

"Um, okay. And that's a problem because . . . ?"

"I need it to get a passport so I can go with you to Aruba. That's why."

"You don't have a passport?" Her friend sounded shocked.

"No, I don't have a passport. I've barely traveled outside of California, never mind leaving the country to go anywhere I needed a passport." Phoenix sighed.

Kim was missing the point. Her lack of a passport wasn't as big a problem as her current lack of the proper identification she needed to *get* a passport.

"Don't worry about it. You have plenty of time to get a passport. We're not going away for months."

"But I read it can take months to get a passport. And that's not the problem anyway. Didn't you hear me? The problem is that to apply for a passport I need my birth certificate, which I can't find. What do I do about my birth certificate?" Phoenix was ready to scream as her frustration mounted.

How could Kim, whom Phoenix knew was an intelligent woman, not understand the enormity of the situation?

"Oh, well, that's easy. You just have to send away for a duplicate birth certificate."

"Wait, I can do that?"

Her heart leaped. If what Kim said was true, it would solve everything.

"Yes. Of course you can, silly. Seriously, you think they expect people to be able to hang on to one little piece of paper from birth until death? That's crazy. Did you think you were the only person in the country ever to lose their birth certificate?"

"No. I guess not." That concept made Phoenix feel moderately better about the whole situation. Could it really be that easy? It was hard to believe. "You're sure I can just get a new one?"

"Sure. My mother lost my brother's. When he got old enough to drive and needed it to get his permit, she just had to apply for a duplicate in the county where he was born. It came in the mail like a week or two later."

"Wow." She could do this. Fix her mess without her parents ever knowing. "Wait. I'm not sure what county I was born in. I only know my parents adopted me in Arizona."

"Just ask your parents."

"I can't do that."

"Why not? Will they care we're going to Aruba? Aren't you going to tell them? How are you going to explain your tan?"

"I'm not trying to hide the trip. I'm trying to hide the fact that I lost my birth certificate. My father thinks I'm scatter-brained as it is, and I doubt my mother has ever lost a thing in her life. I'll have to try to get out of them where I was born somehow. . . ."

"Uh, Phoenix?"

"Yeah?"

"Think about it."

"About what?" She was in no mood for Kim's guessing games.

"Your name."

Phoenix frowned, not understanding what Kim was hinting at and wishing she'd just come out and say it. "What about my name? A Phoenix is a mythical bird."

"And it's also the largest city in Arizona, the state where you were adopted. And it's in . . . hang on a second . . . Maricopa County. At least it is according to the search I just did online."

"You think that's where I was born? Phoenix, Arizona?"

"I think the odds are pretty good. If you really don't want to ask them, I'd try applying for the duplicate certificate in Maricopa County and see what happens. The worst they can do is say you weren't born there."

"Hmm." It was definitely something to think about. And if it kept her from having to admit her mistake to her parents, it would be worth the gamble. "You might actually have a good idea."

Kim laughed. "Thanks for sounding so surprised by that."

"Aw, relax. You know I love you." In fact, thanks to Kim's idea, Phoenix was feeling lighter than she had all day. "But I gotta go."

"Where?"

"My parents' house. I'll call you later." Phoenix figured before she went to the trouble of wasting the time applying for the duplicate in possibly the wrong county, it couldn't hurt to do some recon.

Casually bringing up the subject of her name and seeing

if her mother was just really into mythology, or if Kim was right and she'd been born in Phoenix, could save her weeks of time and needless paperwork.

Fingers crossed, she staunchly ignored the mess she was abandoning for now and grabbed her car keys.

Chapter Three

Phoenix pulled her used but beloved Volkswagen Bug along the curb in front of her parents' yard.

She cut the engine and glanced at the house where she'd lived the first twenty-three years of her life. In fact, this had been her home from the day they'd brought her here from Arizona right up until a couple of years ago.

That's when, armed with her degree in education and a burning desire to prove she could make it on her own, she'd gotten a teaching job, saved what she needed for her security deposit and first month's rent, and moved out to her own place.

Her father's car wasn't in the driveway. He'd be back from work shortly, but her mother would be home.

Breathing in, she prepared for the mission ahead of her.

It should be easy enough for Phoenix to get her parents to confirm where she'd been born. Once she'd done that, she could request a duplicate birth certificate, get her passport, and no one would be the wiser about the little mishap with the original paperwork.

If she could get her mother to confirm Kim was right that she'd been born in Maricopa County, that duplicate certificate could be winging its way to her in mere weeks.

She hated lying to her parents, but this wasn't exactly lying. It was really more like selectively withholding information. She might have been irresponsible in losing her birth certificate in the first place, but she was handling replacing it, and that proved she was responsible after all.

Good thing the kids she taught couldn't see her now. This deception, and her pretty weak justification of it, wouldn't set a very good example for her students. The impressionable youth she'd been tasked to educate by the State of California would never know she was both disorganized and deceitful.

With her purse hooked over one shoulder and her guilt resting heavily on both, she let herself into the house.

Once inside, she called out, "Hey, Mom. I'm here."

"I'm in the kitchen, sweetheart." The response came from the back of the house.

Phoenix walked in the direction her mother's voice had come from. She found her standing over the stove in front of a large pot.

The enticing aroma that filled the room had her mouth watering. "Mmm. That smells good."

"Just stuffed peppers. Nothing special." Her mother waved off the compliment. Wiping her hands on a dish towel, she turned away from the stove to face Phoenix. "I didn't know you were coming over."

"I, uh, didn't know either. I was out running errands and thought I'd drop by." Phoenix pushed down the guilt over that little white lie. Though the truth was she hadn't known she was coming over until she'd discovered her birth certificate missing. It just happened that her errand was to get information from her parents. "I'm sorry. I should have called you first to let you know."

"Don't be silly. You know you're always welcome anytime. Do you want to stay for dinner?"

"That would be great. Thanks." She'd been so busy tearing her place apart, she hadn't even thought about food.

Besides that, there was no way she'd say no to one of her mother's meals. She realized she hadn't eaten since an early lunch and her stomach grumbled in protest.

Phoenix could get by in the kitchen. She could cook well enough that she didn't have to rely on fast food for sustenance every night, but she wasn't a chef—or a homemaker—even near the caliber her mother was.

The kitchen smelled amazing, but she shouldn't be surprised. It always did about this time in the afternoon.

Her mother routinely started cooking early in the day. Every meal made in this house by her mother was orchestrated to perfection. Timed so that when her father arrived home after work, the food would be ready and waiting to be served the moment he was ready to eat.

"Want some tea?" Her mother paused with her hand on the handle of the kettle.

"Sure. Thanks." Sitting down over a mug of tea would be the perfect way to casually bring up the subject of her birth. Or at least the topic of her name, which would hopefully lead to more information.

Her mother filled the kettle with water from the sink and set it atop the gas flame of the burner. "Pick your tea."

"Okay."

Yes, in this house there was an actual tea box. A glossy cherrywood lidded box that housed a dozen different varieties of tea bags, each in its own little section. It was great. Like a fine restaurant. Plenty of choices to meet the taste of any guest or the mood of any one of the family members.

So why did it make Phoenix feel so inadequate as she lifted the lid and perused the choices?

Because her tea—the cheap plain kind that was sold by the hundred—lived in her cabinet inside its original cardboard box. She'd just have to accept she wasn't her mother and never would be.

"What can I take out for you, Mom?"

"Peppermint, I think."

Phoenix grabbed a mint tea bag for her mother and a green tea for herself. She moved to the cabinet and took down two mugs while her mother manned the stove, watching the dinner in one pot while waiting for the kettle to boil.

It seemed like as good a time as any to broach the subject. "So I was researching some things for class. Mythology and stuff."

"Oh? That sounds interesting."

"It is. The legend of the phoenix came up and I started wondering. Did you name me after the bird or was I, like, born in Phoenix, Arizona, or something?" Her heart sped a little faster from the lie as much as from the anticipation that she might get the information she needed.

"Actually, yes." Her mother grabbed the kettle as the steam began to pour from the spout.

"Yes, what? Which one?" Which suggestion had her mother agreed with? The bird or the city? Phoenix's heart pounded. She was so close to the information she needed.

"You were born in Phoenix. Well, at least the adoption agency we worked with was located there, and though it was a closed adoption, they did tell us that you were born at a local hospital. But I always did love the legend of the mythological bird rising from the flames." Her mother shrugged. "Your name made sense on many levels. Now, convincing your father of that was another matter. He wanted something traditional. But when he saw you, and you were so beautiful, he was a big pile of mush and I got my way."

Phoenix's heart skipped a beat at the answer. She barely heard what her mother was saying after she'd confirmed the adoption agency's location and that they'd said she'd been born in a local hospital. It wasn't exactly hard-and-fast confirmation that she had been born in that county, but it was close.

Close enough for her to apply for the birth certificate. And if the county clerk or whomever she'd have to contact said she hadn't been born there, then she'd apply to the next closest county until she found where in Arizona she'd been born.

"Do you want sugar?" Her mother's question pulled Phoenix out of her thoughts.

She glanced up and realized her mother had already poured the boiling water into her mug. "Um, yeah. But I'll get it. You sit down."

Though she was dying to get home and right to work on ordering that duplicate, it would have to wait. She'd eat dinner and then make her escape as soon as she could without seeming rude.

She had to get online and research this birth certificate application business.

Chapter Four

Justin ran the back of one hand across his forehead and let out a breath. It was a hot day. Then again, moving hay was a hot, dirty job no matter what time of year it was, but they were finally done with work for the day.

Tyler had already headed back to the barn. He'd gone to meet the blacksmith they'd called to come to check on the stallion that had a hoof abscess.

Justin's boss, Rohn Lerner, was hoping if they pulled the stallion's shoes and clipped his hooves shorter, the abscess might work its way down. Recovery was much faster and neater if the infection drained from the bottom of the hoof rather than burst through the top by the pastern.

While Tyler dealt with the lame horse and the black-smith, Justin and Colton had been left to finish stacking the last of the bales in the hay shed to store them for winter use.

That was fine with Justin. He knew from experience that the Arabian stallion they'd been training could be tempera-mental, and he was a kicker. There was a good chance that Tyler had gotten the worst end of this deal.

"Phew. I'm glad that's done."

Justin glanced up at Colton's comment. "You ain't kidding."

While wiping his hands on his jeans, Colton wandered

closer. "So I'm gonna head home, shower, and then get dressed to go out. It's two-for-one beer night at the Two-Step. You're coming, right?"

"Nah." Justin shook his head. "Thanks, but I think I'll pass."

Colton drew his brows low. "Not that I'm complaining, but you haven't wanted to do anything lately."

"That sounded like complaining to me. Besides, what do you care?"

Justin shouldn't argue with him because Colt was right.

It had been two weeks since Justin's near meltdown in the bar, and he wasn't feeling much better. In fact, he was even more of an antisocial bastard, if that was possible.

"I care because we're friends." Colton frowned.

"Yeah, right." Justin screwed up his mouth with doubt. "You care because now that Ty is all bowed up with Janie every night, you got nobody to go out trolling for girls with."

Colton wobbled his head from side to side. "Eh. I guess there is that, too."

That elicited the first laugh from Justin all day. "At least you're honest about it."

Colton lifted one shoulder. "Anyway, you know where I'll be if you change your mind. I'll even pick you up so you don't have to drive, if you want."

"That's a very generous offer. . . ."

"But?" Colton prompted Justin to continue when he let the sentence hang.

"I'll let you know if I change my mind and decide to go."

"A'ight. Good enough. I'm heading out. Maybe I'll see you later." It seemed, with that final comment, Colton was going to let the subject drop. Justin couldn't be more relieved.

"Maybe," Justin called after Colton, who'd already turned toward where the trucks were parked.

Colton didn't bother turning around as he raised an arm to acknowledge he'd heard.

Justin reached for the handle of his own vehicle and swung the door open. As he settled in the driver's seat, he saw dark clouds hanging low on the horizon. There'd be a storm rolling in tonight if he wasn't mistaken.

Hopefully, it would just be a little rain. Thunder made his mother nervous. Tornadoes, even more so.

A bad storm meant she'd sit up all night, not sleeping a wink. She'd be exhausted in the morning. She always seemed worse when she didn't sleep. He'd noticed that over the past couple of years.

With the anniversary of his brother's death coming up next month, it was already like walking on eggshells at home as he tried not to do or say anything that might set off a major bout of depression.

Meanwhile, he had his own issues to deal with. His mood felt as dark as those clouds in the distance.

Maybe he should go out with Colton. Get drunk and get laid and knock himself out of this crappy mood. So far, sitting alone and stewing for the past couple of weeks hadn't helped. His trying to be there to cheer up his mother hadn't worked to make either of them feel better.

The wind began to kick up and he heard the sound of distant thunder rumble through the air. He sighed. He needed to get home.

His mother would need him.

The only question was, could he hold on long enough to support her while not cracking himself? He'd need to do something to keep sane and soon, before he wasn't fit to be near anyone, including his mother.

He fired up the engine and spun the truck toward the road headed for home.

They didn't live too far from the ranch, so it didn't take

long for Justin to reach home, or what had become his home again after he'd had to move out of his own place and back in with his mother. That had been shortly after his brother's death, when he'd realized his mother couldn't be alone.

Big fat drops of rain began to strike the glass of his windshield as Justin pulled into the house's driveway. He realized they'd gotten that hay put up in the shed at Rohn's place just in time. If they'd left the job until tomorrow, it would have been soaked.

Justin parked the truck behind his mother's car in the drive, blocking her in. That was all right. She wouldn't be going anywhere tonight. She rarely went anywhere during the day. She sure as hell wouldn't be leaving the house on a stormy night.

He sprinted to the house, trying to avoid getting wet. Inside the front door, he shook the water off his hat and then hung it on the hook.

"Hey, Mom. I'm home." Justin's announcement didn't elicit a response.

He walked through the kitchen, dark except for the waning light filtering through the windows. He noticed there wasn't anything started for supper.

Continuing to the living room, he found her on the sofa in front of the television, wrapped in a blanket in spite of the warmth of the day.

"Hey."

It took her a second to look up. Long enough that he wondered if she'd heard him. Finally, she glanced at him and said, "Hi."

As she turned her focus back to the television, Justin sat next to her. "What do you want for dinner?"

"Nothing. I'm not hungry." It was her usual response. A clap of thunder had her jumping. "There's a storm coming."

"Just a few storm clouds. It'll pass." He noticed for the first time what she was watching on television. The Weather Channel.

A banner that read *Storm Alert* in bright red text spanned the width of the screen. Leave it to the media to make an event out of anything, including a simple thunderstorm.

He drew in a breath and stood, knowing she'd sit there all night watching the live weather radar and worrying, and there was nothing he could do about it short of unplugging the TV.

"I'm gonna throw something together for dinner for myself."

"I'm sorry. I can do it—" She flipped the blanket off and moved to get up.

Sometimes, on the better days, he saw her guilt when she realized he was pulling both his own weight and hers. That he'd work a full day at the ranch and then come home to cook, clean, and do laundry. On those days she'd try to make an effort to function normally.

"Stay. I got it. It's fine." He moved toward the kitchen, too hungry and not in the mood to watch her wander aimlessly around the kitchen, taking twice as long to do something as it would take him because she couldn't focus her mind.

He'd defrost some of the chili he'd seen in the freezer. If he delivered a bowl to her where she sat, she'd eat at least some of it, just to make him happy. That would have to do for now.

The best he could do was get some food into her. Then he'd convince her to take one of the pills the doctor had prescribed for her after his brother's death. The ones that calmed her and made her sleep.

They were out of refills on the prescription and the bottle was getting dangerously low, but she took them so infrequently, there were still enough left to get her through the next month, when she'd need them most. After that, he'd have to convince her to go to the doctor again and get more.

Hell, maybe he should be taking the meds, too. Though he preferred to self-medicate with the good old-fashioned, tried-and-true medicinal properties of booze.

Five minutes in the microwave and dinner was ready.

Justin looked down at his culinary creation as he carried the two bowls to the living room. He had managed to put together a decent-looking dinner for them, and in just a few minutes.

It was amazing what a guy could do with a microwave and some incentive.

Dinner consisted of hot chili, smothered in the shredded Cheddar cheese he'd found in the fridge. It wasn't gourmet, but it would fill the hole in his stomach fine.

More importantly, the food should warm up his mother, who looked inexplicably chilled on a day Justin had spent sweating. Of course he was warm because he'd been doing physical labor, while it looked as if she hadn't moved more than to go from her bedroom to the sofa.

When he returned to the living room, she still sat right where he'd left her—on the sofa.

"Dinner's ready."

"Thank you, but I'm not hungry."

"Mom—"

"Justin, you eat. Don't worry about me," his mother cut him off while not touching the bowl he'd put in front of her on the coffee table.

"Momma, I'm going to eat. I promise you that. But I want you to eat, too." When she didn't look as if she was going to do as he'd asked, Justin added, "Please? Just take one bite and make me happy."

She sighed but finally nodded. "Okay. Thank you. It looks good."

"It *is* good." As Justin talked, his mom took one bite. "I might not be a gourmet like those chefs you watch on that cooking channel you like, but I do know spiced beef."

"You do. So did your father." She forced a smile, but it faded quickly with her mention of his father. "His specialty was chili, you know."

He watched her reach out and put the bowl back on the coffee table after only taking that one bite.

"Dad was who taught me how to make chili, though I do add my own secret ingredient . . . mostly because he wouldn't reveal his." Justin tried desperately to salvage the meal by bringing up a good memory from the old days, when his father and brother were both still alive.

He wanted to be able to reminisce with her. About his dad. About his brother. Remembering things that would make them both smile and help them heal. But she obviously wasn't ready for that. She remained silent as she pulled the blanket closer around her.

Frustration and anger roiled through him. At times like this, he wanted to shake the sad out of her, while at the same time he wanted to hug and comfort her until all the hurt went away.

He was the son and she was the mother, dammit. This role reversal messed with his head as much as his inability to help her no matter what he did.

His own appetite ruined now, Justin stood. One glance at the weather radar on the screen showed him that the storm had moved past them. Clear skies were over their corner of Oklahoma.

The rain had stopped. He could see that through the window, and he hadn't heard any thunder since before he'd made dinner.

He grabbed her bowl to carry it to the kitchen with his. "I'm going out for a little bit. You going to be a'ight?"

The only indication she'd even heard the question was the dip of her head as her eyes remained glued to the television.

"A'ight. I'll see you later, then."

She didn't respond at all this time. That reinforced his confidence that he could leave her. She probably wouldn't even notice he was gone.

It was better he go anyway because he was angry, even though he had no right to be. He strode to the kitchen, tossing both bowls onto the shelf of the fridge uncovered. He reached for his keys and was about to head out the door when he changed his mind. He was in the mood to wallow in his own misery, and he did that best while in his brother's truck.

Justin tossed his own truck keys onto the counter and reached for the hook where the keys to his brother's truck hung.

Much more of this and he was going to be as broken as his mother. Then what the hell were they going to do? They'd be two depressed, damaged individuals who couldn't even get out of their own way, forget about earn a living or maintain a home.

He needed a break. Rohn would give him the time he needed to get out of town for a few days.

After all the stock he'd broken for the man, on top of everything else he did around the ranch, his boss owed him at least a couple of days off.

Of course Justin would have to call his aunt to see if she'd come check on his mother while he was gone. Maybe she'd even stay at the house while he was away. He'd feel better knowing someone was there with his mother at night. The sisters could have a girls' night. Just because he was trying to escape from all humanity didn't mean his mother craved the same.

It calmed him even thinking that he was going to get away for a few days. He could drive to . . . hell, he didn't know where. Anywhere would be fine.

He'd been ready to crawl out of his own skin the past few weeks. He only hoped he'd be able to stand his own company for long enough to get out of town.

His boss would have to understand Justin's need for the time off. Rohn had lost his wife to cancer over five years ago. It had taken nearly that long for the man to recover. At least he hadn't dated in all that time. Not until this summer, when Rohn's old high school friend, Bonnie Martin, had come back to town. Now the two were engaged and Rohn acted like a new person.

Surely Rohn would realize that as the two-year anniversary of Jeremy's death approached, Justin would need some personal time.

As the ranch came into view, Justin figured he'd know Rohn's answer either way soon enough.

Chapter Five

Phoenix turned her key in the lock and flipped open the metal door of the mailbox. She peered inside and saw the small box was stuffed full.

Knowing it would be mostly junk mail and the rest bills, she sighed as she reached in and grabbed the bundle. Unfortunately, there was nothing she could do about the junk mail or the bills.

She closed the door and pulled out the key before turning toward the stairs leading up to her apartment.

One flight up and another turn of a key—this one for her tiny apartment—and she was home. The new school year started in a week and a half and in preparation, she'd been at school almost every day this week, in meetings and setting up her classroom. All the things it took to prepare for another school year.

It was exhausting, but more than that, it meant her summer break was almost over. The same old feelings she'd had as a child hit her just as hard as an adult.

Phoenix wanted to hold on to the last days of summer, even as they slipped through her grasp. In that respect, students and teachers were no different.

Mail in hand, she flopped backward onto the sofa. Flipping

through the stack, she was about to write the whole pile off as junk when she saw an official-looking envelope from Arizona.

Arizona?

She looked more closely at the return address.

Office of Vital Records, Arizona Department of Health Services.

It took a few seconds before realization hit. Her duplicate birth certificate. She'd applied for it close to two weeks earlier, long enough ago that she'd forgotten about it.

Tearing into the envelope, Phoenix held her breath, more than anxious to see what was inside. It could just as easily be a sorry, no-duplicate-for-you letter. But as she pulled out the papers, she saw the heading on one page and let herself breathe again.

Certificate of Birth.

She glanced over the document, across fields listing the county, state, and city of her birth. Date of birth. And mother's name.

The name typed into that field stopped Phoenix in her tracks.

Bonnie Martin.

Her adoption had been closed, meaning she didn't know her birth parents' names and they didn't know who had adopted her. All parties had agreed to no exchange of information during the adoption process and no contact afterward.

Phoenix had never even heard her birth mother's name. It certainly hadn't been listed on her original certificate. That one had listed her adoptive parents.

Though, now that she thought about it, *that* certificate must have been modified and the one in her hands was a copy of the real original, filled out by Phoenix Baptist Hospital at the time of her birth.

She looked closer at the rest of the information.

Instead of her name, she was listed as *Female Martin*, leading her to believe that her birth mother, Bonnie Martin, whoever she was, had given her baby away immediately. Even before she'd named her.

Why? What had inspired this woman to give up her baby so quickly? So completely.

The space for the father's name was blank. That was probably the answer right there. Bonnie had been an unwed mother.

Phoenix had never been one of those adopted children who thought much about her natural parents. The people she'd called mother and father for as long as she could remember were her real parents as far as she was concerned. But seeing her birth mother's name had her wondering about things. Asking questions she'd never thought she needed or wanted to know the answers to.

In the age of the Internet, it was easy enough to open a browser and do a search. Too easy.

Ignoring the overwhelming feeling niggling at the back of her consciousness that she could be opening a Pandora's Box, Phoenix hauled herself off the sofa. She headed for the desk against the wall by the window and pulled out the chair.

Sitting, she stared at the closed laptop.

When she'd first walked through the door, she'd been planning to sort through the mail and then investigate what was in the fridge that she could use to throw together dinner for herself.

Hunger took a backseat to curiosity as, bracing herself for what she might find, she flipped open the laptop and hit the Power button. The screen came to life.

Drawing in a deep breath, Phoenix opened a browser and typed into the search field her birth mother's name, followed by the city and state listed on the certificate.

It was a long shot, but she hit Enter anyway.

A page of search results appeared. As her breathing grew short and shallow, Phoenix clicked to open the page for the white pages residential listing of a Bonnie Martin in Phoenix, Arizona.

She stared at the screen, reasoning that this might not be her mother. Martin was a common last name. Not quite like Smith or Johnson, but common nonetheless. But the name Bonnie wasn't so common. The combination of first name and last name, along with the listing in the city in which she was born made her feel this was very possibly her mother.

This Bonnie Martin, who lived on West Meadowbrook Avenue, could very well be the woman who'd carried Phoenix for nine months. The same woman who'd then given her nameless baby away to a childless couple whom she knew nothing about.

The reality of the situation began to feel overwhelming. She'd never cared that she'd been given up for adoption. Why should she? Her parents were wonderful. They had given her anything and everything she'd ever needed. She hadn't missed out on anything growing up. But what would it be like to look into the face of her birth mother?

What would it feel like to possibly see eyes as blue as her own staring back at her? To have a stranger see them together and remark how much they looked like mother and daughter?

More, what would it be like to know her inability or maybe just lack of interest in staying organized was inherited and not just her own laziness, as her father so often insinuated?

Did her love of books come from her birth mother or father? And who was this man who'd contributed to her existence? Had her birth parents been young and in love? Star-crossed lovers who could never be together for some reason she couldn't fathom?

Jeesh. Now she really was letting her imagination run

away with her. Chances were her natural parents' love story was nothing like *Romeo and Juliet*. Her birth was more likely the result of a drunken frat party or a one-night stand lacking in birth control.

She wasn't sure what clerical error had led to her having in her hand the very information she needed to meet her birth mother, but now that she had it, she had to decide what to do.

Did she honestly want to know the reality, the circumstances behind her birth, or was it best to leave things as they had been intended during the closed adoption—a secret?

The ringing of the phone made Phoenix jump in her chair. Dragging herself away from the computer screen, and the key to unlocking the secrets of her past, she stood and dove for the phone.

The ID listed her friend Kim's name on it.

Phoenix hit to answer. "Hey."

"Hi. Why do you sound breathless?"

"My duplicate birth certificate just arrived."

"Well, hallelujah. Now you can apply for the passport and I won't have to worry I'll be in Aruba all alone. Of course then I'd have all the men to myself, so maybe that wouldn't be so bad."

Phoenix moved back to the desk and stared at the information her Web search had unearthed. "Mmm-hmm."

"Um, am I boring you?" Kim asked.

"No. Sorry. Um, it's just that something was strange about my birth certificate."

"Strange how?"

"Well, my original one—"

"You mean the one you lost?"

"Yes." Phoenix rolled her eyes at the interruption, and the reminder she didn't need or want. "Anyway, that one listed both names of my adopted parents and then my full name."

"Okay. And?"

"This one doesn't show any of that. This paper lists a Bonnie Martin as my mother."

"And is that your birth mother's name?"

"I never knew her name. That's the point. It was a closed adoption. Her name wasn't supposed to be given to us even if we asked for it. Ever."

"Oh, boy. Somebody at the department of records screwed up big-time."

"That's what I'm thinking. That first certificate—the one I lost—must have been the one for the adoption, but there was still an original from the hospital where I was born."

"And that's the one the person filling your request for a duplicate copied."

"Exactly." Phoenix nodded.

"Wow."

That was an understatement for how she felt about the whole thing. "So now what do I do?"

"What do you want to do?"

"I don't know." Phoenix flopped against the chair back heavily.

"Well, do you want to meet her?"

"I think I might want to." She'd never been interested in the past before, but now, staring at the name on the screen, things were different.

"What other information is on the certificate?"

"Not much. The name of the hospital in Arizona, but that's about it. There's no father's name."

"Unwed mother."

"Most likely."

"So how will you find her?" Kim asked.

"I Googled her."

"And?"

"There's a Bonnie Martin living in Phoenix, Arizona."

"Oh my gosh. You have to go find her. It's not that far."

Phoenix's eyes widened at the suggestion. "I can't just go there."

"Why not? School doesn't officially start for a couple more weeks. Your meetings are done, right?"

"Yes." Today had been the last one. "But my classroom . . ."

"Ah, jeez. You can hang the new calendar and whatever else you need to do when you get back. How long will that take?"

Her friend was right. There really wasn't any reason not to go. "Okay."

"Really? You're going?" Kim sounded surprised.

Phoenix was pretty shocked by the decision herself. "Yeah. I think I am."

"Yay! I'm so excited for you."

She laughed at her friend's reaction. "Why?"

"Because it's amazing. It's fate revealing this secret and guiding you."

"No, it's more like my lack of organization."

"I don't think so. Everything happens for a reason, Phoenix. The universe made you lose that certificate so you'd have to get the new one. Forces bigger than yourself provided you with your birth mother's name so you can find her."

Phoenix wished she had Kim's faith. In her opinion it was simply a combination of the mistake of one incompetent clerk and Google that had provided her with the name and then the address of her birth mother.

Whether it was the universe or the Web, she could still use the information—if she chose to.

"Why are you not packing already?" Kim's question had Phoenix sighing.

"Because I'm still not sure I'm going to do anything with this information."

"*Pfft.* If we all waited until we were sure to take action, nothing would ever get done. What if you wait a month or a year or more and then get there to find she died just before you arrived? How would you feel?"

"That's horrible." Sometimes her friend had a warped mind.

"It is horrible. You'd never forgive yourself. Don't live with regrets, Phoenix. Go. Follow your destiny."

Phoenix shook her head at the over-the-top drama of Kim's argument. Sometimes it was easier to just do what Kim wanted and not fight it. "Okay. I'll take a road trip."

"Thank goodness. You won't be sorry."

Phoenix blew out a breath. "I certainly hope you're right."

Chapter Six

As Justin turned onto the driveway and headed toward his boss's house, he was in no mood to talk to anyone, but he had no choice. He'd have to take a few days off to regroup so he'd be able to act human again. And to get that time off, he had to talk to Rohn.

Lucky for both of them, Rohn tended to be a man of few words himself. Nope, the older man wasn't a big talker at all, but tonight, after that scene with his momma, even a "Howdy" delivered in the wrong tone could be enough to set Justin off.

Rohn had better give him the days he was asking for because in this mood, Justin was even losing his patience with the animals, and he loved animals. More than people some days. He should probably work on that.

He pulled Jeremy's truck into the long drive that led to the house and barn belonging to the Double L Ranch. Rohn had named the place for his late wife, Lila.

Justin had worked here for years. Since before Jeremy had died. Over the years, Rohn had stood by Justin with whatever he needed.

Through grief as well as Justin's various rodeo-related

injuries, Rohn had given him the time off he needed to heal. He could only hope he'd do the same now.

The moment he turned onto the property, a black and white streak ran at full speed from the house toward the truck. Justin slowed to avoid hitting the crazy dog that had more energy than good sense.

While the dog bounced around him, Justin threw the truck into Park, figuring it was safer to stop where he was than pull all the way to the barn where he usually parked. He didn't want to risk hitting the dumb animal. He wasn't planning on staying long anyway. Just long enough to get permission from Rohn to take those few days off.

Rohn stepped out of the kitchen door and meandered toward the truck. He whistled for the dog, who ignored him in favor of bouncing around the vehicle.

No surprise there.

When Justin opened the driver's side door and stepped down, she bounced as if on springs until he finally gave in and reached down to pat her head.

"Hey, Justin." Rohn finally made it over to him. "Daisy. Come here."

The dog, apparently satisfied that Justin had acknowledged her, ran to Rohn's side. Her herding dog genes finally kicked in, and the dog stared up at him, waiting for the next command. Rohn wasn't her master, but she came to work often enough with Tyler that the dog minded Rohn more often than the rest of them.

"What's Daisy doing here?" Justin asked.

"Janie stopped by. She's inside visiting with Bonnie, and this little girlie decided to tag along." Rohn reached down and rubbed the dog's ear, turning her into a wiggling, tail-wagging bundle of uncontained joy.

Even while feeling like a bastard who didn't want to be amused by man or beast, Justin had to admit the dog was cute. That didn't mean he wanted to deal with the dog's daddy or Tyler's inevitable incessant questions.

Justin raised his gaze to Rohn. "Ty here, too?"

"Nope. He's next door at Janie's place, tinkering with that old truck of his." As he said that, Rohn glanced at the truck behind Justin.

No doubt the man had noticed Justin wasn't driving his own vehicle but instead had his brother's truck. If he did, Rohn didn't comment on it. He didn't comment with words anyway, but he sure as hell said a lot with that one glance.

"What brings you back here?" Rohn drew his graying brows low. "I remembered to give you your paycheck, didn't I?"

"If I said no, would you give me another one?" Justin asked.

"No. My memory might be going, but my bookkeeping is still sharp as a tack. I'd notice the stub in the checkbook."

"A'ight. Then no, you didn't forget to pay me. I was wondering—hoping—I could have a couple of days off."

"Okay."

Justin raised a brow. "That's it? Just okay?"

"Son, I'm well aware this time of year is tough on you and your ma. You need a few days off to be home with her, you got it. No questions asked. Tyler and Colton can pull the extra weight."

Guilt rode him too hard not to be honest with his boss. "You're right about the anniversary coming up. And I will have to be there for my ma. But I was hoping to get away for a couple of days on my own. All alone. Just get in the truck and drive until the scenery ain't familiar. Then turn around and come back home."

"A'ight." Rohn tipped his head. "When you leaving?"

"As soon as possible. Probably not tonight. I wanna talk to my ma and then make sure my aunt can look in on her while I'm gone. Tomorrow morning, most like. By first light."

Rohn nodded. "In that case, maybe we can help each other out."

"Whatcha mean?" Justin asked.

"You know Bonnie's mother?"

"Miss Tammy? Yes, sir."

"Well, she packed up the place in Phoenix she and Bonnie had been living in and she's fixin' to sell it. Now that she's decided to move back into the old house."

"And now that Bonnie is living here with you." Justin grinned.

Rohn lifted his brows. "Watch how you say that, son."

"How did I say it?"

"Like we're some kids, shacking up."

"Nope, you're definitely not some kids." He couldn't help the grin growing wider as he teased Rohn. "But as for the shacking up . . ." He wobbled his head back and forth.

"We're engaged. That's as close as I can get to marrying her right now. I'll make an honest woman of her as soon as she and her mother can get the wedding together. Damn women take forever to plan these things." He shook his head. "If it was up to me, I'd drive to the justice of the peace and be done with it. But if Bonnie wants the church and white dress, then that's what she's gonna get."

"Spoken like a man in love."

Rohn rolled his eyes. "I know, God help me. But I already waited too damn long for Bonnie Martin to become Bonnie Lerner to rush her now."

Justin frowned. "Didn't seem like all that long to me. Seems you two went from friends to, uh, whatever, pretty fast."

Rohn snorted. "Not exactly. Bonnie and I dated for a bit during the summer after we graduated high school."

That information was a surprise to Justin.

Rohn continued. "That was twenty-five years ago, if you can believe it."

"Oh, I can believe it," Justin teased. "I just didn't realize you'd dated then."

"Yup." Rohn looked kind of nostalgic as he nodded. "Even back then, when we were only eighteen, I knew I wanted to marry her."

"So what happened?"

"She moved away to Arizona for college. I went to school around here. Things ended." He shrugged.

The conversation had taken a turn toward the serious suddenly. Rohn drew in a breath and Justin could almost see him shake off the memories of the distant past.

"Anyway, Bonnie's mother is in town now. She had an interview and got the job. Bonnie and I convinced her to stay here for now, in my guest room, but—"

"But what man wants his future mother-in-law living with him and his girl?" Justin asked.

Rohn lifted one graying brow. "I was going to say that because she got a job, she wants to go back to living at their old house, which at the moment has next to no furniture in it. We were deciding if we were gonna just hire a moving company to drive her stuff from Arizona to here or if I was gonna go get it all myself. But if it's a road trip you're looking for, maybe you want the job."

Justin considered that. He hadn't been looking for any responsibilities. Just to escape.

"I'll cover all fuel costs and throw in two hundred extra for your expenses and trouble." Rohn dangled that addition temptingly.

The offer was hard to refuse, considering the price of fuel and Justin's limited funds because he was the sole earner in the household at the moment.

Decision made, he nodded. "A'ight, boss. You got yourself a moving man."

A smile bowed Rohn's lips. "Good. Glad to hear it. I'm assuming that there pickup has a trailer hitch."

Justin glanced at Jeremy's truck and back, nodding. No self-respecting man around there would buy a truck that didn't. "It does."

"Then you can take the small trailer. Just make sure to sweep the horse shit out of it before you put Bonnie's stuff inside or I'll never hear the end of it."

"I don't know about that. We didn't negotiate for shit removal." Feeling lighter just at the prospect of getting away, Justin teased Rohn.

"Let me put it in a way you'll understand. If Bonnie ain't happy, then I ain't happy. And that means—"

"None of us are gonna be happy either." Cringing, Justin finished the sentence for him. "Yeah, I got it. I'll sweep out the trailer before I leave here."

"Good idea. I doubt the real estate agent would appreciate a pile of manure in the driveway in Phoenix."

"You never know. They could put it on the flowers. City people pay top dollar for quality manure."

Rohn laughed. "Yeah, but let's not take that chance. Back the truck on up to the trailer. I'll run in and write down the address in Phoenix for you."

"Get the house key from Miss Tammy, too. I don't want to be arrested in Arizona for breaking and entering," Justin called after him.

"You sure? It'd make a good story." Rohn grinned.

Justin shook his head at Rohn's joke. "Yeah, I'm sure. Thanks."

Rohn raised a hand in acknowledgment and headed into the house, the dog at his heels.

Justin pivoted toward the truck. The visit hadn't gone quite as he'd expected, but this new turn of events could be good. He liked having an excuse to get away. It would look to his friends like he had a job to do, not that he was running off.

And the two hundred in cash wouldn't hurt either.

Chapter Seven

It was peaceful on the road.

Justin realized just how peaceful as the miles between him and home grew, along with the distance that separated him from everything he knew. He should have done this long ago.

Getting away, even for just a couple of days, would help.

With nothing but the open highway ahead, all his troubles seemed to shrink like the passing scenery in the rearview mirror.

A man could think on the open road.

Sometimes that was a good thing. Sometimes not so much.

Right now, Justin's mind had turned to taking inventory of his own life. He didn't like the results.

He lived with his mother. There were reasons for that, but still, it seemed a man of his age should have his own place. It was no wonder he had no girl. Hard to hook up when you were bringing her home to your old bedroom at Mom's place.

He owned his truck—minus the small loan with the bank. And though he'd never gotten around to switching the name on the registration, he supposed he could count Jeremy's truck as one of his possessions, too.

He had a decent job—the hours weren't bad and the pay wasn't too shitty. But really, where was it leading? He had no clue. It just seemed easier to show up every day and let Rohn tell him what to do than to think too hard about the future.

He had friends. Though they'd drifted apart a bit since Jeremy's death. The former ladies' man Tyler had started to act married, always working over at Janie's place, never going out. Ty was now the opposite of Colton, who was still single and wanted to go out all the time.

His boss Rohn was a good guy. Of course Rohn was so busy with Bonnie, he wasn't really present in Justin's life lately, other than to tell him what to do at work. When even your widowed boss had a new woman in his life, it made a man wonder why he was still alone himself. It was enough to make Justin feel even more lonely.

Though, to be fair, Rohn's new girlfriend was really his old one. Justin now knew that Rohn and Bonnie had dated back in high school. He just didn't know the full story of how they'd broken up or how Bonnie had somehow ended up living in Arizona for the last quarter of a century.

But fate must have been at play so that the two had reconnected when Bonnie came back to town to settle her father's estate. Good thing, too. Rohn had gone from grumpy old man to acting more like a teenager. Justin had come up on them giggling in the corner when they thought no one was looking.

At one point Rohn had even gone so far as to dye his mustache to hide the gray. That's what love did to a man, Justin supposed. Love made him do crazy shit like dye his damn hair.

Maybe Justin should be grateful he wasn't in love. That didn't mean he was opposed to some lovin', though.

It had been too long since Justin had had some of that. Way too long.

Hell, maybe this little road trip to Arizona would be a good opportunity to partake of some guilt-free, risk-free lovin'.

A girl couldn't expect anything from a man who was just passing through for forty-eight hours. As long as she knew upfront that he was just in for some companionship for the night, it should be good.

Of course women didn't always think the way men did.

A shame, that. Life would be so much simpler if they did. But women were a different breed.

Then again, there were plenty of differences between men and women he was more than grateful for.

The softness of their skin. The sweet smell of their hair. Those little teeny tiny thong undies they liked to wear. How they licked their lips when they were flirting.

And damn, now he had a hard-on while driving down the road.

Enough of those thoughts. He'd have to move on to something else.

Unfortunately, the something else his mind turned to was that he'd left the area and was far enough away from home that he'd started to lose the radio station. As the signal faded, the static increased.

Crazy as it was, he couldn't bring himself to change the damn station his brother had last left tuned on the radio.

Justin hit the button and turned off the radio completely.

One day he'd get over it. Or he wouldn't. Either way, the quiet wasn't bad now.

Scenery sped by the window at seventy-five miles an

hour. He glanced down at the speedometer and saw he was actually going closer to eighty.

Looking in the side mirror, he saw the highway was as empty behind him as it was in front. He could probably risk a little more speed.

What the hell. Why not? Might as well open up the engine and let this truck breathe a bit. He didn't take the truck out enough, but he'd make up for it on this trip. There was nothing better for an engine than to blow out the carbon once in a while.

While he was at it, maybe it would help blow some of the cobwebs out of his own head. He hit the accelerator harder and felt the thrill of speed fill him. Yup. He should have done this long ago.

Motion behind him caught his attention. Glancing in the rearview, he saw the trailer hitched to the truck sway with the increased speed.

Justin sighed, easing off the gas pedal.

Rohn's horse trailer cost more than he could afford to pay to replace it if he flipped the damn thing by speeding too fast while towing an empty trailer behind him.

Oh, well. It had been fun while it lasted. He slowed to a little over seventy and glanced at the mileage on the counter, and then the time on the dashboard clock.

Two and a half hours down. About twelve more to go.

That was a long damn time. Keeping an eye on the trailer, he hit the accelerator a little harder and allowed his speed to creep back up to close to seventy-five again, hoping to cut at least a part of that time.

It was a long haul. He'd left well before dawn, and driving straight through with minimal stops, he'd hit Phoenix after sunset this evening. That was all right. He could handle it. He'd driven longer for a competition when he'd been riding on the rodeo circuit.

That was another thing he'd decided it was safer to give up—competing. His mother couldn't take the worry that he'd be injured, or worse, killed. And he couldn't afford to miss work. Last year's injury had put him out of work for a few weeks.

He knocked that depressing memory out of his mind and glanced at the passing signs along the highway.

Next stop, Arizona. Or more likely a rest area along the way so he could stretch his legs and take a piss. And maybe buy another energy drink to keep himself alert. That was always a challenge on a solo long-distance drive.

Even so, he wouldn't trade the solitude for company. A man had to do what a man had to do for a little peace. It might mean keeping his sanity.

Chapter Eight

Phoenix kept the windows down in the Volkswagen.

The A/C wasn't exactly working all that well, so she had no choice. Much like her tiny apartment, the Bug wasn't perfect, but it got her where she was going and it was all hers.

Not to mention the used 2003 Volkswagen Beetle had been all she could afford at the time. She'd bought it the year she'd turned eighteen with her own money, which she'd saved from babysitting.

It was old and worn but even so, she loved it. It was good on gas. Easy to park. Very cute in its own little beetlelike way. It was a classic car and had the original body styling that got attention from folks young and old wherever she drove.

Her little yellow car had character—just no A/C at the moment.

That was okay. It felt good driving with the windows open. The wind whipped through her hair as the highway scenery hurtled past.

It wasn't a horrible drive from her part of California to Phoenix, Arizona. Still, it was over four hours, and that was much farther than Phoenix was used to driving alone.

She pretty much only went to work and to her parents' house, with stops in between at the occasional store or restaurant, and Kim's place.

If Kim had been able to come, Phoenix would have asked her friend to accompany her.

Would that have been weird? Meeting her birth mother for the first time with her best friend in tow? It was going to be weird enough as it was.

What exactly did one say in this situation? *Excuse me. You don't know me, but I think you might be my mother.*

Wasn't there a children's book just like that? If she remembered correctly, it was about some animal—or a bird maybe—who wandered around asking every random animal he could find, "Are you my mother?"

That scenario felt a bit too close to the reality of this little road trip. Phoenix stifled a groan.

The situation was certainly going to be awkward, and it wouldn't matter whether she blindsided this Bonnie Martin alone or with Kim as her wingman. But Kim's department head had scheduled a meeting for tomorrow and she couldn't have come even if Phoenix had begged her to.

Phoenix probably should have postponed the trip until Kim was free, but something had driven her forward. Probably the fear that if she didn't do it now, she'd chicken out and never go.

She didn't know where the urgency originated, what force propelled her toward the city in which she'd been born. All she knew was that she was almost four hours into the road trip and there was no turning back now.

Twenty-five years she'd lived happily without knowing anything more than that she'd been adopted by the two people she called her parents. Now she was putting all of that in jeopardy.

She might wind up discovering something she didn't want to know.

Worse than that, what if this was the wrong Bonnie Martin? That would be horrible. And embarrassing. She could walk in there, accuse the woman of having a baby out of wedlock twenty-five years ago, and make a fool of herself.

Or, if it was the right Bonnie Martin, Phoenix's sudden appearance could expose a secret to Bonnie's current family that she'd never wanted them to know—hence the closed adoption.

Every scenario Phoenix's spinning brain came up with seemed worse than the last. Maybe it would be better to just observe the woman from afar for a little while and then decide whether to introduce herself. She could casually ask questions. See what she could discover. Do a little more research online. She'd checked the big social media sites and hadn't found Bonnie, but maybe if she dug deeper, she'd find a profile on one of the lesser-known sites.

Though this all sounded an awful lot like the behavior of a stalker.

Great. She'd probably end up in jail with a restraining order filed against her by some woman with no connection to her whatsoever but who had the unfortunate luck of being named Bonnie Martin.

Phoenix sighed, doubting this entire trip more with every passing mile marker on the interstate.

The letters on the sign on the horizon appeared to grow larger as she moved closer until she could read the words "Phoenix Exit 2 Miles."

The sign, physical evidence of how near she was to her destination, had her insides twisting. It was way too late to turn back now.

The vibrating of her phone in the console startled Phoenix. She reached for it and answered, "Hello?"

"Where are you?" Kim asked.

"Almost there. I just saw the exit sign for Phoenix."

"Oh my gosh. Are you nervous?"

"Yes, thank you. Don't remind me."

"It'll be fine."

"I'm not so sure."

"It will. She's going to love you."

"I'm not so sure about that either." A twenty-five-year-old stranger showing up at the door out of the blue asking about a closed adoption? Phoenix didn't think that made for a cozy family reunion.

"Well, I am sure. Just relax. Maybe pull over when you get to town and get yourself together for a minute before you head to her house."

Phoenix frowned as a thin trail of smoke began to creep from the crack between the car's hood and her windshield. She was nearing the exit ramp anyway, so she slowed and the smoke got thicker. "What the hell?"

"What's wrong?" Kim asked through the earpiece of the phone.

"Something's wrong with the car."

"What else is new? Something is always wrong with that car."

The smoke billowing from under the hood was definitely new. "It's more than the squeak in the brakes or the A/C blowing hot air." She glanced at the dashboard and saw the temperature gauge had moved into the red. "I think it's overheating."

"Oh, no. That's bad. You'd better pull over."

"That's my plan." Phoenix tried to turn on the blinker and navigate the car off the highway, all with only one hand as she held the phone in the other. She really had to buy a hands-free earpiece before she got into an accident or got a ticket. "Listen, Kim, I gotta hang up and put the phone down. I'm going to have to find a service station or something and get someone to help me figure out what's going on."

"Okay. But call me back to let me know what's happening."

"I will. 'Bye." Without even waiting for Kim to say good-bye back, Phoenix ended the call and tossed the phone onto the passenger seat.

She'd gotten a late start and it was already evening. She wasn't sure she'd even find an open service station.

The smoke or steam or whatever it was her poor little car was spewing billowed thick and steady. It obscured her view of the road and made her wonder if she was in danger of the car going up in flames with her in it.

Just up ahead, she saw a long low building. Through the cloud of smoke hanging in front of the windshield she could just make out writing on the sign out front. It read not much more than "BAR" in big block letters. The place looked as if it had seen better days, but to Phoenix it was like an oasis in the desert.

Desperate to park and get out of the car in case it was about to burst into flames, she eased off the road and into the large lot, pulling all the way off into the corner, away from the few other cars there, just in case the worst happened.

Grabbing her purse and phone, Phoenix scrambled out the door. As she backed away from the car, she glanced back at the overnight bag she'd left behind the driver's seat.

Should she grab it or leave it there? Neither seemed like a good option at the moment. She didn't want to crawl into the smoking vehicle any more than she wanted her stuff to go up in flames.

She was just deciding what to do when her phone vibrated

in her hand. Glancing down at the screen, she saw *Home* on the readout.

Groaning, she picked up. "Hello?"

"Hi, sweetie. What are you up to during your last few days of summer break?"

"Hi, Mom. I'm, um, out. I had some things to take care of before school starts again." The guilt assaulted her.

She hadn't told her mother or father anything. Not what she'd accidentally found out about her birth mother or that she was crazy enough to drive all the way to Arizona because of it.

That she'd felt she had to lie to her mother about this trip was a good indication she shouldn't be taking it. Even so, she changed the subject to get her mother into safer conversational territory. "Did I tell you they gave me a different classroom this year?"

"No. Are you unhappy about that?"

"It's fine, I guess. Just different."

She really didn't know where she was going with this line of discussion. All she'd wanted to do was get her mother off the topic of where she was and what she was doing so she wouldn't have to lie about it.

She couldn't exactly tell her the truth while on the phone, standing next to her smoking car. The discussion about how she was in Arizona stalking her birth mother, whose name she'd gotten on the duplicate birth certificate she'd ordered because she'd lost her original, should really happen in person, but that was impossible right now.

Oh, what a tangled web . . .

After this trip, she was never getting herself into a web of deception like this again.

"Anyway, I was calling to see if you wanted to come for dinner tonight. It's lasagna."

Uh-oh. That was her favorite and her mother knew it. She

scrambled to come up with a believable excuse to miss dinner. "Oh, I wish I'd known. I, uh, have a date tonight."

"A date? You didn't tell me about that."

Uh-oh. She had chosen a bad lie—not that there was ever a good one—but now her mother would want to know about this nonexistent man in her life. Then, tomorrow, her mother and father both would want to know how the fictional date had gone.

Her little white lie was rapidly snowballing out of control. She never should have answered the phone in the first place. She could have pretended the battery in the cell was dead or something.

Lesson learned. She would be more careful in the future, but she still had to extricate herself from the mess she'd created.

"Well, it's not really a date. Kim invited me over for dinner along with a few people from school, and she said one of the teachers was bringing her single brother and she was going to introduce us."

Cripes! The snowball was growing into an avalanche.

"Oh. Did Kim tell you anything more about him?"

In the face of yet more questions from her mother, Phoenix realized she needed to end this call. In an attempt at a Hail Mary, Phoenix threw out one last fib. "Mom, can I call you back? Kim is calling on the other line."

"Of course."

"Great. Talk later. 'Bye." She hit the Disconnect button and didn't breathe freely again until she saw the screen go blank.

As she stood next to her steaming vehicle, Phoenix pocketed the guilt over the rapidly growing list of lies she'd told her mother and turned her attention back to the more pressing issue. What was she going to do about her car?

What if she couldn't get it fixed? What if she had to call her parents to come get her?

After all the fibs she'd just told, she couldn't call them. Kim would just have to be the one to come.

But maybe things weren't as dire as she supposed. She tried to look on the bright side as she glanced at the building whose lot she'd landed in. It looked open. At least the neon beer signs were lit. That was a good sign.

The bar didn't, however, look like a place she'd normally ever go in on purpose. Beggars couldn't be choosers. She really had no other choice.

Phoenix locked the car doors, even though the risk of someone trying to take the VW in the state it was in was pretty unlikely. She had opted to leave her overnight bag in the car, though, so there was that to protect. If it didn't burn up, she didn't want it to be taken.

After one more glance at the hood to make sure there weren't any flames amid the waning smoke, she turned toward the building. With any luck, there'd be an auto mechanic having an after-work beer inside.

She could only hope.

Chapter Nine

A road trip always sounded like a good idea in theory. There was the usual excitement of getting ready. Packing a bag. Buying snacks and energy drinks. Mapping out a route. Heading out on the open road.

Then there was the reality. The idea of a road trip was far better than the actual trip itself.

By hour twelve in the cab of the truck, Justin was ready to throw himself out the door and onto the highway. By hour fourteen, the seat had long ago made his ass numb. His lower back ached. He was torn between boredom and sleepiness, neither of which was good when driving.

The sign for the Phoenix exit was a welcome sight.

Neon glowed through the waning light of dusk from a building on the side of the road, calling to Justin like a beacon. He was hungry, thirsty, and he had to piss like a racehorse.

The place didn't look like much, but judging by the sign, he was pretty sure it would provide at least a few things he needed. Those being a beer and a bathroom. Throw in a fat juicy burger and he'd be in heaven.

Swinging the truck and trailer into the parking lot, Justin anticipated the sweet freedom of getting out of the cab.

Barely taking the time to pull the key out of the ignition, he swung the door wide and stepped down onto the blacktop.

The paving of the parking lot had seen better days. There were potholes and cracks, but he'd never been so happy to set foot on pavement as he was then.

Driving his brother's old truck like a bat out of hell to blow off steam for an hour was one thing. Justin had learned that driving it across the country was quite another.

Stretching his back, Justin groaned. From now on, he'd stick to the short trips and use his own truck or one of Rohn's for any long-distance escapes. But he'd made it to Phoenix, so he was halfway done.

He'd take a quick meal break here, then head to Bonnie's house and spend the night. He needed to assess the situation there. He didn't know if there were just boxes or larger furniture that would require another man to move.

Rohn had told him Bonnie's neighbors were friendly, and he could knock on their door if he needed anything. The antisocial side of Justin hoped he'd be able to get everything into the truck by himself, and that he wouldn't have to ask for help or even talk to another living being.

Tomorrow, as soon as the last of the things were loaded into the truck, he'd turn around and head back to Oklahoma.

He wasn't looking forward to fourteen more hours on the road tomorrow, but he sure was looking forward to a cold beer and a hot burger tonight.

Finally being able to feel his legs again as the blood began to circulate, Justin took one stiff step and then another toward the oasis before him.

Justin pushed through the heavy wooden door and inhaled. It looked and smelled like all the other bars he frequented.

The scent of stale beer hung in the air. The lighting was dim, all the better to hide the wear and tear on the old wood and vinyl barstools and chairs. Better for him to hide as well. At least he wouldn't have to worry about running into anyone he knew here.

The bartender was busy with a woman at the other end of the long wooden bar, so Justin decided to hit the head before ordering. That would give the man time to finish with the blonde, and it would relieve Justin's most pressing need.

When he emerged from the bathroom, he saw the bartender still busy in some deep conversation with the woman. The man was probably looking to get some. Not that Justin blamed him.

Another time, another place, and if he'd been in another mood, Justin would be over there talking her up himself. He was a sucker for soft blonde waves. It had been a long time since he'd woken up with some girl's sweet-smelling hair tickling his nose.

The bartender's love life—or sex life—was not Justin's concern. If the guy wanted to flirt, he was welcome to do it. But Justin wanted a beer.

Deciding to give the guy a little reminder that he had other customers, he leaned against the bar. "Hey, bud. Can I get something to eat and drink?"

"Yup. I'll be right there." The bartender said a few more things to the blonde, too low for Justin to hear, before he came to his end of the bar. "Sorry. The lady doesn't take no for an answer."

Justin let out a laugh. "Lucky you."

The older man shook his head. "If it was about that I wouldn't be complaining. Her car broke down outside in my lot, and she's got it in her head that I should go out and see if I can fix it."

"In that case, better you than me." Justin let out a snort.

"Oh, I'm not gonna do it. Believe me. I'm working. I

can't leave the bar unmanned, go outside, and crawl around under a hood gettin' all greasy."

"I hear ya. No guarantee you can fix what's wrong with it anyway."

"Exactly. I got no tools. No lift. No parts. Hell, I don't even have a quart of oil here with me." He shook his head. "Women, right? They just don't get it."

"Nope, they sure don't." Justin swung his head in agreement.

"Anyway, what can I get for you?"

"I was hoping for a beer and a cheeseburger. If you got 'em."

"That I do. How you want that burger cooked?"

"Medium well."

"You got it. The burger comes with fries. That all right?" Justin dipped his head. "Even better."

The bartender nodded. "I'll get you that beer, then I'll put in your order."

"Thanks."

In no time at all the bartender had slid a foamy mug in front of him and then turned toward the kitchen. Justin picked up the beer and drew in a long swallow of the frosty brew.

The worst of today was behind him. Time to relax. The only thing he had to worry about now was getting a full belly and falling asleep at Bonnie's. Unless he decided to get a head start on loading the trailer tonight rather than doing it all in the morning. That would depend on what he found waiting for him inside the house.

He was pretty sure Bonnie and Tammy's place was just a few miles away. It was if the GPS on his phone was right. He figured he could enjoy one beer with his burger and fries and still safely drive. No problem. He wouldn't have more than one, though.

The bartender came back and paused in front of the blonde, who still stood at the end of the bar, probably hoping in vain that someone would help her fix her car.

She'd better not look in his direction. Cute though she was, Justin was in no better position to perform car repairs than the bartender. He had no tools and no parts with him either. And he had a full schedule already. He had a whole house worth of shit to move between today and tomorrow.

The woman needed to drive her vehicle to a service station where a mechanic could take a look at it. If it wasn't drivable, then she'd have to call a tow truck.

"What you decide to do?" the bartender asked the blonde loud enough that Justin could hear from where he sat.

"I think I'll give it a little longer and then go out and try to start it and see what happens. Maybe it'll be better."

The bartender's brows rose. Justin agreed with the reaction, figuring it was pretty doubtful the car had gotten better all on its own. Cars didn't tend to heal themselves.

"And if it's not better?" the bartender asked. Justin didn't miss his doubt-filled tone.

The girl sighed. "Then I guess I'll have to get it to the service station. Can I have a diet soda while I'm waiting?"

Waiting for what, Justin wasn't sure.

"Yes, ma'am." The bartender came to Justin's end of the bar and grabbed a tall glass.

"What is she waiting for the car to do?" Justin asked.

"Cool down. From what she described to me when she came in, it overheated." The bartender packed the glass with ice and then grabbed the soda gun.

Justin nodded. Her car would cool down, and she might even be able to drive it for a little bit before it overheated again, but make no mistake, it would overheat again and it would keep doing so until she got it fixed.

"She check the fluids?" He already knew from their

conversation that the bartender hadn't gone out to check it himself. But maybe the girl had checked the coolant level herself.

The bartender snorted out a laugh while filling the glass with cola. "Look at her. You think she'd know how to check it?"

"Probably not." Justin didn't need to glance at the girl again to answer that. She didn't look the type to get her hands dirty.

She was definitely the kind who was used to having someone else handle these sorts of problems. Whether that other person was usually a hired mechanic or her boyfriend, Justin didn't know, and to be honest, he shouldn't care.

He was just passing through. It didn't matter that it would take him only five minutes to pop her hood and take a look. For once, the problem wasn't his responsibility and he didn't have to deal with it.

"I'm gonna go drop this off with her quick, then I'll see if your burger's up." The bartender hooked a thumb in the direction of the girl.

Nodding, Justin watched the man move to the end of the bar and deliver the drink to the girl. He heard the frustration in her voice when she thanked the bartender for the soda. He fought the guilt creeping up on him.

He supposed he could check the car to see if there was water in the radiator.

Crap. He hated that he'd even thought that.

Nope. He wasn't gonna do it. Wasn't gonna go out there and try, and probably fail, to fix her car. He was firm this time.

Dammit, sometimes not helping was more difficult than just giving in and doing it.

This trip was about moving Bonnie and her mother's stuff. About getting away from all the do-gooders and well-wishers and memories he couldn't escape in Oklahoma.

This trip was not about getting involved with any cute young thing or her problems, even if she did have a sexy voice. And soft blond curls. And an ass that looked damn enticing when she leaned forward to reach for her glass while she was perched on a barstool.

Justin did his best to concentrate on his beer. On the television hung in the corner of the room. The bottles on the shelves behind the bar. Anything and everything so he wouldn't go over there and offer to help that girl with her car.

His efforts worked. The bartender returned with the burger and fries in hand, and then Justin had another goal—filling the empty space in his grumbling stomach.

Still, he wasn't heartless. When the bartender came over to see if the burger was all right, Justin asked, "Is there a service station nearby for her?"

"Oh, yeah. There's a few actually. I already wrote down the number of one and gave it to her. I know the mechanic there. He won't rip her off."

Justin nodded.

Good. He didn't have to worry. She'd get her car taken care of and for a fair price. Feeling satisfied the situation was well in hand, he took another bite of the juicy burger and let the flavor of grilled beef and cheese fill his mouth.

"Can I get you another beer?" the bartender asked.

He shook his head. "I better not. I gotta hit the road right after this. I will take a glass of water, though. Thanks."

"You got it." The man nodded and reached for a glass as Justin glanced at his cell phone.

No messages from his mother or his aunt. That was good. He'd text Rohn when he got to Bonnie's place to let him know he'd found it okay.

Happy with that plan, Justin reached for another salty hot fry. He had to admit, though it didn't look so nice from the outside, the place was pretty damn good.

Too bad sometimes the opposite was true—for bars and women. You couldn't always judge just by looking, because what you saw wasn't always what you got.

Yup, one more reason to steer clear of the hottie at the end of the bar. As if he needed another one.

Chapter Ten

"What's happening? Where are you? Why didn't you call me back?"

While sitting at the bar, Phoenix digested the rapid string of questions fired at her through the earpiece of the cell phone.

"My car's broken." She figured that answer would satisfy Kim for now.

"Oh my gosh. That's horrible. Where are you now?"

"I'm in a bar in Phoenix. I pulled off the highway and into a parking lot when the engine started to smoke."

"That really sounds bad. What are you going to do?"

"Hopefully get it fixed. I think it's still drivable. At least enough to get it to a service station."

"Wow. That seriously sucks."

Phoenix ran a finger through the condensation on the glass as she let out a snort. "No kidding. But listen, I need a favor. If for any reason my mother calls you, you have to lie for me and say we're having dinner."

"What? What are you talking about? And why in the world would your mother call you?"

"I don't know, but just in case, I told her I couldn't come to dinner tonight because I was going to a dinner party you were throwing for some faculty, and that one of the teachers coming was bringing her single brother and you were going to introduce me."

"Jeez. Did you have to make it so elaborate? Phoenix, when you lie, you're supposed to just keep it simple. A dinner party? When have I ever thrown a dinner party?"

"I don't know. I'm sorry. I panicked."

"And a hot single brother, too. Jeez, I wish our lives were half as exciting as your fib made them out to be."

"I know—"

"Why stop at a fancy dinner party for the school staff and their relatives? You should have told your mother I was having Angelina and Brad over to dinner, too."

"All right. I get it."

Her friend continued, "Next time—"

Phoenix interrupted Kim. "I hope there isn't a next time. I hate lying and I suck at it."

"Yes, you do. But you better improve at it and fast."

"Why?" She was never going to lie again after this fiasco.

"Um, hello. You're trapped in Arizona with a broken-down car. How are you getting home?"

"I'm hoping to get it fixed."

"And if you can't? Or if it takes them like a week to fix it? Then what are you going to do? We have classes starting soon."

Phoenix rested her forehead on her hand. Kim wasn't telling her anything she didn't already know.

"I'm well aware of that. If the garage can't fix it, I was hoping you'd come and get me?" Phoenix tacked a question onto the end of that statement. When she heard no response from Kim except for a deep sigh, she added, "Please."

Kim let out a breath. "Of course I'll come get you. You're my best friend. I wouldn't strand you in Arizona."

"Aw, thank you." Feeling guilty for putting Kim out, she

said, "I can always rent a car if you can't get me and the car is beyond fixing."

"Stop. I'll come get you. A girls' road trip. How exciting would that be? How could I miss that?"

"I could do with a little less excitement right about now, but thank you. I appreciate it." Renting a car on top of paying for a hotel room for the night was going to put a serious dent in her vacation savings fund. With any luck, she'd be on her way back home tomorrow and wouldn't have to pay for a room for more than one night.

"What about your mother?"

"I'll keep lying to her, I guess." Though she hated to do it. Her father was going to flip out if he found out the car had broken down. He'd told her not to buy a used car. And especially not one so old.

"I was talking about your *other* mother. Bonnie Martin," Kim reminded her of the reason behind this ill-fated journey.

"Oh." She'd forgotten how much more complex her family tree had recently become. "The car was smoking so badly, I pulled over before I got to her house. I made it to the Phoenix exit, at least, but I stopped at a bar right off the highway."

"You're not going to leave without seeing her, are you?"

"No. It would be pointless to come here, go to all this trouble, and then leave." Phoenix had been so wrapped up in the car problem, she hadn't thought much about her original plans.

Because the bartender couldn't help her, the car repair would likely have to be done by a mechanic. She didn't know what to expect from a service station, but she did know one thing—she didn't want to leave Arizona without at least attempting to get a glimpse of Bonnie Martin.

Phoenix blew out a breath. "I'll figure something out.

Listen, I'm going to go see what I can do with the car. I'll call you to let you know what's going on."

"You'd better."

"I will. Promise. 'Bye."

"'Bye. Good luck."

"Thanks." Phoenix disconnected and laid the cell on the bar.

She looked for the bartender and found him at the other end, talking to the cowboy who'd walked in not long after she had.

He was tall and solid, with plenty of muscles visible beneath the short sleeves of his taut T-shirt. He wore a cowboy hat that gave him the look of a man out of his time.

It felt as if she'd stepped back into some long-gone era and into a time and place where this tall drink of water could have ridden his horse to the local watering hole.

She watched while he devoured the last bite of the burger he'd ordered. The sight had her mouth watering—both from the aromatic food and the tasty-looking man.

Wait until she told Kim about the gorgeous scenery. If Mr. Sexy Cowboy was an example of the kind of men who lived in Arizona, she might consider visiting again. Next time they could make it a girls' getaway.

It would cost less than going to Aruba, that was for sure. And it didn't require a passport—which was part of the reason behind her being stranded in this surreal cowboy bar in the first place.

If Phoenix ever straightened out the mess with her car, not to mention the situation with her birth mother, she'd have to remember to tell her friend all about the finer points of this road trip.

While enjoying the eye candy sitting at the other end of the bar she sucked on her straw. That resulted in a loud slurp that resonated through the bar and told her that her glass was empty.

Both men glanced in her direction. Her cheeks heated as she noticed the sexy cowboy grin.

The bartender walked over. "Can I get you a refill?"

She shook her head. "No. Thanks. I have to get going to see about my car. What do I owe you?"

"Nothing. It's on me."

"Thank you." She would have been more grateful if the man had been able to fix her VW, but it was still nice he'd bought her a soda while she waited for the smoke to clear.

Time to go deal with her car. As the bartender cleared the glass and cocktail napkin from the bar, Phoenix pawed through her mess of a purse and found a dollar bill. She tossed it onto the bar as a tip.

He'd given her both the number of a service station and the soda, so she figured she owed him at least a tip. Besides, it wouldn't hurt to keep the staff on her good side. There was a chance she'd be back in here again if the car burst into flames or something.

Phoenix climbed off the barstool and turned toward the exit. She wished she was dressed a bit sexier when she noticed the cowboy glance up as she walked past him toward the door.

Story of her life. The first cute guy she'd seen in what felt like ages and she met him at a dive bar located in another state hours away from where she lived.

She met his hazel eyes as he treated her to the slightest nod of his head. She smiled back and then the moment was over. She was outside in the dusk.

With a sigh, she walked around the building and toward where she'd parked, luckily under a security light. The car was still there and, from what she could see, no longer smoking.

That was a good sign. She moved closer and held her breath as she glanced through the window.

The interior seemed fine. She'd been half-expecting to see charred and smoldering upholstery, but all looked normal. Another good sign.

She opened the door and took a sniff. No smoke smell. No steam seeping from beneath the hood. So far so good.

Gathering her courage, Phoenix slipped behind the wheel but left the driver's side door open just in case she had to make a quick exit from the vehicle.

Silently praying to whomever was the patron saint of automobiles, she stuck the key into the ignition and turned it. The engine sputtered to life. She glanced at the temperature gage and watched as it stayed down in the cool range.

Phoenix wasn't insane enough to try to drive back to California without getting the vehicle looked at, but she was confident she should be able to make it a few miles.

She had a choice to make. She could drive directly to the service station before it closed for the night, but then be stranded there while her car was worked on. Or she could take a chance and drive to the address she had for Bonnie Martin and hope the car didn't overheat again. Then, in the morning, after she'd spent the night in a hotel, she could head to the service station.

Glancing at the directions she'd printed out from the Web, she made a decision. She'd head to Bonnie Martin's house tonight. There was a very real possibility if she didn't go now, she'd chicken out and never go.

Of course what the hell she was going to say when she got there was quite another story.

Chapter Eleven

Fueled up with the food he'd eaten at the bar, Justin was more than ready for a night of moving boxes and whatever else awaited him at Bonnie's house.

He paid his tab and headed out into the parking lot. He braced himself to see the cute thing from the bar outside, bent over her engine and looking helpless. He knew damn well he wouldn't be able to resist going over and helping her.

Even if she didn't have such a fine ass, he would help her. The sucker in him couldn't turn away from a woman in need.

There were already too many things going on in his life right now, and he was definitely no damn knight in shining armor, so why did he feel compelled to help every damsel in distress? His mother had raised him right, he supposed, but sometimes the overwhelming impulse to act like a gentleman could be damn inconvenient.

Luckily for him, when he stepped out of the bar and into the cooling evening air, the woman and her car were nowhere in sight. Hopefully she'd gone directly to the service station the bartender had recommended.

That would have been the smart thing to do. Unfortunately, not everyone did what was smart, including Justin.

He knew that with a certainty as he reached into his pocket and pulled out the keys to his brother's truck.

He shouldn't have taken the truck on this long-ass trip. For a quick getaway? Yeah, sure. For a long-distance moving job? No way. If Jeremy's truck broke down because he'd pushed it too hard, he'd never forgive himself. Hopefully nothing would go wrong. And if it did, he could always go to Tyler for help fixing it.

With that plan as assurance, he climbed into the driver's seat amid the familiar things surrounding him in the cab—Jeremy's things. The stuff he couldn't bear to part with.

Yup, he was as messed up as his mother in his own way. Which reminded him that he needed to call home when he got to Bonnie's place.

Throwing the truck into gear, he steered the truck and trailer in a wide turn. There were only a few other vehicles in the lot so he had no problem navigating to the parking lot exit and onto the main road.

Next stop, Bonnie's house. He glanced at his cell phone's GPS app and confirmed he was headed in the right direction. Just a few more miles and the first leg of the trip would be done.

One day down, one more to go. He stifled a groan as he thought about the return trip. Driving this distance alone hadn't been as relaxing as he'd thought it would be. In fact, it was downright torture.

He'd thought he wanted to be alone, but his solo getaway hadn't turned out as Zen as he'd thought it would. He probably should have brought Rohn's old dog along for company. Though Cooter had enough trouble getting up the two steps into the house. Forget about hopping into a high truck cab.

Nope. Best to go it alone. He'd just have to make sure to stock up on extra energy drinks for the drive home to stay awake on the road.

A few more times checking the map on the GPS and Justin turned onto West Meadowbrook Avenue. He tossed the cell into the console and started looking for the numbers on the mailboxes to find the address Rohn had written down for him.

The headlights hitting a bright yellow Volkswagen in the driveway caught his attention first. Followed shortly by the girl from the bar, walking away from the front door toward the car in the driveway.

What the hell?

He checked the reflective numbers posted on the mailbox and compared that to what Rohn had scrawled on a piece of paper. Yup, this was the place all right.

The only question was, how did the sweet young thing with car trouble fit into this puzzle?

Maybe she was Bonnie's real estate agent. He figured that was as good a guess as any.

The best thing to do was just ask her. He pulled up along the curb so as not to block her in the driveway. After she left he could back the trailer into the drive so he would be closer to the house. That way he'd have a shorter distance to carry whatever boxes or furniture awaited him inside.

She glanced up and stumbled to a stop when she saw the truck and trailer. He saw her eyes widen even from the distance. She continued to look surprised as he cut the engine, swung the door open, and stepped down from the truck.

After walking around the truck, Justin squinted at the Volkswagen. By the light of the streetlamp he saw it had California plates. Whoever she was, she was definitely not a local, and that ruled out his real estate agent theory.

He ambled up the driveway. When he got closer to the woman, she asked, "What are you doing here?"

Amused by her questioning of him, Justin lifted a brow.

"Well, howdy to you, too. And as for what I'm doing here, I was wondering the same thing about you."

His comment seemed to stump her. "Uh, I was . . . um . . . looking for the homeowner." She tripped over her own words, which only made Justin more interested in who she was and why she was here and acting so nervous.

Moving to her car, he leaned against the door, effectively blocking her escape should she try to make one before offering him an acceptable, believable explanation. For some reason—whether it was her body language or his gut instinct—he didn't believe her so far.

"The homeowner, huh? And who is that?"

"Bonnie Martin." Her correct answer, delivered in a firm tone, threw him.

"And who might you be?" Justin asked.

She hesitated just a second before saying, "Phoenix Montagno."

He would have thought she was lying, but who the hell could make up a name like that?

Had she come back with Jane Smith, there's no way he would have believed her.

"Who are you?" She crossed her arms to mirror his stance and turned the question back to him.

"Justin Skaggs." He gave her a minimal answer, still not certain why she was there or trusting her completely, even if she had supplied Bonnie's name.

"What business do you have here?" Her gaze cut to the truck and trailer as she followed up with a second question.

Justin wasn't quite ready to answer that just yet. "I believe I asked you the same thing."

"I told you. I'm here to see the homeowner."

"Bonnie Martin." He tipped his head in a nod. "Yup, that you did, but you didn't say why."

"That's a private matter."

"So is my reason for being here." He wasn't about to tell this stranger that the house was unoccupied. Not until he had more information on the girl.

Sad but true, even cute-as-a-button girl-next-door types could be up to no good. He figured it said a lot about his maturity that he could ignore the perky breasts beneath the tight T-shirt and remember that. He was pretty proud of himself.

"You're not going to tell me?" A deep frown creased her brow.

"Nope." He grinned.

Justin was enjoying this back and forth with the mysterious and lovely Phoenix. He just hoped she wasn't some sort of door-to-door salesperson or someone else he would find equally annoying.

She blew out a breath and looked totally baffled at his unwillingness to give her information. "Then I guess we're at a standoff."

"I guess we are." He glanced down at her car, which he was still leaning on. At first glance, the vehicle seemed just fine to him. "I see the car *got better*."

He used her own words from the bar to tease her.

"I drove it here." She didn't offer any further explanation.

"So I see." Suspicious bastard that he was, Justin started to wonder if it ever had been broken down to begin with, or if she'd lied for some unknown reason.

There'd been a time, not too many years ago, when Justin would have taken this woman at face value and not cared about more than how to get her alone and naked.

Again, he supposed this was another sign of his maturity.

Sometimes acting like a responsible adult sucked.

Rohn had put him in charge of getting Bonnie's stuff, and along with that he figured came the responsibility for the house. He'd do what was necessary to protect it.

"Well, the homeowner isn't here, but I'll be sure to tell her you stopped by." He had the house key Rohn had given him in his pocket. He pushed off the girl's car and fished out the key. He tipped his hat to the blonde as he passed. "Have a good day."

He moved to the front stoop, opened the storm door, and slid the key into the lock.

"Wait."

The girl's voice had him turning. "Yes?"

"You have the key?" she asked, though it was obvious he did.

"Yup." He pushed the front door open and then slid the key out of the lock as evidence. He let the storm door slam closed and remained outside on the front step.

"And you know Bonnie Martin?" That adorable little furrow creasing her forehead as he confused her was too damn cute. It made him want to tease her more.

"That's how I have the key." He held it up, letting it dangle between two fingers for her to see.

He still had no intention of giving her too much information. Not until she gave him some in return. Fair was fair, and he had a few trust issues with this girl, thanks to her evasiveness when it came to answering his questions.

She took a step toward the house, while he stayed on the stoop, waiting to see what she had to say next.

Finally, she said, "How do you know her?"

He decided to give her a tidbit of information in hopes of getting more back. "Mutual friends."

"You're driving a truck with Oklahoma plates." She glanced at the truck again and then back to him.

"Yup." He nodded. The woman could see that clearly herself, both from the plates and from the location beneath the name *Double L Ranch* painted on the trailer. "You wanna tell me why you're so interested?"

"I'm just, you know, interested in speaking with Ms. Martin."

"I'm getting that. My question is, why? Who are you? And what has you driving all the way from California just to see her?"

"I told you, that's—"

Justin nodded. "None of my business. Yes, so you've said before. I'm afraid I can't answer your questions if you can't answer mine. Now, if you'll excuse me, it's been a long day and I still got stuff to do."

He waited a beat. When she didn't offer a valid explanation for her presence or a reason for not answering what should be simple questions, he gave up. Drawing in a breath, he took one last look at the cute but evasive girl by the car and then turned back to the house.

Inside, he saw the house was packed and ready, just as Rohn had promised. Boxes were stacked in various piles around the living room furniture.

He should have been taking inventory of the house. Seeing whether everything would fit in the trailer, how neat he'd have to be while packing it all in. Determining if he could lift the sofa by himself or if he'd have to get the neighbors' help.

That was what Justin should be concentrating on.

Instead, he leaned against the wall to one side of the front window and peered at the driveway through the crack in the blinds.

Phoenix remained in the driveway. Looking torn as she stared at the house.

Justin pulled out his cell. He scrolled through his contact list until he found Rohn, then hit Call.

"Hey," Rohn answered after a few rings. "You there yet?"

"Yeah. I just got to the house. Let me ask you something. Is there any reason that a young lady driving a car with

California plates would be stopping by here and asking for Bonnie?"

"Um, I don't know. I could ask her. Hang on."

Justin heard the jostling of Rohn's phone. Some mumbling through the line and then Rohn was back. "Bonnie says she doesn't know anyone from California. About how old would you say this woman is?"

"Midtwenties, I guess." Though nowadays, between makeup and Botox and all that other cosmetic stuff a person could get, it was getting harder and harder to tell how old or young anyone was.

"That age would be about right for her to be a former student of Bonnie's. Is it possible maybe she's back in town and looking to visit?"

"Maybe." It was possible, but Justin wasn't sold on that explanation.

Rohn's suggestion made sense, except for one thing— why wouldn't she have just told him if that was the reason she was here? He'd never liked school much himself, but he would understand a good student—one who actually enjoyed classes—wanting to catch up with a favorite teacher. Especially if she'd moved out of state and was back visiting for a short while.

"Sorry I couldn't help you more." Rohn's voice put an end to Justin's guessing.

"No, it's fine. I figured I'd call and ask. Just a shot in the dark." Justin was the one who was sorry he couldn't get to the bottom of this mystery for Rohn and Bonnie's sake.

He'd tried and failed to get some answers. The one thing Justin hated most was not being able to finish what he set out to do.

"Did you have a chance to look around? You think you'll be able to handle everything okay there?"

Justin pulled himself away from the mystery out in the

driveway and turned back toward the living room. "I haven't had a chance to look around much yet."

He eyed the sofa. If it wasn't an open-up sleeper kind—which were always hella heavy—he'd probably be able to wrestle it into the trailer alone. He'd brought Rohn's hand truck with him. If he tipped it up on end he could maybe strap the sofa and the other heavy pieces on to that and manage to get them all loaded one at a time.

"Remember, if you need help, go next door. Bonnie's mother already called the neighbors. The husband works during the day, but if you catch him after work, he said he'd be happy to help."

Which meant Justin had to get moving. He didn't intend to spend more than one night here. "A'ight. Got it. I'll let you know when I'm taking off tomorrow."

"You do that. Thanks again for doing this."

Justin let out a snort of a laugh. "Thanks for paying me to."

Rohn laughed as well. "Money well spent. My hip hurts if I have to sit in the truck as far as Elk City. No way I wanted to take that drive."

"You would have done it for Bonnie, though."

"Yeah, I would have. Now stop being a smart-ass and let me get back to her. She's making supper and I promised I'd help."

Justin cocked a brow, remembering a few of Rohn's failed attempts in the kitchen. "She knows you can't cook, right?"

"Yup. She sure does and she loves me anyway. Go figure. I'll talk to you tomorrow. Have a good night. Call if you need me."

"Okay. 'Night." Justin disconnected the call and shoved the cell in his pocket.

He should go check out the bedrooms. See if there were huge mattresses and dressers he would have to move so he could go grab the neighbor before it got too late. Instead, he moved back to the window. He peered between the blinds at the driveway.

He'd be lying to himself if he didn't admit his surprise at seeing the woman and the car gone. A small part of him was a bit let down by the discovery. It was probably just the intrigue of the situation that interested him. It had broken up the monotony of his very long day on the road. And Justin really hated not having answers to his questions.

He let the blinds fall back into place.

His disappointment couldn't stem from anything else. Of course not. A girl like that, so full of secrets, one who couldn't even give him a straight answer to a simple question, would only spell trouble. On top of that, she obviously lived in California. You couldn't get much farther from Oklahoma. So it definitely wasn't that he wouldn't mind coming across her again.

Teasing her was amusing. That was all. If he'd push himself to go out more, the way Colton was always suggesting, he'd meet plenty of girls. He just hadn't felt like going out lately. Maybe it was time he made the effort.

After one more glance outside, Justin heaved a sigh and turned to explore the rest of the house. He had a moving job to do.

Chapter Twelve

Phoenix stared at her tablet, waiting for the new browser to open.

She logged in to the hotel's Wi-Fi. Thank goodness even cheap hotels had free Internet nowadays.

Hopefully another search would provide more info because so far the day couldn't get much worse.

Her car overheating. No one being home at the address she had. Then there was Mr. Cowboy Hottie being all evasive and basically blocking her way, keeping her from getting to see Bonnie Martin, wherever she was.

Things hadn't gotten much better after she'd left either. The mechanics at the service station had all left for the day by the time she'd finished bantering with the cowboy who thought he was so witty.

Any repairs would have to wait until morning, but she knew she definitely had to get the problem taken care of before she tried to drive home. The temperature gauge on her car had been well into the red by the time she pulled into the hotel parking lot. She could only hope it would be a simple fix a mechanic could handle in the morning.

There was a lot she had to do tomorrow. Get the car fixed. Try one more time to see Bonnie Martin. Not necessarily in that order.

In the meantime, she was stuck in a slightly shabby but affordable hotel room for the night. She had her tablet and she had Wi-Fi, and she was very well versed in Web searches. She used the Internet often in the course of her job. Tonight she intended to use it to discover anything and everything she could about Bonnie Martin of Phoenix, Arizona.

She started with social media. Phoenix calculated that if Bonnie Martin was her mother, she could be anything from forty to sixty years old. That was a wide range, but nowadays everybody left some sort of trace on the World Wide Web, no matter what their age.

Heck, even her mother had an Instagram account now.

This Bonnie Martin should have some sort of profile somewhere. Even if she was married and had a different name, most people posted their maiden names so classmates from high school could find them when it came time for reunions and stuff.

Phoenix pawed through the biggest, most popular social media site first. There was a Bonnie Martin in Iowa and one in Alabama, but none in Arizona. She moved on to the next site. Then the next, searching members' names and locations, all while knowing the search might be futile if Bonnie had chosen not to list her maiden name online.

But no, she must still use the name Bonnie Martin because that's what Phoenix had found when she'd done her original search and located the address in Arizona.

The hottie cowboy flashed into her mind, as he had more than once since she'd left the house. He'd said he knew Bonnie and he was driving a truck with Oklahoma plates.

She'd searched Bonnie Martin in Phoenix, Arizona, but

she hadn't searched Bonnie Martin in Oklahoma. Armed with that idea, Phoenix set her fingers on the keys and typed in the search.

The search results filled half a Web page. Heart pounding, Phoenix clicked on an obituary from a small town Oklahoma newspaper. Local resident Tom Martin had died earlier that summer, leaving as a survivor his only child, a daughter, Bonnie.

Things were starting to make sense now. The pieces were falling into place. Why there wasn't all that much to find about Bonnie Martin in Arizona. Why there was a cowboy from Oklahoma who said he knew her.

There was plenty to find on Bonnie in Oklahoma. Phoenix searched further and found Bonnie Martin in the list of graduates at Stonewall High School.

That was the year before Phoenix was born. Her birth mother hadn't been long out of high school. Pregnant. Unmarried. But why had she left her family and come all the way to Arizona to have her baby? And by all indications, she'd stayed out here.

Was it for a job? Or for college maybe?

Phoenix switched gears. Now that she had a specific date range to research, she started searching the students of Arizona universities about the time Bonnie would have graduated. It didn't take too long before she found her listed in the member profiles of the Arizona State University Alumni Association.

The facts listed about her said Bonnie was a teacher.

A teacher, just like Phoenix.

She looked at the current picture posted on the alumni site. It was like looking at a picture of herself, twenty or so years in the future. This was where she'd gotten her own blue eyes, and she had Bonnie's blond hair.

It was as if she'd found a missing piece of herself.

But it wasn't enough. She wanted to know more. Was Bonnie hopelessly disorganized? Did she like to read? Was she clumsy, or funny?

Phoenix had to know.

That settled it. She was meeting this woman, come hell or high water. She wasn't leaving Arizona until she did. And no one and nothing was going to stand in her way. Not Mr. Oklahoma Sex on Wheels. Not one faulty German-engineered Volkswagen engine. Not even her mother, whose call she'd already dodged.

Too excited not to tell someone, Phoenix spun, searching for her cell phone on the bed. She grabbed it and scrolled through the contacts to find Kim.

She stood, too antsy to sit, and paced the small room while listening to the phone ring in her ear. Finally Kim picked up.

"Phoenix, you know I can't talk right now. I'm in the middle of the fancy dinner party I'm throwing for all my colleagues from school. Remember?"

"Ha, ha. Very funny. Listen, I found something and it's pretty amazing."

"What did you find? Tell me."

"Bonnie's father—I guess that makes him my grandfather—lived in Oklahoma."

"Then how did she end up in Arizona?"

"She went to Arizona State, and you won't believe this—she's a teacher just like me. And she's got blond hair and blue eyes. I have to meet her."

"So go meet her."

"I'm going to. At least I'm going to try. She wasn't at the house today, but I'm going back tomorrow. First thing in the morning."

And nobody was getting in her way this time. She didn't care how big the cowboy or his truck, she was determined this time.

Chapter Thirteen

Justin carried another box to the truck. He had to put it down on the floor of the trailer just inside the door, then hop up inside. Things were getting tight. Each box he brought out was like one more puzzle piece he had to place just right. The good news was that he was down to the final room of cardboard boxes. Most importantly, all the big stuff had gone in first. The mattresses, the dressers, and the sofa.

Now he just had to fit the remainder of the boxes in the empty spaces between the big things.

Fortunately, the neighbor had been in good shape. He was probably Rohn's age, but he was strong and healthy and had no problem helping Justin with the heavy stuff. The guy had gone above and beyond last night.

Apparently, Bonnie and her mother were well liked in this neighborhood. The cookies and pies they said Tammy baked and brought over to her neighbors had gone a long way to win her goodwill.

The neighbor's wife had even tried to feed Justin, which he'd said wasn't necessary. But he had accepted the cold beer they offered him, all while feeling guilty because he was the one who should be buying them a cold one for the help.

He looked around the dark interior of the stock trailer. Rohn had been right that the smaller trailer would work—the big stock trailer would have been overkill, and hauling it would have made the drive even more miserable than it already had been—but this one was going to be packed to the ceiling.

He bent to pick up the box from the floor and turned with it in his hands. Where to put this one? It was like a game. A giant game with oversize pieces that weighed close to fifty pounds each.

What the hell was in this one? He grunted as he heaved it into a space over his head. He spotted the letters written in black marker on the cardboard that spelled out *Books*. That explained it.

Books were heavy shit.

Next time he offered to move someone, he'd make sure the person was less of an intellectual. More fluff between the ears would mean lighter boxes to haul, he figured.

Though he remembered helping an old girlfriend of his move. She'd had what had to be close to two dozen boxes filled just with shoes and boots. At least they'd weighed less than this library of books Bonnie owned. She was a teacher. Books came with the territory, he guessed.

Satisfied that the box was secure in its perch on top of the end table that was on top of the sofa, Justin turned toward the doorway. He bent and then hopped down to the ground.

He stopped dead when he saw the flash of yellow in his peripheral vision.

There was only one thing that particular color yellow and it had him smiling. The Volkswagen's engine went silent and he waited for the driver's side door to open.

Was he irresistible? Or was it the need to see Bonnie that drove this girl to come back again? He could only hope he was the lure, though he shouldn't be hoping anything of the kind, for all the same reasons he'd come up with the night before.

Even so, a man could be curious, and he was enjoying the distraction she provided. That seemed safe enough.

He ambled down the driveway toward the curb where she'd parked. Finally, the door opened and she stepped out, shading her eyes against the glare of the morning sun.

"What are you doing?" she asked.

"Considering I've got an invite to be here and I'm pretty sure you don't, you sure do ask a lot of questions and demand a lot of answers."

"How do I know you have an invite? And how do you know I don't have one?"

He could respond to her challenge easily enough. "For one, I have the keys. For the answer to the second part, I made a phone call last night, and it seems Bonnie doesn't know why anyone from California would be looking for her. So . . ."

He let that fact hang in the air and watched her react to it. She sputtered for a few seconds. "Just because she didn't know I was coming doesn't mean she doesn't know me."

"Ah." Justin nodded, intrigued.

The cute frown he'd grown to enjoy appeared again across her brow. "I still don't have any proof you are who you say you are or that you're supposed to be here."

"A'ight. That's easy enough." He dug his cell phone out of his pocket, scrolled through the contacts, and found Rohn's house number. He hit Dial and handed it to her. "Here you go."

Her eyes widened. "What are you doing?"

"Calling Bonnie. You can ask her yourself."

She didn't take the phone. In fact, she took a step back from him as he held it out toward her.

He cocked a brow. "You'd better take it. It's ringing."

"Hang up." She looked panicked and he became even more interested—and suspicious.

He heard the muted sound of Rohn answering the phone and brought it to his ear. "Hey. Good morning."

"Good morning. How're things going there?"

"Good." Justin kept his eye on Phoenix as he talked, planning to grab her if she made a run for it. There was no way he was letting her go before he got some answers.

"You get everything loaded?"

"Almost done. The neighbor helped with the big stuff. I'm just getting the last of the boxes loaded, then I'll be hitting the road."

"That's great."

"Yup. It's a little later in the day than I'd like, but I figure I can make it back tonight."

"Justin, just get a damn hotel room."

"I shouldn't—"

"Justin, listen to me. You're hauling a full trailer. You did a thirteen-plus-hour drive in one shot just yesterday. Don't try to do it again today. Put some miles in today and then stop for the night. Get yourself a good dinner and a decent night's sleep and finish up the drive in the morning."

"But that means I won't be at work tomorrow."

"Ty and Colt and I can handle it just fine. I'll pay you for the time. Just take the second day. I don't want to have to scoop you and all of Bonnie and Tammy's stuff off the side of the interstate when you wreck."

"I've never gotten in a wreck."

"Let's keep it that way."

Justin sighed. "Fine. I won't drive straight through."

"Good. And thank you."

"You're welcome. See you tomorrow. Before lunch."

"Whenever you get here you get here."

"A'ight. 'Bye."

"'Bye." Justin disconnected the call and raised his eyes to Phoenix. He shoved the cell into his pocket and crossed his arms. "Now back to you. Talk."

"Why should I?"

"Because you're hiding something."

"Even if I was, it's not for you to know."

"It is if you want my help."

"Your help?"

"It's obvious you're hot to speak with Bonnie. You tell me why, and if I think it's a good reason, I can make that happen."

She shook her head.

Justin let out a sigh. "A'ight. Suit yourself."

He turned toward the house. He had to finish up. Even if he did plan to get a room tonight and take two days getting home, he still didn't want to get too late a start.

Besides, he had a feeling she wasn't going anywhere. He hadn't missed the way she kept looking at the stuff in the trailer. She was interested in what was happening and he had a feeling she wasn't the type to leave without getting answers any more than he was.

They were a lot alike. He hated a mystery himself.

Correction—he enjoyed solving a good mystery. It was the unsolved ones that drove him batty.

This one he hoped would resolve itself shortly. Right now, his plan was not to give her anything until she gave something up in return.

He went into the house and eyeballed the last stack of boxes. Reading the writing on them, he saw two out of the four remaining were marked *Books*. Then the final two were marked *Fragile*.

He'd stack the heavy boxes of books first and then maybe

put the two fragile ones in the cab of the truck with him if he had to.

He wondered how fragile they were. And how careful a job Bonnie's mother had done wrapping the stuff in them. He'd have to wedge them real good so they didn't move but be sure not to crush them in the process.

This moving stuff was tricky on a good day. It was even trickier when he had an audience. He saw her watching him when he came out the front door, one box in his hands. The damn things were too heavy to carry two at once, though he had considered trying.

"You still here?" He slid the box onto the floor of the trailer and hopped up inside.

He chose a spot for the heavy box, grunting as he picked it up and heaved it into place. Wiping a forearm across his forehead to catch the bead of sweat there, he turned his attention back to her. "No answer, huh? No more questions for me either?"

"Would you answer if I asked?"

"Maybe I would. Give it a try." He grabbed the bottle of water sitting on the floor inside the doorway, cracked off the cap, and took a long swallow. "Go on, shoot."

"Where are you taking all this stuff?"

"Oklahoma."

"Who does it belong to?"

"The homeowner."

"And who is that?"

"I thought we already determined that yesterday."

"Bonnie Martin."

"I guess, though I'm not sure if it's hers or her mother's."

"Why are you answering my questions now when you wouldn't before?"

"Because I figure it's either give you a few harmless tidbits of information you'd be able to find out on your own

anyway or have you follow me all the way to Oklahoma."
He shrugged. "If you weren't lying yesterday and your car
really is acting up, I don't need you breaking down while
you're tailing me. Then I'd probably feel bad and help you,
and I really don't have time for that right now."

She pouted at his scenario. "I wasn't lying. It overheated."

"Then why aren't you at the service station getting it
fixed?"

"Because I wanted to see Bonnie Martin."

"Why?" he asked.

"I can't tell you."

He nodded and eased off the edge of the truck he'd been
leaning against. "Then it seems we're done here." He turned
back toward the house.

"Wait."

He paused and turned to look at her. "Yes?"

"Can't you tell me where she is?"

"I could."

"Will you? Please?"

Justin folded his arms. "You first."

She looked miserable. So much so, he started to think
she might actually have a good reason to see Bonnie. He
waited. He figured if he stood there long enough, eventually she'd have to say something. Finally, she drew in a big
breath.

"I have good reason."

"I'm sure you do. What is it?"

"I can't tell you."

Rolling his eyes, Justin shook his head. "Nice meeting
you, Phoenix."

"Wait." At that single word from her, Justin halted one
more time. Finally, she said, "I'm afraid it's a secret."

That was interesting. He met her gaze. "You're not sure?"

"I know it was supposed to be kept a secret, but it got

exposed by accident, so now I know, but I don't know if anyone else does."

"All righty." That wasn't too confusing. When she didn't continue, he said, "I'm still not giving you anything more on Bonnie until I know what you're up to."

"That's the problem. We want the same thing."

"How's that?" he asked, not getting what she was hinting at.

"You're keeping Bonnie's whereabouts from me to protect her and I'm trying to protect her by keeping her secret from you."

"The secret you accidentally found out."

"Yes." She seemed relieved he'd finally gotten it, when in reality he didn't understand shit.

"So if this secret is between you and Bonnie, why didn't you take the phone and just talk to her?"

"Because you were right when you said she doesn't know who I am. I mean, she knows me, but she doesn't know me as Phoenix Montagno. Well, she doesn't know me now, but we're connected, I swear to you. At least, if my guess is right we are. Then again, I could be wrong."

"I've been with a lot of confusing women in my life, but I have to say you are by far the worst."

"I'm not trying to be." The glassy shine of tears in her eyes told Justin she was speaking the truth.

When one big fat tear spilled down her cheek, he couldn't smother a cuss. "Shit. Don't cry."

"I'm sorry." She swiped away the wetness with one hand. "It's just been a very emotional week."

He let out a snort. "Yeah. I can understand that." He watched her for a few seconds as she tried to control the tears that kept coming anyway.

"What do you want from me here?" he asked.

"I want to know where Bonnie is."

He sighed and gave in. "Oklahoma."

"Is she coming back?"

"I don't think so. The house is going up for sale. I'm moving out the last of their stuff and bringing it to her and her mother."

"How far a drive is Oklahoma?"

"Fourteen hours, give or take." He glanced at her car. "With you stopping every time you overheat, that'll only take you like a month or so."

Phoenix bit her lip as her face crumpled with the look of a woman about to have a breakdown.

"Look, there's nothing to get upset about. You don't have to drive to Oklahoma. I told you I'd let you talk to her on my phone."

"I can't do that."

"Why not?"

"I don't know if she wants to talk to me." The tears began to flow again.

"Christ." Justin sighed. Tears were his weakness. "What do you want to do?"

"I want to meet her. Get to know her. But I don't want her to know who I am."

"Okay, now you really do sound a little like a crazy stalker. You do see that, right?"

"I'm not a stalker." She looked up at him. "I swear. I just need to see her."

For some reason he believed her. "A'ight. I get that. So how about this? You get your car fixed, then when it's running good, you take a trip to Oklahoma. Or fly there. You're not moving a house full of shit the way I am. You can take a plane."

"I guess." She raised her eyes to him. "Or I could go with you."

His eyes widened at that suggestion. "Excuse me?"

"You're driving there already."

"Yeah. So?"

"I could leave my car at the service station here. While they fix it, I drive to Oklahoma with you. You introduce me to Bonnie as a friend of yours. Once I meet her and spend a little time with her, I can rent a car and drive back here to get mine at the service station. I could get a flight, but they're pretty expensive last minute, so driving would probably be cheaper."

He could see by the glazed look in her eyes that she was deep into her plans. Plans that included him not only driving her but lying to Rohn and Bonnie when he got there by saying she was his friend, all so she could, for some undisclosed reason, get to know Bonnie, even though Bonnie didn't know her.

"No." He shook his head.

"What?"

"No. I'm not driving you or introducing you as my friend."

"Why not?"

"Well, first of all, I already told them you were here looking for Bonnie."

"Oh." That seemed to stump her. "What did they say when you told them that?"

"That Bonnie didn't know anyone from California. And that maybe you were an old student of hers."

Her eyes widened. "That's perfect. I could pretend to be an old student."

"Again, you're missing the point. I'm not lying to Bonnie and my boss."

"Your boss?"

"Bonnie's fiancé is my boss."

She glanced at the lettering on the trailer. "From Double L Ranch in Oklahoma?"

Shit. Now she knew exactly where Bonnie was. All she'd have to do was dial Information on her phone. Rohn's listing was public. Of course it was. He was operating a business. It had to be.

For the first time she smiled when she realized the same thing. She could get to Bonnie with or without his help.

"The way I see it, I could rent a car and go on my own, or I could go with you. I really hate driving alone. And if I go with you, you can keep an eye on me. Make sure I'm not a crazed stalker."

There was no proof this chick wasn't crazy, but what she'd said was accurate. The one way for him to keep an eye on her, and thereby protect Bonnie and Rohn, would be to keep her close to him.

As much as he hated to admit it, he said, "*If* I bring you with me . . ."

Her expression brightened. "Yeah?"

"I said *if*."

"Okay. Go on. If I go with you, what?"

"I'm not lying to Rohn and Bonnie that you're my friend or anything like that."

She drew in a breath. "Fine."

"I mean it," Justin warned.

"I know you mean it. I can tell. You're not the kind of guy who says something he doesn't mean."

"Really? So now you think you know me?" He crossed his arms over his chest.

"No. No more than you know me. But I suppose fourteen hours in the truck together will fix that."

"Jesus." Justin groaned and glanced at the sky, not believing he was actually going to do this. His peace and quiet had just been wiped away in one fell swoop.

"So you'll take me?" She looked hopeful.

"Yeah, I'll take you. For Bonnie and Rohn. Not because

of some misplaced noble nature you think I possess. Which I don't. Get that through your head right now."

"Okay." Her smile told him she didn't believe him.

He smothered another cuss. "If I'm taking you, you better help me finish loading the truck."

"No problem. I've very strong."

"I don't care how strong you think you are." He led the way to the house. "Take the light boxes that say *Fragile*, not the one box marked *Books*. It's too heavy for you."

"Not noble my ass." She mumbled the smart-ass comment, but he heard it anyway.

He glanced at her over his shoulder. "I heard that."

"Good." She smiled.

Annoyed at her and himself, he grumbled all the way to the boxes on the floor. "And we're dropping your car off at the service station because I'm not going to try to fix it myself."

"I never asked you to try."

"I know." He bit out the response because she was right. She hadn't asked, but his own damn conscience was nagging him to do just that.

He was going to regret this decision to take her with him. He felt that deep down to his bones.

Chapter Fourteen

Phoenix watched Justin expertly pull the truck and trailer along the curb, as if he'd been driving the oversize vehicle for most of his life. Thinking about it, she realized he probably had. Especially if Justin worked on a ranch.

Just because the guys she knew drove economy-size cars that made sense in California didn't mean the rest of the country wasn't hauling big rigs.

There were probably all sorts of things Justin did that would surprise her. Things she'd only seen in movies. She'd have to ask him about them.

There'd be plenty of time. According to what he'd said, they'd have fourteen hours alone in the cab of his truck on their journey to Oklahoma. They'd have time to talk about all sorts of things.

Why wasn't she worried about spending that much time with a stranger?

There was a definite flutter in her belly, but it seemed to stem more from anticipation and nerves similar to what she'd feel on a first date with a guy.

This was definitely not a date. But hell, being captive in a tight space with a hot cowboy was probably a better way to get to know a man than some forced social situation like dinner.

She was really jumping the gun, because there were a ton of other things she should be concerned with instead of this hot cowboy.

First on the list—her car.

She opened the door and stepped out of the car, taking the keys with her. She turned to catch Justin's attention and motioned that she was going into the station. He nodded and remained in the truck. Smart. It wasn't like he could leave something so large parked along the curb on the main street. There was probably some sort of law against that.

As she pushed through the door of the service station and stepped inside, a bell tinkled above her head.

"Can I help you?"

"Yeah. The bartender at the place right off the interstate suggested I come here. My car—the yellow VW Beetle parked in your lot—keeps overheating."

The man, dressed in navy blue overalls with the name *Ben* embroidered on the chest, glanced past her through the glass door.

"Out-of-towner? You got California plates."

"Yeah." She hated to admit that. Was he going to charge her double, knowing she couldn't do anything about it because she wasn't local?

"I'll take a look at it, but I can't say how long it'll take to fix. If I have to order a part, it could be two, maybe three days. That gonna be all right? How long you here for?"

"Actually, two or three days would be fine. This is only the first leg of my trip. I'm heading to Oklahoma for a couple of days." She motioned to the truck and trailer. "My ride's waiting for me now."

The mechanic followed her gaze and nodded. "Nice rig."

"Uh, thanks."

"All right. Let me get some contact information." He slid a clipboard with a form and a pen attached toward her. "Once you fill that out, you and your ride can take off. Just leave me the keys."

"Okay."

"I'll take a look at it and call you with an estimate of the cost and how long it'll take me."

"That would be wonderful." She finished scribbling her name and phone number, her home address, and her license plate number, and then slid the form back toward him. "Thanks so much."

"Sure thing."

Phoenix turned to go as he said, "Uh, I'll take those keys."

"Oh my gosh. I'm so sorry." She was scattered on a good day. The day she was heading to Oklahoma to meet her birth mother, riding shotgun with a hot cowboy, forget about thinking at all.

She slid the keys across the counter to the man. He reached for them while saying, "You got everything you need out of the car?"

It was a valid question. She probably would have forgotten her bags if Justin hadn't already transferred all her belongings to the cab of his truck.

But the mechanic didn't need to know that, so she was happy to report, "Yup. I got everything. Thank you."

He tipped his head in a nod. "No problem. I'll be in touch."

"Thanks."

She pushed through the door and headed for the curb. Justin had the window rolled down. "What'd he say?"

"He'll take a look at it today and call me with an estimate."

Justin tipped his head. "A'ight."

She walked around to the other side and opened the passenger-side door. She had to hoist herself up into the high cab with the grab bar on the doorframe, but finally she was settled in the seat.

"You tell him the bartender recommended him?"

"Yes, I did." She pulled the seat belt across her and then frowned. "How did you know that? Did I tell you?"

He looked as if he didn't want to answer her but finally said, "The bartender told me."

"Why?"

"A boring day shift, a cute customer with car trouble. What else did he have to talk to me about? I guess you were the highlight of his shift." Justin shrugged and flipped on the directional signal.

Meanwhile, all Phoenix could think about was that Justin had referred to her as cute. "Did he say that?"

Justin concentrated on the side mirrors before pulling out into traffic and then asked, "Did he say what?"

"That I'm, you know, cute?"

Grinning, he shot her a look. "Why? You interested? He's a bit old for you, no?"

"No, I'm not interested." She felt her cheeks heat.

She let the subject drop. She could only hope he would, too. She'd been baiting him to see if he'd been the one to think she was cute, but it had backfired on her. All she'd done was look foolish and make him laugh at her.

She sucked at flirting. It was going to be a long drive if she continued to be so ridiculous in the small-talk department.

"So, tell me about yourself." His question surprised her.

"What do you want to know?"

"Eh, I don't know. How about how you know Bonnie?"

Phoenix scowled. "I thought we agreed you were fine not knowing that."

"Oh, I never said I would let it go, just that I'd drive you even if you didn't tell me—you know, to keep an eye on you because of you being a possible crazed stalker and all." His grin told her he didn't really believe that and was teasing her again.

"How about you tell me about yourself?"

A dark expression settled on his brow. "I don't like talking about myself."

So much for that. She'd hoped to turn the tables on him, but he hadn't gone for it. A few minutes passed in silence. Finally, she had to say something. She'd caused the conversational drought by asking him about himself. She felt the need to fix it.

"So, what's the Double L Ranch like?"

He glanced at her and lifted one brow high beneath the brim of his cowboy hat. "You really wanna know?"

"Yeah, I do." To her own surprise, she wasn't just being polite. She really did want to know, especially if Bonnie was connected to the ranch somehow.

"Well, it's mainly a cattle operation. But Rohn—he's the owner—has a pretty successful rough stock business going, too. And of course we also deal with trained stock. We buy green horses and then saddle break them to be pleasure horses. And we train cutting horses. As far as competitive rough stock, his bulls are good, but I'd say his broncs are probably his bread and butter."

Most of what Justin had just said had gone right over Phoenix's head. When he stopped talking and glanced across the cab at her, she realized she'd yet to respond. She nodded. "Oh."

His wide grin told her he'd caught her in a lie, pretending she knew what he was talking about. "What part you need explained to you, city girl?"

City girl? She wasn't sure whether to deny it, however true, or feel honored he'd given her a nickname. She opted not to respond to the name and answer truthfully. "Pretty much all of it."

He laughed. "Yeah. I figured."

"How?"

"That glazed expression in those big blue eyes of yours was a dead giveaway."

He'd noticed her eyes were blue . . . and she had to stop letting her mind run away with her every time she was near this guy. It could very well be her imagination that he looked at her a bit longer, a tad deeper, than necessary.

This was a ride only, and he'd taken her to keep an eye on her. Even so, she could enjoy listening to his cowboy speak.

She did just that as, still looking amused, he launched into an explanation of the difference between rough stock and trained stock. Then moved on to a rundown of the different events in a rodeo and all the kinds of animals the ranch would truck in to supply for the competitions.

He seemed to relax when he talked about the animals and the ranch. The tension she'd noticed in his shoulders eased until it disappeared. The tight control he seemed to hold on personal information about himself eased a bit, too, as little tidbits about himself slipped out along with his explanation of his job at the Double L.

She liked this Justin much better than the elusive, hard version she'd first met yesterday—the guy at the bar who'd ignored her while he ate his burger and the even harder man who'd walked into Bonnie's house and closed the door without giving her the answers she needed or wanted.

This Justin might actually answer some of the dozen or more questions she had about Bonnie and her mother—Phoenix's grandmother—if she asked. But it seemed she didn't have the nerve to dig for more answers. Or maybe she just didn't want to bring back the guy from yesterday, or even this morning. She was enjoying this friendly, smiling incarnation too much, and with another dozen hours or so in the truck, it wasn't worth risking annoying him so he withdrew into himself. She didn't want to spend the rest of the long ride in silence.

Justin was in the middle of regaling Phoenix with a tale about a black Arabian stallion and some cowboy he worked with by the name of Tyler when she felt her phone vibrate in the bag she held in her lap.

She ignored the signal. It could be her mother calling. What would she say to her mother or to Justin? She couldn't see him sitting there while she lied to her mother, pretending she was home in California. Just as she couldn't risk having her mother hear she was in a truck with a strange man.

That would really open a can of worms. How would she explain it?

Sometimes it didn't feel like she was twenty-five, working and living on her own. Mostly she still felt like she was a preteen looking to her parents for approval at every turn. Looking for their guidance as well.

Maybe that was why she didn't know how to diagnose car problems or do anything else on her own. Her father had babied her. Her mother had sheltered her. And she'd let them.

Not anymore. At least not on this trip. Look at the results of her not seeking her parents' approval. She'd gotten into a truck with a stranger for a trip that would take her halfway across the country. They definitely wouldn't approve.

Justin glanced at her. "You gonna answer that?"

"Um." She cringed. A person never realized how loud the vibrate mode on a cell phone was until they were hoping another person didn't hear it.

He raised a brow. "Well, now. This is interesting."

"What is?"

"You dodging that there call." He tipped his head toward

her bag, which had thankfully stopped vibrating where it rested in her lap.

"It's nothing."

"Oh, I think it's something." His grin widened.

"It's probably just my mother."

"Uh-huh."

"I'm serious. It's got to be my mother. Who else do you think I'd be dodging?"

"That I don't know. Any more than I know why you'd be avoiding your poor momma and not answering her call. That's just not right."

She let out a huff. "I have my reasons."

"I'm sure you do. What would they be?"

She was attempting to come up with a smart comeback when the phone started to vibrate again.

She watched his smile widen further.

"You're not even gonna look? That's even more telling."

"Why?"

"Because it's like you know who it is."

"No." It could as easily be Kim being nosy as it was her mother checking up on her. But now Phoenix wanted to know who it was. The curiosity was too much for her. She let out a huff. "Fine. I'll check to see who it is."

"Don't look on my account." He focused his eyes on the road, but she could tell he was most definitely laughing at her as she opened her purse and pawed through the contents until her hand connected with the cell phone. It had stopped vibrating by the time she'd retrieved it, but she could see by the readout that she had two missed calls, both from Kim.

"So?" Justin asked.

"It wasn't my mother."

"Interesting. Who was it? Your boyfriend, I bet."

"I don't have a boyfriend."

"You don't? Hmm. Yeah, that makes sense."

"What? Why does that make sense?" She was definitely feeling insulted at that comment.

"Don't get your panties in a twist. I'm just saying no man would let you go carousing around the country in a broken-down old car alone. At least I wouldn't if you were my girlfriend."

"I'm too busy for a boyfriend right now." She skipped over the male chauvinism and moved on to making sure he knew she wasn't incapable of attracting the opposite sex. She just chose not to at the moment.

"Oh, really. Busy doing what?"

"Teaching.

"Teaching? So you're a teacher?"

She bit back a curse when she realized she'd played right into his hands. She'd given him plenty of information about herself in the past few minutes alone, all unintentionally. He now knew she was dodging her mother's calls, she had no boyfriend, and she was a teacher. Not bad for just a small effort on his part.

However, if he thought she would spill what he really wanted to know—why she wanted to see Bonnie—just because she was spilling some other tidbits, he was sadly mistaken.

She decided to turn the tables on him and do a little digging of her own. "So you really wouldn't let your girl-friend take a road trip alone?"

"Alone? Nope."

"So what, are you one of those overprotective guys who locks a girl away and doesn't let her out? What is she doing while you're gone? Waiting at home baking pies like a good little girl?"

"Baking pies?" He cocked a brow. "Can't say I'd object to some pie, but no, I got no girl waiting on me with any form of pastry." His gaze cut to her. "You find out what you wanted?"

Her heart pounded. He'd seen right through her.

"What?" Her voice sounded higher than she'd thought it would.

"You were snooping around to find out if I had a girl."

"No—"

"It's a'ight. Women are naturally nosy."

She raised her brows high. "And you haven't been snooping around asking me all sorts of questions, including about boyfriends?"

He shrugged. "Just wondering who let a helpless girl like you go wandering around."

"A helpless girl like me." Her eyes went wide at the insult.

"Yup. One who wouldn't know a dipstick from a Popsicle stick."

She couldn't argue with him there. She didn't know cars, but it was still insulting.

"That why you avoiding your mother? She didn't approve of your little field trip? She didn't sign your permission slip?" He grinned.

"I told you, I'm a teacher, not a student."

"I know. That's why I thought my joke was extra clever." She smiled in spite of herself, shaking her head as she did.

"It's all right, you know," he said.

"What's all right?"

"That you like me even while I annoy the hell out of you."

"I'm starting to see that's just part of your charm."

"Exactly." He glanced at her and then back at the road in front of him. "We're gonna get along just fine."

"As long as I don't ask you about Bonnie Martin."

"Oh, you can ask—I'm just not gonna answer. Unless, of course, you tell me your little secret."

She shook her head, not joking this time when she said, "I can't."

"Then neither can I." His gaze flicked to the cell still in her hand. "So come on. Who's calling you?"

Phoenix rolled her eyes. "My friend Kim. She's probably wondering what I did about my car. I kind of have her on standby to come get me if I can't get the car fixed."

"Don't you think you should let her off the hook for now and tell her you won't be needing a ride for at least a couple of days?"

"Yes."

"And you're not doing that because . . . Oh, I know. You don't want to have to tell her you hitched a ride with an incredibly charming though annoying guy while I'm listening."

"Don't flatter yourself." She turned to the window to hide her smile, not wanting him to know that was exactly why she didn't want to talk to Kim in front of him.

"How about this? I need a break to get out and stretch my legs. There's a truck stop coming up in a couple of miles. I'll pull over and you can call your friend back and talk in private."

"I don't have to talk in private."

"Maybe not, but this way you can feel free to—hell, I don't know—tell her how cute I am and all." Justin grinned wide.

"Yeah, all right. I'll make sure to do that."

He laughed and, slowing, flipped on the turn signal. After checking the side mirrors, he eased the truck and trailer into the right lane of the interstate.

She could use a bathroom break after all she'd had to drink that morning at the diner where she'd had breakfast. She hadn't wanted to ask him to stop, but between free refills on her hot tea and then all the water she'd had, she definitely was happy he'd offered. And yeah, she did want to call Kim back so her friend wouldn't worry and wouldn't keep calling.

She wouldn't admit it to Justin, but Kim would probably have something to say about her hooking up with him for the ride. Phoenix never knew with Kim. She could just as easily freak out that her best friend had gotten in a truck with a stranger who could be a murderer for all she knew as she could get jealous Phoenix was in a truck with a hot stranger.

Either way, Justin was stopping, so she'd get a chance to pee and call, definitely in that order. Now that her bladder had heard they were stopping, that need seemed more urgent than before.

He slowed further as they neared the sign for the exit to the rest stop. Maybe she should grab something to eat, too. It was getting near lunchtime.

Amazing how quickly the couple of hours had passed, but there were many more to go.

Justin pulled the truck into the extralong spaces she'd always noticed were at rest stops but had never had need to use. He stopped there and cut the engine. "So I'll meet you back here in say fifteen minutes?"

"Okay." She reached for the door handle, then turned back. "If I'm late, you won't leave without me, will you?"

If the line at the food place was long she might not make it back in time.

He raised one brow. "You planning on being longer than that?"

"No, but there might be a line."

"I won't leave."

Was he lying? She didn't think so, but still, it made her worry. "I won't be late."

He laughed. "I said I wouldn't leave."

"I know." She opened the door, realizing she really didn't

know. Not him or what he'd do. Phoenix hadn't even called Kim yet and her friend's unspoken doubts were already infecting her brain.

Phoenix decided to multitask to save time. She dialed Kim as she headed toward the restrooms.

"Hey. About time you called me back. I was worried."

"Sorry. I didn't mean to make you worry."

"Where are you?"

"Um." Phoenix glanced around, but she couldn't exactly answer the question. "At a rest stop on the interstate somewhere between Arizona and Oklahoma."

"What?"

She realized how much had happened in a very short time. None of which Kim knew. "I'm going to Oklahoma to meet Bonnie Martin."

"What made you decide to do that?"

"The guy from Oklahoma."

"Guy? Do tell."

Phoenix rolled her eyes. "There's nothing to tell. The fact is, Bonnie Martin is selling her house in Arizona and apparently never coming back. This guy is moving all her stuff to where she is in Oklahoma. Kim, she's living there with her mother. Do you know what that means?"

"No, what?"

"I can meet both my birth mother and my grandmother." Phoenix didn't have any living grandparents. Even her memories of them before they'd died were vague because she'd been young when she'd lost them, one at a time. That was one thing she missed, a lot. It hit her when Kim talked about her own grandmother cooking something special. Or her grandfather saying something funny.

"That's wonderful about your grandmother, but let's get back to this guy."

"He's driving me there because my car is in the shop."

"Okay. I need details."

"What kind of details?"

"Start at the top and work your way down, and don't leave out any of the important parts in between."

Phoenix shook her head. Typical guy-crazy Kim question. At least it seemed she wasn't going to be subjected to a lecture about taking rides from strangers.

She made it to the door of the ladies' room and said, "All right. But I have to make it quick. He gave me fifteen minutes to use the restroom, get something to eat, and get back to the truck."

"Ooh, a taskmaster, is he? I like a forceful man."

Phoenix sighed at her friend. She had some pretty strange ideas about the opposite sex.

Unfortunately, Phoenix didn't have all that much to report.

Justin was adorable, yes, with his suntanned skin and his sexy cowboy hat covering his light brown hair. Then there were those hazel eyes that crinkled at the corners because, when he did smile, he smiled so wide it reached all the way to his eyes.

And he was nice and tall and muscular, and had a bit of a swagger in his walk that only accentuated the whole cowboy-ness of his boots and jeans. But besides that, Phoenix didn't know all that much about him.

Only that he was kind enough to give her a ride. And he talked about animals with more enthusiasm than any other subject. And that he spoke about his boss with a reverence usually reserved for a father. And that as much as he joked and complained about his coworkers, she could tell he really did love the guys and enjoyed working with them. Tyler and who was it? Colton.

What he didn't mention at all was his own family. Which only made her wonder if he didn't have anyone to call his own.

Then there was his secrecy when she asked questions about Bonnie. But that was probably her own fault. As he'd said, he'd share with her when she opened up with him.

"Um, hello? You still there?"

"Oh, sorry. Yeah. I'm just in the bathroom." And she'd been distracted by thoughts of Justin.

One of the stall doors opened and Phoenix moved to fill the vacancy.

"Aw, jeez. I'm all for multitasking, but please just use the bathroom and then call me back."

Phoenix laughed. "Okay. Probably safer that way anyway."

All she needed to do was drop her phone in the toilet. Then she'd really be in trouble.

"Ya think? But you're not getting off the hook. I still want to hear about Oklahoma hottie."

She laughed. "All right. I'll call you right back. 'Bye."

It wasn't going to be a hardship to talk a little bit about Justin, as long as he didn't hear her. If he did, his ego would make the trip unbearable.

In spite of everything, she was having fun. And if the end result of her trip—meeting with Bonnie—turned out as well as the journey to get there . . . that would be amazing.

Chapter Fifteen

It was late in the day, but he hadn't checked in with his mother yet today.

Though he'd never admit it to Phoenix, he had to be honest with himself—her company, uninvited though she had been, was making the hours pass more quickly than he'd ever imagined.

That was one reason why the day had gotten away from him and he hadn't thought to call until now.

It was late afternoon, and though Phoenix hadn't asked, he figured it was time to make another pit stop even though it had only been a couple of hours since the last one. He didn't mind stopping.

Driving long distance, not to mention hauling a trailer with a full load, was tough, and he could use a break himself.

Besides, it would be a good opportunity to make the call in private. He didn't want an audience for this.

It was a risk to call at all. He knew that one phone call could ruin his relaxation and his good mood, but that wasn't going to stop him.

Even if he had taken this trip to get some much needed time away from the overwhelming crush of responsibility that weighed on him at home, he still needed to check in. It was the responsible thing to do, and for better or worse, with his father and older brother gone, his mother was his responsibility now.

While Phoenix was in the bathroom, he hit the button on his cell phone to dial the house. He waited through the series of rings, but no one answered the phone. Finally, the automated message came on.

"Dammit." He said the word aloud and received a stare from the man pushing past him into the men's room.

Now he had to worry about his mother because she wasn't answering the phone. Why wasn't anyone answering? Where was his aunt? His mother's sister was supposed to be there keeping an eye on things in his absence. He'd asked her before he'd left, and she'd agreed. She knew as well as he how his mother could swing from good to very bad on a second's notice. One thing, a single memory, could trigger her descent.

Pissed now that he couldn't even trust family to be responsible, he ended the call and tried his mother's cell phone.

No answer.

Heart pounding, he scrolled to his aunt's number and placed one more call. Again, it went to voice mail. In a panic now, he considered what to do.

He was still hours away. There wasn't much he could do. He could call the sheriff's department and ask them to stop over and check out the house.

That seemed extreme. He'd hate to embarrass his mother like that. He knew everything might be fine. Or all hell could have broken loose. He could call Rohn and ask him to take a ride over.

Drawing in a breath to calm the panic riding him, Justin did his best to think things through. He glanced at the readout on the phone. He'd leave messages for his mom and aunt to call him right away, and if they didn't get back to him in half an hour, he'd consider calling . . . somebody.

Shit.

He made the calls and then headed back to the truck, intent on getting closer to Oklahoma.

His stride was fast, his boots hitting the pavement hard, as he headed for the truck. He found Phoenix already there, waiting next to the passenger door for him, a to-go cup in her hand.

"Hey. I beat you." She smiled.

"Yup. Sorry. I locked it."

"It's all right. I wasn't here long."

He dug in his pocket for his brother's keys and then clicked to unlock the doors so she could get in.

He strode around the truck, trying his best to ignore how closely she seemed to be watching him, as if she'd picked up on his changed mood. Of course there was a good chance he was being paranoid and imagining it. In any case, he didn't feel like talking, so he hoped her soda pop would keep her mouth busy.

He hoisted himself into the driver's seat and shoved the key into the ignition.

She didn't try to make conversation as he pulled onto the interstate and punched the accelerator.

It didn't matter how fast he sped, he wasn't getting home any time soon. Still, it made him feel better.

The miles passed and the truck's cab remained silent. He was grateful for that as he kept one eye on the clock on the dashboard.

She glanced sideways at him. "Can I turn on the radio?"

He'd had it turned off since she'd gotten in this morning, knowing from the trip out that he got nothing but static on the station it was set to. But they'd been on the road for hours and they might be in the zone to start picking up the station. It was syndicated, so it spanned a couple of states.

"All right. Sure."

She reached out and hit the Power button. The song playing was barely audible above the static. She reached her hand out again, and Justin panicked. "No. Don't touch that."

She glanced at him, her hand still heading for the dial. "It's all static. I can find a station that's clear."

He reached out and intercepted her, hitting the Power button and turning the radio off. "No."

"I'm sure there's some station—"

"Just . . . leave it off."

This had been a bad idea. All of it. Taking his brother's truck to begin with. Picking up a passenger. Trying to drive while his mind was miles away in Oklahoma as he worried about where his mother was, what she was doing, why she hadn't answered the phone.

Just as he thought that, his cell lit up. There was a text. It was dangerous to check the text, but he couldn't stop himself. He opened it and saw a message from his aunt.

We're fine. Will call in a bit.

Taking a deep breath of relief, he tossed the cell back in the console. The worrying had exhausted him. He was still shaking a bit. Time for a break.

"I'm going to pull off at the next town and stop for the night."

She turned to frown at him. "I can take a turn at the wheel if you're tired."

"No."

"Why not? Because I'm a woman?"

"No. Not because you're a woman." Great. He'd insulted her.

"Then why not?"

Thank goodness there were plenty of reasons for Justin to cite without his having to admit to her that he hadn't let another person behind the wheel since Jeremy had died.

"Because you're used to driving a car small enough to fit in the bed of this truck, that's why. No way you can handle a full-sized pickup hauling an overloaded trailer. That's for one. For another, it's Rohn's trailer and Bonnie and her mother's stuff and I'm responsible for it, so no."

"I could handle it."

"Well, you don't have to. There's an exit up ahead and the sign says there's lodging and food and fuel. We can gas up the truck, get dinner, and a good night's sleep and start fresh in the morning."

She let out a breath but didn't voice her displeasure, even though it was clear to him that she was unhappy.

If she'd just listened to him and left the damn radio station alone, they probably wouldn't be having this debate.

Even so, he felt bad. He was in no state of mind to argue with the girl right now, but he didn't want to hurt her feelings. "I'm sorry. I'm not trying to insult you or anything. I just don't feel comfortable turning over the wheel."

Enough said. There really was no more need for explanation.

"It's not that. I was just hoping we wouldn't have to stop."

He shook his head. "Nah. We got a late start. If we drove straight through, we wouldn't get there till after midnight."

She sighed again. "All right. Can we try to find someplace on the cheaper side?"

"Uh, I'll try."

"Okay, thanks."

She must be worried about money. He supposed she

had incurred a few unexpected expenses over the past twenty-four hours. The repairs to her car, for one. The cost of getting back from Oklahoma to Arizona for another.

He could offer to let her stay in his room. He doubted she'd say yes, but at least he'd feel better about making them stop if he offered.

"If cost is a problem, I guess you could share with me. Nothing, you know, inappropriate. I'm just saying if you don't have the money for a room." He glanced at her. "I'll get one with two beds. When the guys and I are on the road competing or hauling stock, we cram three or four guys in a hotel room, so it's no big deal."

"That would be fine. Thank you."

He lifted his brows, surprised she'd agreed so readily. "You sure? It's not gonna be a problem?"

"Yeah, I'm sure. You're giving me—a perfect stranger— a ride when you don't have to. I trust you."

He snorted. "Well, you probably shouldn't."

"Why not?"

"A woman trusting a man is a good way for her to get herself into trouble." And now that the offer had been made and she'd accepted it, he had to think this was one of the dumbest ideas he'd ever come up with.

First, he still had to talk to his mother. He supposed he could step outside to make that phone call. But more than that, this sexy-as-hell woman was going to be sleeping just a few feet from him. Looking all soft and warm under the covers. Smelling all sweet and girlie, just how he liked. Taking a shower in the same bathroom so he'd have to picture her wet and soapy and naked.

Crap. How was he going to get a wink of sleep with all that in his head?

The road to hell was surely paved with good intentions. He'd heard that said, but now he fully understood the meaning.

Miss Phoenix Montagno was going to be his roommate for the whole night, after which he'd have to be in the truck with her again for another half a day. Whether he touched her or not, the fantasy of it was already tormenting him

This was a bad idea. The pressure in his jeans told him that already.

Chapter Sixteen

Justin walked down the row of doors, each one painted the same obnoxious turquoise color. The numbers got higher until he finally stood in front of the one that matched the key tag in his hand.

"This is it." Justin pushed the key into the lock and turned the knob. The door swung in. "Home, sweet home."

For better or worse.

It wasn't the nicest place. Then again, it wasn't the worst one he'd stayed in, either. There had been hotel rooms when he'd had to do a few shots at the bar, then go back to the room, close his eyes, and try to forget how bad the accommodations were just so he could sleep.

He entered the room first and flipped on a light, glancing back at Phoenix, standing in the doorway silhouetted by the setting sun. "What do you think? Is this okay?"

She nodded. "Yeah. It's fine."

He followed her gaze to the twin beds. There were two, just as he'd requested, but they were separated by barely two feet. Only the width of the night table stood between them.

A room this small didn't have the square footage for more space between the beds. About now she was probably regretting saying she was all right with sharing.

He knew he sure was, but he wasn't half as worried about spending a sleepless night with this girl just feet away as he should be. His mind was still back in Oklahoma and on the fact that his mother and aunt had yet to get back to him after that one text.

He pulled his phone out of his pocket again and checked to see if he had a signal. He did. Not the strongest, but enough to get a call or text through. He opened his text messages and sent one to both his mother and his aunt.

Call me!

Hitting Send, he glanced up as he shoved the phone in his pocket. "I'll go get our bags."

"I'll come help."

"No need. I got 'em."

She smiled. "Thanks. But you don't have to take care of me."

Sure he did. He'd taken her with him and now she was his responsibility, on top of all the others he had. The same ones he was trying to get away from for just a few damn days. And that had turned out to be a shit idea. Now he had to worry about where his mother was and what she was doing.

His anxiety about his mother rose as his mood plummeted further. Scowling, he said, "I'm not taking care of you. I'm just carrying your damn bag."

She pulled back a bit in reaction to his harsh words and tone. "Okay."

Shit. He'd known he wasn't fit for company on this trip. Sometimes he should listen to the little voice in his head when it talked to him. Instead, he'd gone against his instincts.

Meanwhile, in spite of his worry, his little head—the

one in his pants—was very interested in Phoenix's close proximity. And that was a whole other set of problems for Justin to deal with. He wasn't prepared to resist his attraction to her. He was too weak at the moment.

Too worried. Too stressed out. Too tired. Too . . . everything.

Sinking into a woman and forgetting everything else but the feel of her was too damn tempting. If it was any other time, another situation, another woman, he'd let himself. But Phoenix came with a load of secrets, and he didn't know if he wanted to get any more tangled up with her than he already was.

He had his own secrets, and after sex, some women wanted to talk. Phoenix was definitely one of those talkers. She liked to ask questions and she didn't like not knowing the answers.

His hours with her so far had proven that to him.

She'd be even more interested in his life, his feelings, his secrets, if he let himself take things further with her. He might be in the mood to fuck, but he sure as hell wasn't in the mood to talk. So that settled that.

This was a bad idea all around. The room. The road trip. Getting involved in whatever was between Bonnie and Phoenix. This was Rohn's problem, not Justin's. He should dump all this on Rohn's doorstep and leave.

That idea was the first bright spot in Justin's dark mood for the past couple of hours.

That's what he'd do. The moment he arrived in Oklahoma, he'd dump Phoenix and the trailer on Rohn's doorstep and go.

With that plan firmly in place, Justin headed toward the truck to get the bags and start the ill-advised overnight hotel stay.

They'd have to eat and then eventually go back to the

room. It was way too early to go to sleep. He sure as hell wasn't going to suggest they go to a bar. Alcohol clouding his judgment was the dead last thing he needed tonight.

He'd just walked in through the door, one bag in each hand, his own duffel and some floral thing that looked like a carpetbag from some old movie in his other, when he felt his phone vibrating in his pocket.

He dropped the bags, thinking afterward he probably shouldn't have done that. He didn't know if Phoenix had something breakable in hers.

It was too late to worry about that as he stepped outside on the walkway, pulling the door almost shut behind him. He wrestled the phone out of his jeans and glanced at the readout.

He saw his aunt's name. That it was not his mother calling had his hand shaking as he answered. "Hello?"

"Hi, Justin. How are you?"

He let out a laugh. "I'm fine. Where have you been? Is Momma all right? You didn't answer my calls at the house or on either of your cell phones."

"Good Lord, don't sound so upset. We were in the movie theater with our phones on silent. We can't have a bunch of calls or texts making noise in the middle of the movie."

He drew in a stuttering breath and let it out slowly. He should be happy they were okay. He shouldn't be angry they'd made him worry. He tried to remember that and keep his tone steady as he said, "Next time, can you maybe shoot me a text to tell me what you're doing?"

"Ugh. I hate texting."

He rolled his eyes. "Then call me. You know I worry."

"I know you do, but we're both just fine."

"How's she doing?" he asked.

"She's doing good."

"She eating?"

"Oh, yeah. We cooked together last night. A big lasagna. Garlic bread. Even a salad, so we didn't totally blow our diets with a carb fest."

He was lucky his mother ate at all nowadays, so he'd be fine with her eating as many carbohydrates as she wanted. But he knew his mother's sister was trying to reassure him. He should be grateful for that.

"Thank you for staying there."

"It's not a problem. Long overdue for us to have a girls' only couple of days."

"A'ight. I appreciate it anyway." He drew in a breath and tried to focus his thoughts now that he knew they were both okay. "I stopped for the night, but I'm planning to be home by lunchtime tomorrow."

"That's fine. Take your time. We're good here. I took the day off from work today and I was already off tomorrow."

His little trip had inconvenienced her. "Thank you for taking off."

"Eh, the boss owes me. No problem at all."

Even if it was a problem, she probably wouldn't have told him. That's the kind of woman she was. His mother had been happy and joking just like her sister once upon a time. Before life had beaten her down. He wished she could be happy again.

It was good for her to be with her sister. Aunt Phoebe was full of life. Single, though by divorce not widowhood. Working a good job. Living on her own. Having fun. Aunt Phoebe was a good example for his mother.

"So is she around? I'd like to say good night."

"She's actually already gone to bed."

It was barely suppertime. "Already?"

"She said the movie wore her out."

"Did she eat supper?"

"I offered to heat up leftovers from last night, but she said the popcorn and pop at the theater filled her up."

Justin's mood plummeted as quickly as it had lifted. It was always one step forward, another step back with his mother. One good day, then a bad day. Hell, more like a good couple of hours followed by a run of darkness.

"A'ight. I'll call you when I hit town tomorrow and am on my way home. Please call if you need anything."

"We won't need anything. And you're too far away to do anything if we did, so just enjoy your trip."

He knew she'd meant her comment to relieve his worry. All it did was have him clenching his jaw in anger. "It don't matter how far away I am. If you need anything, I can have three men over there in a matter of minutes."

If he knew anything it was that Rohn, Tyler, and Colton would be there for him if he needed it. Janie and Bonnie, too, if it was something that only a female could deal with. And hell, if it was worse than they could handle, there was the sheriff's department. He had friends all over town and he wouldn't hesitate to call in a favor.

"We're fine. I love you. Have a good night, Justin."

He drew in a breath to calm himself. "Love you, too. Good night."

Still determined that he could and would be able to handle any problems, even if he was miles and hours away, Justin pushed back into the hotel room with enough force to send the door slamming against the wall.

Phoenix let out a little yip as he startled her. She was standing by her bag not far from the door. No doubt she could hear anything and everything he'd said on the phone.

He only hoped she had enough good sense to keep any comments or opinions or, heaven forbid, questions to herself.

"You hungry?" It was a diversion to keep her from questioning him, though he actually was hungry.

"Yeah, sure. I could eat. It's about dinnertime anyway."
He nodded. "Let's go."
"Where?"
"We'll figure that out when we get there."
"Okay. Sounds good to me." She was on her best behavior.
"Good. Come on."

Chapter Seventeen

Phoenix watched Justin's stiff back ahead of her as he led the way to the truck.

He was wound tight as a drum, and she wasn't talking about his tight butt cheeks moving beneath the denim of his jeans as he walked. She could definitely see the stress he was under.

The question remained, why was he so stressed? She didn't know, just as she didn't know who had been on the other end of that phone call that had seemed to agitate him so much.

She climbed into the high cab of the truck for what must be the fifth or sixth time that day. The perplexing truck with the even more complicated man behind the wheel.

Why did he jump down her throat, and look as if he was panicking, all because she wanted to change the station on the radio? Did he have some sort of obsessive-compulsive disorder involving the radio? That wasn't the only odd thing she'd witnessed today. That phone call was also pretty mysterious.

Phoenix shot Justin a glance, not daring to ask all the questions pinging through her head. He was right. If she wasn't willing to tell him her secrets, she couldn't ask him about his.

"What?" he asked as he glanced in her direction. He must have noticed her staring at him.

Phoenix shook her head and tried to look innocent. "Nothing."

He raised a brow. "Didn't look like nothing."

She shrugged. "Not sure what you're talking about. I'm just waiting to see what this town offers for food. That's all."

"A'ight." Whether he believed her or not, he let the topic drop. After a few minutes had passed, he slowed the truck and finally came to a stop along the curb. "Here's a place. It's early, but they look open. Whatcha think?"

He turned in his seat and looked to her for an opinion.

Little did he know that Phoenix was so far out of her element, she couldn't even form an opinion about the restaurant.

She wasn't even sure what state they were in. Texas, maybe? She didn't think they'd crossed into Oklahoma yet. But they'd left New Mexico a while ago.

Traveling across the country. Staying in a cheap hotel room. With a stranger. A male stranger at that. It was all crazy.

The only travel she'd ever done was with her parents, and a couple of school trips. That was nothing at all like this little journey. Those trips were all very safe. Supervised. Well planned and laid out, minute by minute on an agenda.

Never had any trip been in a truck, with a radio she couldn't change, while pulling a trailer packed with the belongings of a woman who might possibly—no, most probably—was her birth mother.

She didn't know much of anything and Justin wanted her opinion on the restaurant? Had he asked her opinion on anything at this point, including if the sky was blue, she might hesitate. "We can give it a try. I'm not picky."

"No?" He looked skeptical.

"No." She frowned. The fact she was there with him at all was proof of that.

"A'ight. Then let's go on in and eat." His words sounded like a challenge.

Phoenix stiffened her back and reached for the door handle. "Fine. Let's go."

She stepped down onto the pavement. Way, way down because the truck, fuzzy radio stations and all, was very high.

Justin stalked around the hood of the truck and met her on her side of the vehicle. "Got everything out that you need?"

She had her purse, which had her phone and wallet inside. That was all she'd need for dinner. "Yup."

He nodded and spent a few moments locking the doors and then even pulling on the handle to check whether it was locked. She would have expected him to double check that the trailer was locked, because that's where Bonnie's belongings were, but he didn't.

More odd behavior.

The truck didn't look like anything special. Heck, he didn't even keep it very clean inside. She hadn't missed the can of chewing tobacco under the dash, even though she'd never seen Justin use any. That was in addition to some other odd things lying around that could easily be thrown out or at least stashed in the center compartment.

They walked into the place, which was oddly similar to the bar in Arizona where she'd first seen Justin.

Just inside the door, Justin moved to the bar, where two guys sat waiting, she guessed, for the two draft beers the female bartender was pouring.

"You serving food?" Justin asked.

"Sure are." The girl nodded as she slid the glasses in front of the two guys. "You want a table?"

Justin turned to Phoenix. "Table or bar?"

"Whatever you want is fine."

He hesitated for barely a second. "Table."

Phoenix didn't contradict him. "All righty."

"Can we just take a seat?" he asked the bartender, a bored-looking female who was probably wishing she was out with her friends rather than working.

"Yup. Menus are on the tables. Server's not in yet, but I'll come over and take your order."

"Thanks." Justin dipped his head in a nod, apparently oblivious to how the girl was checking him out. Phoenix hadn't missed it, though. Not that she could blame the bartender. Justin was a good-looking guy.

His hand on her lower back steering her toward a corner table caused a strange feeling inside her. Especially after she'd just been thinking about him as a man rather than just the source of a ride.

With him touching her, this felt much less like two people who happened to be eating together and more like a date.

She was being silly. He just wanted to sit in the back away from the other people so he was steering her in that direction. No big deal. Definitely not a date. That was crazy. He pulled out her chair and she repeated the this-is-not-a-date mantra to herself as she sat.

Her heart fluttered as she glanced up at him. "Thanks."

"Sure." He moved around to the other side of the table and pulled out his own chair, apparently unaffected by her adolescent reaction to a man simply acting like a gentleman.

He grabbed the menus from where they were stashed behind the ketchup bottle, the Texas Pete Hot Sauce, and the salt and pepper shakers made out of mini Corona bottles. He handed one to her. She took it and tried to digest what was written there.

Luckily, it wasn't too hard. There was the typical bar fare, mostly beef, and everything came with French fries.

She decided on a hamburger, figuring she couldn't go wrong with that. It was cheap and it would fill her up. Because this wasn't a date, she had every intention of paying for her own meal. Even if he was paying for their room. She decided to say something about that.

"Thank you for covering the room cost."

"Not a problem. Rohn told me to stop, and he gave me extra money for expenses." He shrugged.

"Well, I appreciate it anyway. So thank you."

"You're welcome."

The bartender came flouncing over. The girl took her time sashaying closer to Justin. "You decide yet?"

She'd asked him directly, but Justin looked at Phoenix. "Ladies first."

Phoenix felt quite a bit of satisfaction over his deferring to her. "I think I'm gonna have a cheeseburger. Medium."

He grinned. "Great minds think alike. That's my usual order. But since I just had that yesterday, I think I'll go with the homemade pot pie." He glanced at the bartender. "Is it really homemade?"

The bartender smiled at the extra attention she was getting from him. "Yes, sir. I saw the chef making it myself today."

"A'ight, then. We're set."

"Anything to drink?" Again the question was directed right at the object of the server's attention. Justin.

"You want something to drink?" Once again, Justin asked Phoenix for her order before he would place his own.

"I don't know. What are you having?"

"I'm having a draft. We're barely a mile down the road, so I figure I can have one."

"Um, okay. I'll have a draft beer, too. Thanks."

"Sure." The girl wasn't quite as receptive to Phoenix's thanks as she was to Justin's.

There was a small feeling of petty satisfaction that she was sharing a meal and having a beer with Justin while it was so obvious the girl was interested in him. Phoenix probably shouldn't feel that way, but she couldn't help it.

She watched the girl walk away toward the door of the kitchen and then turned back to Justin with a smile. "I think we make a good choice of places."

He laughed. "Not sure there was much more in this town to choose from. We'll see when the food arrives."

"At least the beer should be good."

"Let's hope. If it's cold, then it should be good." He watched the bartender, tracking her with his eyes as she headed to the bar and the taps before he frowned and focused solely on Phoenix. "Hey, did the service station ever call you about your car?"

"No. I didn't see a call." She'd forgotten all about that. And it was definitely something she couldn't let slide. She needed that car to get home so she could start school. "Let me check. Maybe I have a message."

She reached into her purse and riffled around for her phone. It was down deep at the bottom, but she finally connected with it. Setting it on the table, she punched in her code and looked for a new message alert.

"Nothing. And no missed calls either."

He extended his hand. "Give me."

"Um, okay."

"You have the number?"

"Yeah." She searched the bag again and emerged with

the battered but still legible cocktail napkin on which the bartender in Phoenix had written the number.

Justin took the napkin and punched in the number. "You remember the bartender's name from yesterday?"

"Um, Joe, I think? Maybe."

He nodded and then pressed the phone closer to his ear. "Yeah, hi. I'm calling about the yellow Volkswagen Beetle we dropped off for service this morning. We were told we'd be getting a call with an estimate."

He was quiet for a second, but she could see by the set of his jaw, he wasn't happy about what he was hearing.

"Uh-huh. So he didn't get a chance to look at it today." Justin shook his head. "Sometime tomorrow really isn't going to work for us. Um, does the owner happen to be there?"

He paused a few seconds before continuing. "A'ight, because Joe at the bar personally assured me that you guys could get the job done fast and at a fair price."

Justin paused again, then nodded. "I'd appreciate that. Yeah, that's the one. It's registered under Phoenix Montagno. Thank you."

He hit to disconnect the call and then laid the phone down on the table. He slid it back toward her. "They're putting it up on the lift now. A mechanic is gonna take a look at it and they'll be calling back with an estimate before close of business tonight."

"Wow. I doubt they would have done that for me."

"Because you're too nice." He smiled.

"No, because I'm female."

He shrugged. "Maybe."

"Probably. Definitely."

"A'ight. Fine. If I need to call a business where a woman would do better like, hell, I don't know, a beauty salon or something, you can do it for me. Okay?"

"Okay, it's a deal. If for any reason you need to call a beauty salon, I'll happily do it for you."

"Good." He grinned.

She was simply happy that he seemed to be in a better mood.

There were lots of mysteries surrounding this man, but if he was good, then she was, too.

The beer arrived and Justin thanked the server, which had the girl beaming as she turned back for the bar.

But it was when he lifted his mug in a toast and his eyes met hers that Phoenix's heart kicked into high gear. "One day down, one more to go."

She lifted her mug in a toast and then took a sip, even if the sentiment wasn't exactly true. "One more day for you. You'll be home tomorrow."

"And you'll be farther from home. I know." He nodded. "However, you'll be in the same town as Bonnie Martin, and I know—though I still have no idea why—that'll make you happy."

Would it? She still had no idea what she was going to say to the woman. It wasn't as if she could walk up and say, "Hi, Mom."

She was still considering that when Justin asked, "How long are you going to stick around Oklahoma?"

"I don't know how long I'll be staying. I do have to get back to California pretty soon. I have a couple of days, though."

"I guess you could look into taking a bus back to Arizona so you won't have to drive alone in a rental car. Or maybe take the Amtrak."

She didn't want to talk about leaving before she'd even gotten there. It was a lot to think about. Meeting Bonnie. How she was going to get home.

Then there was Justin—a small part of her would be

unhappy to think about never seeing him again. Though, if Bonnie was her mother, and if she wanted to build some sort of relationship between them, there was a chance she'd be coming back to Oklahoma again.

And those were a lot of *ifs* to get past. Not to mention the biggest one—if Justin was at all interested in seeing her again.

They got along pretty well, though. Forget about dinner dates or movies. Phoenix was beginning to see the best way to get to know someone was by traveling together.

Hell, if two people could survive a road trip, normal dating would be a breeze.

Chapter Eighteen

Feeling stuffed from dinner and a little sleepy from being so full, Justin pushed the door of the hotel room open. "It's not the Ritz, but . . ."

Phoenix followed him inside. "It's fine. Really."

"Well, it's ours for the night, so we might as well get comfortable." Justin realized that might have sounded suggestive. "You know, to get some sleep."

"Yup." She nodded.

Still not confident he'd defused the sexual tension he felt, he added, "Tomorrow's going to be another long drive."

"Mmm-hmm," she agreed, not moving from where she still hovered near the door. "So do you want to go in the bathroom first?"

"Uh, sure." Justin glanced at the bathroom. "Unless you want to get in there first? That's fine, too."

"No. I think I'll sort through my bag before I go in. I kind of just threw things in this morning. I have to, you know, find my toothbrush and stuff."

"A'ight. I'll go first." He turned toward the door and then realized he needed his stuff, too.

He couldn't come walking out of the bathroom wearing nothing but a towel. He turned back toward the bags he'd dumped by the door before they'd gone out to eat dinner and grabbed his, carrying it to the bed by the door. He paused before he put the bag down.

"You have a particular preference on the bed?" he asked, and then scrambled to add, "I mean which one you want."

He tried his best not to think about her preferences as far as what to do in bed.

"Nope." Phoenix shook her head. "Whichever is fine."

"A'ight. I'll take this one, then." He'd rather be by the door.

If anything went down, he wanted to be the one to deal with it first, not her. Yeah, he might be paranoid, but you never knew what could happen on the road.

He unzipped his bag and reached inside. His hand connected with a clean T-shirt, and though he never slept in a shirt, he took it out anyway, thinking tonight might be a first for him. He didn't think Phoenix would be comfortable with him being shirtless.

As he pushed a pair of socks aside and reached for his shorts, he had to wonder what Phoenix was going to be wearing tonight. That was a bad thought. He shouldn't be thinking things like that.

He found the bag he'd tossed inside that contained his deodorant, toothbrush, toothpaste, and razor. He grabbed the whole thing to take in with him. For some reason, he had the urge to shave. Why, he didn't know.

Dammit. He did know why.

It was because he was sharing the room with Phoenix.

Because he hadn't bothered to shave while he'd been in Arizona, he was walking around looking scruffy. His beard only grew in a little bit. That was one issue with having lighter-colored hair, unlike Tyler, whose hair was so dark brown it was almost black. Ty could grow a full beard in a couple of days, while Justin would only have sporadic stubble.

He was thinking too hard about all this shit. He didn't

have to make excuses. A man could shave when he wanted to, dammit.

Mad at himself, he grabbed the bag. "A'ight. I'm heading in."

"Okay."

Leaving her out there in the room, staring into her bag, he turned and closed himself into the bathroom.

He flipped on the shower and let the steam from the hot water fill the room before he realized the water was much too hot for him. He flipped the hot down and the cold up. It seemed he couldn't even manage to shower without messing it up.

That's what thinking with the little head did to a guy. He had to stop it. If not, he'd end up wrapping both his brother's truck and Rohn's trailer around a tree when he tried to finish the drive tomorrow.

Justin somehow accomplished an event-free shower, after which he shaved and managed not to even nick himself during it.

He brushed his teeth, slapped on some deodorant, and towel dried his hair. He did everything he normally did before bed and then that was it. He had no more reason to hide out in the bathroom, except that he wasn't sure he could handle it if Phoenix looked all cute and cuddly in bed. Or worse, if she looked sexy in some skimpy nightie. That would do him in for sure.

Crap.

Better to find out sooner rather than later either way. He gathered up his shit, tossed his towel onto the hook, and opened the door.

Lucky for him, she wasn't even undressed yet. That was a relief.

Instead, she stood next to the bed with her phone in her hand. She glanced up when he exited the bathroom. If he wasn't totally off base, she was looking pretty relieved that he was clothed.

"The service station just called."

Good. Something to talk about that he could sink his teeth into, and it had nothing to do with sex. "Yeah? What'd they say?"

"He thinks it'll be an easy fix. Some hoses or something. But he should be able to do it tomorrow, so it'll be ready whenever I get back there."

"Great. I'm glad to hear it."

He was happy the car was an easy fix. That was a no-brainer.

What surprised him was how odd he felt when he thought about her leaving. They barely knew each other. He liked spending time with her, but he sure as hell wasn't in the market for a relationship—not long-term and definitely not long-distance.

So why did he care if she left sooner rather than later?

It had to be because he needed to get laid. He was definitely thinking with the wrong body parts at the moment. That's what long periods of abstinence did to a healthy young man, he supposed. Sad but true.

He wrestled his focus back to his present dilemma. The two of them standing in a cheap hotel room with nothing to do besides the obvious things a man and a woman could do in a room with not much more than a bed in it. "Uh, so the bathroom is all yours."

"Okay. Thanks."

"Water's nice and hot in the shower. Good water pressure, too."

"Good." She nodded.

"Well, enjoy." Why was he babbling like an idiot?

"Thanks. I will." She grabbed her stuff and headed into the bathroom.

When the door finally closed behind her, he blew out a big breath.

Yup. It was going to be a long night.

He tossed his dirty clothes as well as his small bag of bathroom supplies into his duffel bag and then stood there, at a loss. If he'd been alone he would turn on the TV to see if there was anything decent to watch.

That sounded like as good a plan as any.

It took him a minute to figure out where the network stations were, and the movie channel, which surprisingly came free with the room despite the bargain price he'd paid. He flipped through a bit and finally settled on a sitcom that, stupid or not, made him laugh.

Some days back home, laughter could be a real lifesaver.

That thought reminded him of his mother. He dug into his bag and found the jeans he'd taken off. The phone was in the pocket where he'd left it. He took it out and laid it on the nightstand next to his bed so he'd hear it if she called or texted.

Thoughts of his mother brought to mind the conversation with his aunt. How she had told him his mother had gone to bed while it was still daylight without having eaten dinner.

That reminder of his depressing home life was enough to knock any ideas of Phoenix and her hot little body right out of his head. That was definitely for the best for everyone involved.

Chapter Nineteen

Amazing as it was, Justin managed to sleep somehow.

In spite of the soft sounds of Phoenix's steady breathing in the bed next to his, he'd eventually drifted off. Of course he'd also woken up with a morning hard-on so huge he had to wait for it to go down before he could take a piss.

Good thing it was still dark when he woke. He'd been able to hightail it to the bathroom without Phoenix seeing the tent in his shorts.

He did notice how she blushed when they bumped into each other while trying to pack up to leave the hotel. How she avoided making eye contact with him while they'd both been in their sleeping clothes. Not that she was wearing anything seductive. At least, her shorts and T-shirt shouldn't have been sexy, but in his current state of self-denial, seeing Phoenix in her sleep attire had nearly broken him.

Thank goodness the awkward night was over. That was one huge hurdle he'd gotten over, and he was more than happy they'd both made it through unscathed. Or at least untouched.

It was the dawn of a new day, and time to hit the road again . . . after a quick take-out breakfast from the fast food joint by the entrance to the interstate.

Finally, they were on the last leg of this eternally long road trip.

Even after spending a restless night passing in and out of sleep and haunted by thoughts and fantasies of Phoenix, he somehow managed to hold up his half of a casual conversation with her as he drove. She was easy to talk to, once he got his head on straight and stopped picturing her in positions he shouldn't be thinking about.

So far, the morning had consisted of long runs of conversation punctuated by bouts of silence as they both watched the scenery speed by.

It was during those long lapses of silence when Justin's mind began to wander. That's when it went to bad places regarding Phoenix. He tried his best to ignore that he was driving down the road fighting a hard-on just because she was sitting next to him talking about her job.

He had figured asking her about her teaching was a safe topic. He'd wrongly assumed that hearing her talk about her first-grade students would distract him from his naughty thoughts about her.

Seeing her in a professional light shouldn't make him want to pull over and take her right there in the cab of his brother's truck, but it did.

He imagined striding into her classroom after school was finished for the day, when all the kids had gone home and there was no one left except maybe a janitor sweeping the hallway. He pictured her sitting at her desk wearing a pair of reading glasses, which he didn't even know if she needed or owned. He'd haul her up against him, crush his mouth over hers, and then have his way with her right on top of the desk. Schoolbooks, papers, and all.

"Justin?"

"Huh?" He turned his head to see her before dragging his eyes back to the road ahead. She must have said something that required an answer and he'd been so deep into his fantasy, he'd zoned out and hadn't even heard her.

"Where's your head?"

He lifted one shoulder. "Nowhere. I'm sorry. I guess driving this long is kind of hypnotic."

"I know you don't want me to, but the offer still stands. If you need me to take the wheel for a while, I don't mind."

"I know, but no, thank you. I'll be fine." If he could keep his mind off her and him getting sweaty together.

She drew in a breath. "All right."

"No argument?" He shot her a look of surprise.

"Nope. I know the answers already. My car is small. Your truck is big. It's not your trailer. I got it."

He glanced in her direction in time to see her eye roll. "That's all true, you know."

"Yeah, I know. I just want to be of some help to you. You're doing me the favor of driving me all the way to Oklahoma."

"You are a help. You're keeping me company. That's keeping me awake and alert."

She let out a laugh. "I don't know about that. You didn't even hear what I was saying."

Because he'd been imagining hiking up her little teacher's skirt—Justin stopped that thought in its tracks.

"I just got some stuff on my mind." He glanced at her when she didn't respond. "I'm sorry. What were you saying before that I missed?"

"Nothing important." She hesitated. "I know something is bothering you. I could tell from that phone call you took last night. And I just wanted you to know if you want to— need to—talk about anything, I'm here to listen."

He lifted his brows. "That goes the same for you, you know. If you want to discuss Bonnie or whatever."

She rolled her eyes again. "I get it. You won't tell me

your secrets until I tell you mine. I know. We've been over this before."

"And yet I still don't know anything about what's really going on with you and Bonnie."

"And neither do I, about what's going on with you and whoever got you upset on the phone."

"Then I guess we'll both keep our secrets to ourselves."

"I guess we will." She turned to look out the window.

Justin shook his head. That little discussion had effectively put an end to the small talk. He saw that clearly as the miles passed and she remained silent.

"I was just calling home to check in on my mother and my aunt. Nobody answered the house phone or their cells or my texts and I got worried. That's it. It was no big deal." At least, the part he was willing to tell her was no big deal. He kept the rest to himself.

"Oh. Okay. I understand how you'd worry, being so far from home. It's scary when people don't answer their cell phones. Where were they? Why didn't they answer?"

"It turned out they were at the movies and had their phones on silent."

She shook her head. "See? Something so simple. Nothing to worry about, but just because we count on people being attached to their phones twenty-four/seven, we worry when they don't answer."

"Exactly." He smiled, pleased. She was back to her chatty self. That was good. There were too many miles left to travel for them to sit in stony silence. It was a risk, but he took it anyway and asked, "So I told you something about me. Your turn."

She shot him a sideways glance. "I don't remember making that deal."

"It was an unspoken agreement."

"Okay. Here's something about me. I have no clue what

I'm going to do when we get to Oklahoma. Not where I'm going to stay for the night. Not what I'm going to say to Bonnie Martin. I've got pretty much nothing."

"You've got me," he reminded her. "But I can't help if I don't know what's going on."

She sighed. "I know."

"I know a hotel right in the middle of town that doesn't charge too much a night. Does that help you any?" Justin asked.

She smiled. "Yeah. That'll help. Thanks."

He'd give anything to have his old apartment back. If circumstances hadn't made him move back home with his mother, he'd be more than happy to offer Phoenix a spot on his sofa for the night.

Yeah, right. His sofa.

He knew damn well he couldn't resist her for two nights in a row.

She sighed again. "I guess I'll have to rent a car to get around while I'm there."

Rental cars could be expensive if she didn't find a deal. It wasn't as if his small town had a rental place in it. She'd have to get the car from the city.

It took him about a second before he felt bad stranding her in town with no ride. "You can use my truck while you're in Oklahoma. You can't take it to Arizona, but you know, while you're in town just to get around, it's fine."

She turned in her seat to stare at him. "This truck?"

"No. My other truck." He could handle driving Jeremy's truck to work for a couple of days. He was getting used to it after this trip. He'd finally stopped being assaulted by the nearly debilitating memories every time he opened the door.

This trip had been good for something after all.

"Oh. Okay." She paused and then said, "Am I allowed to change the radio station in that one?"

He couldn't help but laugh. "Yes."

"All right. Thank you. I'll be very careful, I promise. I won't wreck it."

Justin snorted out a laugh at that. "I certainly hope not."

He might be obsessed with preserving Jeremy's truck, for obvious though most likely unhealthy reasons, but he was almost as careful of his own truck. He was still paying the bank for the loan on it, so it would suck if she did crash it.

"So, since I'm supplying you with a truck to drive during your stay, I think that should buy me one other piece of information. It's worth that, no? What do you think?"

"Oh, so this is a quid pro quo situation?"

Lucky for her, he happened to know what the little scholarly sprinkling of Latin in her snarky response meant. "Yes, it is. I give you something and you give me something in return. Come on. One fun fact about Phoenix. Or Bonnie. Or why you're so interested in my boss's fiancé. Anything you'd like."

"That's right. You told me Bonnie was engaged. Tell me more about her fiancé."

That fact was obviously of interest to her. "Not much to tell. She and Rohn got engaged this summer."

"Rohn, owner of the ranch where you work. Hence the Double L Ranch trailer filled with her stuff."

"Yup." He nodded. "I take it you don't know Rohn."

"No." That was all she said, though he could almost see the thoughts flying through her brain, she was thinking so hard.

He'd just about given up on getting that one more piece of information she owed him in exchange for the truck loan when she drew in a huge breath and turned in her seat to angle toward him.

"Can I trust you not to say anything? If I tell you a secret that has to do with Bonnie, even though she's engaged to your boss—heck, especially because she's engaged to your boss—will you promise not to say anything to anyone?"

This conversation had gotten real serious real fast. He wished they were having it anywhere else besides a moving truck where he had to divide his attention between her and the interstate.

Even though it looked as if he was about to get some answers, he wasn't sure he liked the direction they were going. "You'd be putting me in a sticky situation having to keep secrets from Rohn. Can I ask you why?"

What she was asking him to do wasn't a small thing.

Rohn had held his job for him when he'd been injured bronc riding and couldn't work for almost a month. He'd given him all the time he'd needed to deal with his brother's death and his mother's current problems.

His loyalty lay with the man who'd stood by him for the past few years, no matter how bad things got in his life.

"This information. It's not really mine to tell. It's a secret that Bonnie's kept for years. By all indications it's something she wanted to remain a secret. And hell, I'm not even one hundred percent sure she's the Bonnie Martin I'm looking for. Even if she is, maybe she's already told her fiancé. I can only hope she has, because if she hasn't and I just show up . . ." Phoenix let the sentence trail off.

He still didn't know what the hell she was talking about, but he did begin to see the enormity of whatever it was she was hiding.

This was obviously going to require his attention. He flipped on the signal, slowed the truck, and merged into the right lane. There was no place safe to pull off the highway, but he sure as hell didn't want to be driving in the fast lane when she sprung whatever it was she was hinting at on him.

Convinced he could drive the speed limit and not swerve

off the road whenever she made her big revelation, he said, "All right. I won't tell."

"Swear it."

He raised a brow at her demand, finally saying, "I swear on my father's grave, I won't tell your secret."

"Okay." After a second, she said, "I was adopted and I'm not certain, but I'm pretty sure . . . I think Bonnie is my birth mother."

Justin absorbed that information.

He didn't know enough about Bonnie to guess whether Phoenix's assumption was right or wrong.

Bonnie had appeared in Rohn's life only a couple of months ago. He didn't know if she'd been married in the past or if she had kids. He knew nothing about her life in Arizona other than the fact that she'd taught school there.

In fact, he'd only just learned that she and Rohn had dated in high school.

"I'm not sure why you're so worried. Even if it's true, what makes you think it would be such a huge secret?" he asked.

"Because it was a closed adoption."

"I'm not sure what that is."

"That means neither party, not the birth mother or the adoptive parents, and definitely not the child, is ever supposed to know the identity of the other. The official records are sealed. They're not supposed to be opened. Ever. Bonnie chose a closed adoption twenty-five years ago. That means she didn't want anybody to know."

"Or it means she just didn't want you to know. Not everyone else in her life."

"Thanks." There was hurt coloring Phoenix's tone.

"I meant, maybe she wanted you to concentrate on your future and not on your past."

"Aw. That's nice. I never thought of it like that."

He smiled. "Glad I could help."

"But as sweet as that idea is, I don't think that's the reason. If I'm right, she wasn't long out of high school and was about to start college when she got pregnant. There was no father listed, so she must have been single and alone. That's why I'm not sure she told anyone at all."

"I'm still confused. If the records were closed, how did you find out?"

"That's the crazy part. I had to apply for a duplicate birth certificate because I couldn't find my original—the one that listed my adopted parents—and when it came, it was a copy of the real original. The one from the hospital where I was born, instead of the modified one created after the adoption."

"Wow. Somebody screwed up."

"Exactly. It was from a hospital in Phoenix and had Bonnie Martin listed as my mother. No father. And I didn't even have a name yet."

"Did it have contact information for Bonnie? An address or something?"

"No. I Googled Bonnie Martin in Phoenix, Arizona, and found the address of the house where I met you."

"Phoenix, Martin is a pretty common name. It's not like, I don't know, Montagno." Justin hated to burst her bubble, but it was true.

"I know. That's why I don't know what to do. What to say. She could think I'm a nutcase if she's not the right Bonnie Martin."

"You're traveling halfway across the country and you're not even sure you're chasing the right woman?"

She sighed. "I know. It's crazy."

"No. It's kind of nice, you trying to find her."

"Even though she never wanted to be found."

"There is that." He cringed. "But hey, maybe she's changed

her mind over the years. Twenty-five years is a long time. Lots of room for second thoughts."

"But if it is her, she's moved on to a new chapter in her life. Maybe she doesn't want her new fiancé to know she had a baby out of wedlock and gave it up."

A memory hit Justin of Rohn saying that Bonnie had gone away to Arizona for college and they'd lost touch. If she'd gotten pregnant and carried the baby to term before giving her up, and she was trying to hide what had happened, it made perfect sense she wouldn't keep in contact with people from home or come back to visit during that time. She and Rohn would have lost touch.

Phoenix might be right. This could very well be something Bonnie wouldn't want Rohn to know on the eve of their new life together.

"Shit. This is tough."

"I know."

"Maybe it's not her." That wouldn't be the best scenario for Phoenix, but it sure would be the easier thing for Bonnie and Rohn and Justin, who was now the keeper of this secret.

"Maybe. But I looked her up on the ASU alumni site. I saw her picture. We look a lot alike."

Justin glanced at her again. Crap. She was right. They did.

Phoenix's eyes lit up. "You know her. Do you see a resemblance?"

He drew in a bracing breath. "You do have the same coloring."

And figure, right down to the cup size, though he'd never admit to Rohn he'd noticed.

"There's more. She's a teacher just like me."

"Yeah. She is." There was nothing concrete, but the circumstantial evidence seemed to be piling up.

"So what do I do?" Phoenix looked completely at a loss.

"I guess you get Bonnie alone and ask her. Privately, so

that if it is a secret and she doesn't want Rohn to know, he won't. That's her choice. Her right." As much as Justin hated doing it with every fiber of his being, he'd have to lie to Rohn, or at least withhold the truth.

"Okay." She pressed a hand to her chest. "But tomorrow, not today. I don't think I can do it today. I'm not ready."

"A'ight. I'll drop you off at the hotel before I bring the trailer to Bonnie's house. I'll stop by later with the truck. You'll just have to drop me home afterward."

Justin discounted having Tyler or Colton follow him over without a second thought. He didn't want to involve anyone else in the deception. The fewer people involved the better.

"I don't know how to thank you, Justin."

"Don't worry about it." He'd spent the whole trip trying to get her secret, and now that he knew it, he wished he didn't.

Chapter Twenty

"So, this is it. My hometown." Justin slowed the truck to the posted speed limit, which after being on the interstate for hours felt more like crawling. "What do you think?"

"I like it." In fact, Phoenix was pretty sure she loved it. The whole atmosphere.

It was a quintessential small town, right down to Main Street lined with mom-and-pop shops, just like on TV or in the movies. Nothing like where she'd grown up in California. There wasn't a Starbucks in sight.

Justin laughed at her response. "That's because you didn't grow up here."

"That's probably true." People rarely appreciated what they had in their own backyard. The old saying was correct that the grass was always greener on the other side of the fence.

"So I'll take you to the hotel first, then drive over to Bonnie and her mother's house?" His tone said that the decision was hers.

It was tempting to ask him to take her with him to meet Bonnie now. Justin would drive her wherever she wanted. She knew that. What she didn't know was if she was ready to confront Bonnie or this issue yet.

"That sounds good."

"Are you sure you're going to be all right here alone with no vehicle until I get back?" He shot her a look of concern.

"Of course. I'll be fine."

"We can stop and grab you something to eat first."

"Justin, you don't have to worry about me."

"If we pick up something, I won't. There's a sandwich shop in town. We can get something there. You don't have to eat it right away if you don't feel like it."

He'd thought of everything. Besides, she wasn't sure she could stomach a fast-food hamburger after having fast food for breakfast and a hamburger for dinner last night.

"A sandwich sounds perfect. Thank you."

They drove for about a mile before he pulled the truck into the lumberyard lot and shifted into Park. "The sandwich shop is right next door. Are you okay running over yourself? I don't want to leave the truck here in case I'm in the way, and I can't park this thing on the street."

"Don't be silly. Of course I'll be okay."

"I hope there's no line. The owner of the lumberyard is kind of nosy. I don't need him asking about the cute young thing riding shotgun with me."

His calling her a cute young thing had the blood rushing to her cheeks as she opened the door.

"I'll be as quick as I can." She climbed out of the high truck.

His comment had her practically bubbling over as she ordered her food from the teenager manning the counter.

She paid for the sandwich and the bottle of water—probably half what she'd pay for the same thing back in California—and returned to the truck.

There was no nosy lumberyard owner in sight as she

pulled open the door and climbed back inside. "Got it. Turkey, bacon, lettuce, tomato, and sliced jalapeno cheese."

Justin lifted a brow. "Wow. That sounds good."

He'd never shut off the engine, so all Justin had to do was shift into gear and drive in a big circle to get out of the lot.

"Anybody bother you while I was gone?" she asked.

"Nope. And I don't see Rod's truck so I guess he's not here. We got lucky."

Phoenix nodded. "Good."

Before she knew it, he was pulling into the entrance of a small hotel. The kind where each of the rooms opened up onto the parking lot. She looked at the slightly dilapidated long low building and felt alone. Justin hadn't even gone yet and she was feeling lonely.

She turned to him as he reached for the key in the ignition. "You don't have to park and come in."

He cut the engine and pulled the key out in spite of what she'd said. "The truck's fine parked here. I want to make sure you get checked in okay."

She glanced around the parking lot. She really doubted they were filled up. There were maybe three parked cars. "I'm sure there's a vacancy."

"I'm coming in anyway. Then I'll grab your bag and see you settled in your room before I go."

There was no fighting a gentleman. Phoenix was beginning to see that. She didn't mind. It was actually kind of nice.

As they walked toward the office, he said, "It might be a little while before I can get back. I have to drop off the trailer at the Martins' house, then go home and swap trucks."

"It's okay. They have HBO in all the rooms." She glanced from the sign by the road to Justin. "See, I'll have plenty to do."

"I'll give you my cell phone number before I leave. Just in case."

"Okay." That she'd have his number made her ridiculously happy, which was completely silly.

It made sense for her to have his number, just in case. There were any number of legitimate reasons why it would be totally appropriate to text Justin and for him to respond. But all she could think about was that knowing she could text him would make leaving less hard and tonight in the hotel less lonely.

In the office, she stepped up to the counter. "Hi, I'd like a room."

The man's eyes shifted to Justin. "King bed?"

"Uh, whatever. He's just dropping me off. I'm checking in alone."

The man looked skeptical at that but moved to start tapping on the computer. "How many nights?"

That was a good question. "Um, I'm not really sure. Definitely one, probably two. I don't know. Can we make it just for tonight for now and I'll get back to you in the morning?"

He sighed. "All right. But checkout is at eleven."

"That's fine. I'll decide before then."

"Parking a vehicle?"

"No. Well, not right now, but I will be later."

He slid a paper and pen toward her. "Fill this out with the make, model, and license plate number, as well as your name and address. And please initial by the rate."

She glanced at Justin for help. Justin leaned down and filled in the parts of the form that pertained to the truck, which had the desk attendant's brows rising.

He didn't believe Justin wasn't spending the night with her. She shouldn't care what the front desk attendant at some cheap hotel in Oklahoma thought about her, but for some reason she did.

"That it?" She slid the paper back after filling in her contact info.

"I just need a credit card and a photo ID."

"Oh, of course." In her distress over this guy's opinion of her, she'd forgotten all about paying. She slid the two items toward the man and turned back to Justin. "Sorry I'm holding you up."

He shook his head. "Don't worry about it. It's fine."

Finally, the man gave her back her card and ID along with a key card. "Room one-ten."

"Thank you." Grateful the check-in was over, she scooped it all up off the counter and spun on her heel. "Let's go."

Justin led the way, holding the door open for her as she stalked through.

The moment they were out of earshot, she spun to him. "I told him I was staying here alone and still he was behaving as if I was lying. Did you see that?"

He grinned. "Yes, I did."

"What are you laughing about?" Hands on her hips, she frowned at him.

"You, getting all embarrassed just because he figures we're staying here together and didn't want to admit it."

Her frown deepened. "But it's not true."

He shrugged. "It was last night. You and I shared a room. Remember?"

"Yes, but we didn't, you know, do anything."

"No, we most certainly did *not*." He put extra emphasis on the last word.

"I just think that considering he's in the hospitality industry, he should hide his opinions, no matter what they are." Phoenix stopped her rant long enough to process the tone of Justin's last statement.

Had he wanted something to happen between them?

Unaware of her inner turmoil, Justin continued, "Don't worry about it. You'll never have to see him again after tomorrow, so who cares what he thinks?"

He might have moved on, but her mind hadn't. Not now that he'd put the thought of their being together into her head. Whether he'd intended to do it or not, the idea was planted firmly.

He grinned wider. "I still think it's cute how flustered you are."

For the second time in less than an hour, Justin had called her cute. A girl could get used to that. She *was* getting used to it. To him. Everything about him. The gait in his cowboy boot swagger. The twinkle in his eyes when he teased her. The sound of his voice. The smell of him—a mixture of deodorant and good clean man.

Dammit, she definitely shouldn't get used to any of it. She remembered too late exactly how far California was from Oklahoma. It wouldn't matter that she had his cell phone number and they could text since they'd still be ridiculously far from each other.

And now she was thinking about sending texts to Justin. Hot ones, at that.

Sexting with Justin. Jeez, she definitely shouldn't be thinking about that.

It was a very good thing he had to get going to drop off the trailer. She needed to take a cold shower or something. She really couldn't have him in the room with her. It would be way too tempting.

And after he left, she was going to steer clear of any romance movies on TV. She didn't need some sappy chick flick putting more ideas in her head.

She already had plenty of bad ideas of her own.

Chapter Twenty-One

Justin got into the truck and drove away from the hotel before he changed his mind and decided to stay.

He reached for his cell and speed-dialed Rohn. The man answered on the third ring.

"Hey, Rohn. I'm on my way to Bonnie's house with the trailer."

"Okay, great. I was just going to call to see about your ETA. I'll meet you over there at her place."

"Um, I was planning on just unhooking and leaving the trailer in the driveway, if that's okay. I mean, I'll help you unload tomorrow if you want, but I kind of wanted to get home right away to check on Momma."

"Of course. You go. Do what you need to do. I think I'm still gonna head over to the house to take a look inside the trailer. I want to see what I'm in for. Was there a lot of stuff to move?"

Justin laughed. "Yeah."

"Was it a lot of furniture or mostly boxes?"

"A sofa, a recliner, a breakfront, a couple of dressers and mattresses. Some of the heaviest books I've ever had to lift." Justin let that all sink in before Rohn got any ideas that he was going to start unloading the trailer by himself.

Rohn groaned. "A'ight. We'll deal with it tomorrow. With the four of us working, it shouldn't take all that long."

"Nope. Not with all of us it won't."

"Thanks a lot for doing this, Justin."

"No problem at all. It was my pleasure."

Unloading the furniture was no problem. But the blushing sweet thing with the secret—the one in the hotel room with the king-size bed—yeah, she might be a problem.

"Will I see you in the morning or do you need a day to recover?" Rohn asked.

"I'm a little stiff and I'll be more than happy to get out from behind the wheel, but I should be good to work in the morning."

"I'll see you in the morning, then. Have a good night."

"A'ight. You too."

Justin made short work of backing into Bonnie's driveway. He didn't bother to even shut off the truck while he unhooked the stock trailer. Instead, he just hopped down and strode around to the back while the engine idled. He'd been hauling stock to rodeos for Rohn for long enough that he could uncouple a trailer from the hitch in his sleep.

Hell, after some trips he'd been so tired it felt as if he *had* been sleepwalking by the time they got back to Rohn's to unload the stock.

Hoisting himself up and sliding back behind the wheel, he was more than happy to be almost home so he could get out of this vehicle. He loved his brother and he loved this truck, but it had been a long three days of driving.

He'd have to get into his own truck and drive back to Phoenix and the hotel in a little while, but he'd be okay with that once he stretched his legs for a bit. Grabbed something to eat. Talked to his mother.

His anxiousness to get home had him driving through

town as fast as he dared. Not pulling the trailer anymore made it easier to speed.

He turned into the driveway shortly and was happy to see his aunt's car was still there so his mother wasn't alone. He parked Jeremy's truck off to the side so he'd be able to get his own out later.

Finally, he was home, and it felt really good to put his feet on the ground.

He went through the back door and tossed the keys onto the kitchen counter. "Mom? Aunt Phoebe?"

"In here." It was his aunt's voice he heard from the living room.

He walked in and found her seated alone on the sofa with the television on. There was a bottle of wine open on the table with two glasses beside it.

"Hi, Justin. How was your trip?"

"Long. Where's Momma?"

"She went to lie down. The wine gave her a headache."

He drew in a breath and let it out. This was why he needed to be around. His mother had a myriad of excuses to go hide in her room, to stay home and sit in the dark all day rather than go out. He knew they were just her way of covering up that she was too depressed to go out.

His aunt, however, was easier for his mother to fool.

And giving her alcohol? He wouldn't have done that. He knew from experience that even just a glass of wine wasn't a good idea. Drinking seemed to bring his mother down. He could watch the decline in her mood with every sip she took as old memories replaced present-day life in her mind.

Even so, he couldn't be ungrateful. His aunt had done him a favor, and though his mother was lying down in the middle of the day, at least she was home and safe.

That was all that mattered.

"Thank you for staying with her."

His aunt stood. "Of course. Any time. It was fun."

He couldn't imagine that was true if his mother had spent most of the time in bed. "I still appreciate it. It eased my mind knowing she wasn't alone."

"I know." She moved closer to press a kiss to his cheek. "You're a good son, Justin. She's lucky to have you."

"I guess." He hugged his aunt. "I'm going to throw something together to eat. You want to stay?"

"I think I'll go home. Get myself together, do some laundry before work tomorrow. There's leftover lasagna in the fridge you can microwave."

"Mmm. Thanks. I will."

His aunt disappeared into the den, which they used as a guest bedroom. Justin tried to forget that was because they hadn't been able to clean out Jeremy's old bedroom. It was still exactly as he'd left it. Like a shrine.

She returned with an overnight bag. "Tell your mom I'll call her tomorrow."

If she made an appearance any time before tomorrow, he would. "Will do. Drive safe."

"I will, sweetie. Love you."

"Love you, too."

She waved before pulling the door closed behind her. Justin sighed and moved to the coffee table. He grabbed the two glasses and the bottle. His mother wasn't getting better. It had been two years and, if anything, some days she was worse now than she had been shortly after Jeremy had died.

That thought left him needing to see for himself that she was okay. Leaving the glasses and bottle on the counter in the kitchen, he headed for the bedroom.

Easing the door open, he peeked inside.

The curtains were drawn shut and the room was dark except for the nightlight plugged into the outlet inside the bathroom just off her room.

Listening, he knew she wasn't sleeping. He could tell by her breathing.

"Mom, you asleep?" He kept his voice low so as not to wake her if he was wrong. He moved farther into the room. "I just wanted you to know I'm back from my trip, but I have to run out for a bit in a little while."

She rolled over to face him. "Okay."

"Do you mind? Do you want me to stay here and sit with you?"

"No. I think I'm just going to turn on the television for some noise and try to go to sleep."

He drew in a breath. "Okay. Aunt Phoebe left, but she's going to call you tomorrow."

"Okay, baby. Go do what you have to do. I'll be fine."

She always told him she was fine even when she wasn't. But he had no proof to the contrary, and he knew she would stay in her all night even if he were home.

He had to get the truck to Phoenix.

Fighting the guilt that he should be staying with her after having been gone for so long, he said, "Call my cell if you need anything while I'm gone."

"I won't need anything."

"Promise you'll call if you do."

"I will. I promise."

"A'ight. I'll be home later."

"Okay." She rolled over and pulled the covers higher around her. She was deep in her cocoon and there was nothing more he could do.

Tomorrow he'd get back on her to get up and dressed, to eat at least one decent meal if not three, and to get some good sleep—when it was actually night, not as a series of naps that spanned the whole day.

He rose from the bed and headed for the back door. He

grabbed his truck keys from the hook, spotting Jeremy's set lying on the counter.

Was he just as bad as his mother when it came to moving on with his life?

He hadn't let Phoenix change the damn radio station in Jeremy's truck. He must have seemed like a lunatic to her. And the napkin—he remembered her reaching down to the floor to pick up an old fast-food napkin she'd found there. She was going to hop out of the truck to throw it away. He'd grabbed it away from her and stashed it in the console rather than let her throw it out.

A paper napkin. All because Jeremy had left it.

His mother couldn't go on in the state she was in, but he realized that neither could he. He had to do something about his mother, though what that might be he had no idea. But as for himself, that was one change he could make. He was in control of his own actions. If he was going to make a change, it was up to him and him alone.

Jeremy had had no choice. His life had been taken away. But Justin was alive. Young and healthy. He could live life to the fullest. And he was going to, starting today.

Chapter Twenty-Two

The brisk knock on the hotel room door had Phoenix jumping off the bed and rushing to press her eye against the peephole.

She saw Justin standing there. Well, mostly just his chest and chin because he was so tall, but she knew who it was.

Frowning, she had to wonder what had him knocking so urgently. She reached to flip the safety latch and then opened the door.

"Hey, what's—?" She didn't have time to finish her inquiry as he backed her into the room and let the door slam behind him.

He cupped her face in his hands and leaned low until his lips were mere inches from hers. "Phoenix."

In shock, she managed to say, "Yeah?"

His eyes narrowed as he moved closer. "I've been thinking of doing this since last night."

He closed the distance, and then his warm lips were covering hers. Her thoughts focused on his words. He'd wanted to kiss her, just as she'd wanted to kiss him.

The amazing part was that they'd both been thinking the same thing. Thankfully, he'd done something about it when she hadn't had the guts to.

He deepened the kiss, pressing closer until she was up against the wall with him against her. She let out a sound that could only be described as half frustration and half satisfaction as she sank deeper into his kiss.

Justin pulled back just enough to lean his forehead against hers. He let out a breathy laugh. "I guess the front desk clerk saw this coming, huh?"

"Yup."

He groaned and pushed himself off the wall and away from her, putting some space between them so she could think clearly again. She didn't want the space. She wanted Justin's lips back on hers.

"You eat yet?" he asked, changing the subject.

"No. I took a shower and then I was looking for something to watch on television." She waved a hand in the general direction of the TV, playing along though there was no audience.

"I brought the truck for you." He hooked a thumb in the general direction of the parking lot.

"Thank you."

"You're welcome." He kicked at the carpet with the toe of his boot.

She watched him as his focus darted around the room. She could see the conflict inside him. "Why are we talking about everything except the obvious?"

He finally raised his gaze to hers. "Because I'm trying to get my head back on straight."

Phoenix moved closer and rested her hands on his chest. "I like your head just the way it was when you walked in here and kissed me."

He cocked one brow up. "You could have just as easily screamed, slapped me, and thrown me out the door."

"But I didn't."

"No, you didn't." He brought his right hand up to her

face and, cupping her face, ran a thumb across her cheek. "Why not?"

"Because I liked it." She rose up on tiptoe, putting her mouth within kissing distance of his.

He groaned and hauled her up against him with one hand pressed to her lower back while his mouth covered hers.

She was very happily kissing him when he broke contact to say, "Starting something when you're leaving so soon is stupid."

"I know. I don't care."

Apparently, he didn't care either. He slammed his mouth back into hers while lifting until her feet left the ground. He carried her to the bed and tumbled them both onto the mattress.

A distant sound she finally identified as Justin's cell phone ringing in his pants distracted her. He pulled away from her mouth and rolled off, just when she was really enjoying the weight of him on top of her.

"Shit. I'm sorry. I have to see who this is." He reached into the pocket of his pants and pulled out his cell. He glanced at the readout, then, after letting out a big breath, tossed it, unanswered, onto the bedside dresser.

"You don't have to answer that?"

"No. It's just one of the guys from work."

As if he could read the doubt in her face, he said, "I thought it might be my mother." He drew in a breath. "You know what, I should probably get back home anyway. She's there alone and I didn't say I'd be out long."

"Oh. Okay." Phoenix tried to hide the surprise that he was leaving her bed to go be with his mother.

She remembered his being concerned about her on their drive. She couldn't fault a guy for worrying about his mother, even if he did seem to worry an awful lot.

Coming from a girl who had two mothers, one she

had yet to meet, maybe she couldn't really judge what the appropriate amount of concern was.

He stood and adjusted the visible bulge in his jeans. "You won't mind driving with me back to my house and then coming back here on your own?"

She'd never been in this town before and had no idea where she was going, and she'd never driven a truck before. But if he was okay with it, she supposed she had to be. "Um, no. It's fine."

"A'ight." He stood and hovered by the door, and she guessed it was time they got going.

"Just let me put on some shoes and grab my room key and my bag with my driver's license." She was babbling to cover her shock.

He stood and watched her rush around the room. He was leaving all right, and anxious to get moving apparently, just moments after he'd kissed her lips swollen. Was it really because of his mother? Was there something else he didn't want to tell her? And was that really just his friend on the phone?

There was only one thing she was sure of, and that was that she'd have lots to think about tonight.

Make that lots to obsess over.

Chapter Twenty-Three

Justin didn't know whether to pat himself on the back or kick his own ass for the amazing kiss and amazingly stupid feat of dragging himself away from Phoenix.

He sat behind the wheel of his truck, driving back to his house while she rode in the passenger seat. That part was familiar at least.

"So it's basically one main road with just one turn to get to my house. When I get out and you're headed back, just turn back onto the main road and drive until you see the hotel." The least he could do was make sure she didn't get lost after driving him home.

"Okay," she agreed, even if she did look a bit concerned about it.

"You sure you'll be okay? I can call a friend to come pick me up if you're worried."

"No, I'll be fine."

He glanced at her. When he decided she would be all right, he moved on to the next subject. "So, tomorrow . . ."

She turned to look at him when he let the sentence trail off. "Yeah?"

"What are your plans?"

"I don't know."

"You'll have the truck, and there are plenty of places right near the hotel for you to grab something to eat." They both knew she was worried about more than eating, but he said it anyway.

She smiled. "You don't have to keep trying to feed me."

"I know." It had become a habit, he guessed. "I'll be heading over to Rohn's early. Right after sunrise for morning chores."

"Okay."

"Bonnie's been sleeping over at Rohn's because there hasn't been much furniture in her and her mother's house. But now that the trailer's there, I figure they'll both head over to start unpacking."

He glanced over and saw her biting her lip. She raised her eyes to meet his. "So you think I should go over there to meet her?"

Meet seemed like too mild a word for the situation. For what Phoenix was about to do.

"Maybe. Hell, I don't know." He shrugged.

"I don't know either." She sounded torn between being relieved to have company in her confusion and frustrated he didn't have any answers for her.

They'd almost reached the turn to his home. He felt the pressure to get everything settled before he cut her loose for the night. "When I get inside, I'll text you the address of the house Bonnie and her momma own. Let me know what you're planning on doing when you figure it out. Okay?"

"I will."

"And text when you get back to the hotel so I know you made it a'ight," he added.

"Okay."

He nodded and flipped on the blinker. Back to the directions. "So here's the turn. When you come out of my house and get to the corner, you're going to turn left to get back on the main road."

"That's easy enough. I think I'll be able to handle it. I'm just glad this didn't turn out to be some sort of huge monster truck. I was a little worried."

"Sorry. I should have told you what to expect. I wouldn't have offered if it was—" He glanced over and saw her smiling.

"I'm just teasing you. I'm fine." She sounded confident enough that he finally believed her.

"Okay. So this is it. Home sweet home." He slowed and pulled along the curb, threw the truck in reverse, and backed into the drive so she only had to drive straight out.

He put it in Park but left the engine running. It was too tempting to sneak her into his room and make out with her the way he used to when he was a teen. But this was a different time, and his mother a different person. "Be sure to let me know when you get to the hotel."

"I will."

He got out and stood by the open driver's window while she hopped from the passenger to the driver's seat.

"The adjustment for the seat is right under there." He watched as she moved the seat up until she could reach the pedals. "You good?"

"Good." She nodded, her hands on the steering wheel. "Thank you again for the loan of the truck."

"No problem. Don't wreck it."

"I won't." She hesitated before continuing, "Have a good night. I hope things are all good with your mom."

He dismissed her concern with a wave of his hand. "Yeah. It's all good. I've just been away for a while, you know?"

"I know." She nodded. "Okay, so I guess I should get back before it's dark."

"Oh, yeah. The lights are right here on the dash. And the high beams are on the directional." He waited while she looked where he indicated to be sure she could find everything.

Damn, everything would be so different if he didn't have responsibilities. He'd be deep in this woman by now, doing exactly as the hotel clerk assumed they'd be doing. Instead, he was sending her away, alone, and in his truck no less.

He pushed off the truck and took a step back. "Okay. You get going. Good night."

"'Night, Justin." She concentrated on shifting into Drive and then, with a wave, flipped on the blinker to turn out of his driveway.

He stood and watched until his truck was out of sight before he sighed and turned back toward the house.

He'd never gotten to eat, so that was first on the agenda. He cut off a nice-sized slab of the leftover lasagna and used a fork to lift it onto a plate. He put that in the microwave and let it heat while he went to the fridge to get something to drink. He grabbed a bottle of water even though after walking away from Phoenix he really needed a beer.

As the microwave chugged, heating the pasta, sauce, and cheese into a molten mass that had the kitchen smelling so good his mouth began to water, he heard his mother's bedroom door open.

Shortly after, she was standing in the kitchen doorway. "That smells good."

As if he was dealing with one of the horses at work, he didn't jump on her comment, though that's exactly what he wanted to do.

His mother being hungry, and taking the initiative not only to get out of bed but come into the kitchen felt so monumental, it was all he could do not to shove her into the kitchen chair with a plate and fork in front of her.

"I know. I love Aunt Phoebe's lasagna." He didn't ask her if she wanted any. If he did, she might say no.

Instead, he simply took the steaming, laden plate out of the microwave when it dinged and then reached into the cabinet for another plate. He cut the one slice into two and put half onto the second plate. After grabbing two forks from the drawer, he carried both dishes to the table and set them down.

Ignoring his mother as best he could, he dug into his own dish and worked to restrain himself when she sat in the chair opposite him and pulled the dish and fork closer to her. She took first one bite and then another.

He hid his smile behind a forkful of lasagna. Maybe things were going to be okay after all. He tamped down the hope, knowing she had good days and bad. If he expected nothing, he couldn't be disappointed. But for now, she was up and eating and that was a good thing.

The phone in his jeans rang for the second time in the past hour. Thinking it could be Phoenix, Justin stood and wrestled it out of his pocket to glance at the readout. He groaned when he saw the name Colton.

He glanced up to find his mother watching him. He tossed the phone onto the table unanswered. "Sorry about that. It's just one of the guys from work. Probably wanting me to go out tonight."

"You should go. You hardly go out with your friends at all anymore."

"But I just got home after being away. I thought I'd spend the night here with you."

She waved his offer away with the flick of one hand. "Don't be silly. There's a new episode of my favorite show on tonight and I missed the last one, so I figured I'd catch up and watch that before the new one airs."

"Yeah? What show?"

"You know the one set in England at the turn of the century?"

He smothered the groan that threatened to emerge. He hated that show.

"Yeah, I know the one you're talking about. Good show." His attempt to sound enthusiastic came out sounding less than stellar.

His mother actually smiled. The expression was so rare, it threw him, and he didn't know what to do or say next.

"Go out, Justin. Otherwise you're going to have to sit in the living room with me and watch two hours of a show I know will put you to sleep."

If he was lucky it would put him to sleep. That was the best-case scenario. Worst case, he'd actually stay awake and have to watch the show. That would require more endurance than he thought he had.

Still, he was reluctant to leave her, even in a good state. He lived in fear daily that he'd come home and find her curled up in a ball in her dark room. He always wondered if he could have prevented the downward slide in her mood if he had been here.

"I think I'll stay home with you."

"Justin." She put her fork down and leveled her gaze on him. She looked so much like her old self he couldn't help but hope there was light at the end of the tunnel. "Go out with your friend. Have fun. Act your age for once, instead of like an old man."

"Hey, I don't act like an old man." He feigned insult.

His phone beeped once. A text message. He glanced down and saw it come across the screen.

At the hotel. Safe and sound. I'm sure that new dent will come right out.

She'd signed it with a smiley face.

His heart sped. He wasn't in the mood to go out with Colton, but he sure was in the mood to see Phoenix.

"Your friend?" his mother asked.

Justin nodded. It wasn't a lie. After all the time they'd spent together, all she'd shared with him, it felt as if Phoenix was a friend. Of course, he'd like to make that friends with benefits.

He glanced across the table. "You sure you don't mind if I go out?"

"No. Now text back right now and tell them you're coming."

He smiled. "Yes, ma'am. I will." He picked up the phone.

Feel like company? I could come over to check out that dent.

He signed it with a smiley face himself, which was so unlike him, he nearly laughed.

The reply came back so fast it had him almost shaking with anticipation.

I'd love company.

He had to finish eating and set a good example for his mother. Then shower and grab clean clothes. But then . . .

Yeah, he couldn't think about then. He'd end up getting a hard-on right there in the kitchen. He punched in the text.

Be right over.

Putting the phone down, he picked up his fork. "So next time, you think you can convince Aunt Phoebe to make some meatballs, too?"

"Mmm, meatballs would be good. I'll do my best." His mother swallowed another mouth of food and Justin's mood soared. She was talking. Eating. Smiling.

The light at the end of the long dark tunnel seemed even brighter.

Chapter Twenty-Four

Justin was nervous, which was crazy. He wasn't eighteen. Far from it. He was almost twenty-eight and he'd been with more girls than he could count on two hands, and yet as he drove Jeremy's truck toward Phoenix's hotel, his stomach was jittery, his mind spinning.

He shouldn't start something with her when she was leaving so soon. He also shouldn't start something with her if she could be Bonnie's long-lost daughter, a secret Bonnie had possibly kept from Rohn for the past twenty-five years.

Complicated didn't even begin to describe this situation, or Phoenix, and yet Justin pushed his brother's truck past the speed limit to get to her.

With any luck, they'd both have a little fun and then he'd get her out of his system.

Of course maybe she'd just want to watch movies on television.

That might be better for everyone involved. It was insane to keep thinking and wondering and planning when he had no clue what she wanted.

Even if he had barreled into her room like a bull out of the chute and kissed her before, that didn't mean anything. He'd taken her by surprise. She'd had lots of time to think about it since that happened. Time to change her mind about inviting him back into her bed once he'd been dumb enough to leave it.

All because of that phone call. He sighed and realized he'd never gotten back to Colton.

Oh, well. He'd just tell him he came back from the road trip and fell asleep. Claim he was exhausted from the three days on the road, and that he hadn't heard the phone.

One more lie added to the pile he'd have to tell if Phoenix didn't get over her trepidation and confront Bonnie about the adoption sooner rather than later.

Before he knew it, he was at the corner before the turn into the hotel.

The sun was beginning to set behind the building, painting the sky with a splash of color as he flipped on his directional signal and turned into the parking lot.

He smiled when he saw where she'd parked his truck. She'd pulled all the way to the end of the lot, into a corner spot under a security light. This must be her city girl effort to protect his truck from dings or thievery.

Maybe it hadn't been as crazy or rash a decision to lend her his vehicle while she was in town. She was treating it with more care than he did on most days. He was still smiling about that when he knocked at her room.

She opened the door almost immediately after he knocked. Since he'd texted, he knew she'd been expecting him, so the speed with which she answered didn't surprise him. What was unexpected, and what he found very interesting, was that she'd changed into her nightclothes.

They'd spent the night in the same room yesterday, so he'd seen her in sleeping clothes already, but that had been unavoidable because they had been sharing a room.

Today was a different story, yet apparently she had no

qualms about getting comfortable with him. He liked that idea. A lot.

"Hey." Phoenix stepped back from the door to let him in.

"Hey." He echoed her greeting.

Too late, he thought how he should have picked up something on his way over. Beer. Food. Something.

Arriving empty-handed seemed rude, but as she raised her gaze to his and he saw the heat in her eyes, he had to think his hands wouldn't be empty long. They could be filled with Phoenix's soft curves. He'd be more than happy with that.

"I'm glad you came back." She bit her lip as she visibly struggled to maintain eye contact.

"So am I." He took a step forward and rested his hands on the spot where her narrow waist flared out to the hour-glass-shaped curve of her hips. She took a step closer in response. "Very glad."

He lowered his head toward hers, intent on getting back to where they'd left off, when she said, "Can you stay for longer this time?"

"Do you want me to stay?"

"Yes." She bit her lip after saying it.

"Then I'll try my best to stay." It sure as shit would take a lot to make him leave.

"Just your best?" She shot him a doubt-filled look as she teased, but Justin knew behind every joke was an ounce of truth. He couldn't blame her if she was insecure because he'd left before, but he knew one way he could reassure her.

"Mmm-hmm. Now hush up so I can kiss you." There were better uses for both of their mouths.

The crease of doubt and concern disappeared from her forehead as she leaned just a bit closer. "Okay."

That was easy. He leaned in and closed the final distance

between them, covering her lips with his as he ran his hands down lower.

The feel of the soft fabric of her shorts sliding over the bare skin of her buttocks sent a thrill through him, and he was happy she'd changed.

He breathed in the scent of her. She smelled clean and fresh, like bar soap and scented lotion. She must have taken advantage of the selection of tiny bottles that came with every hotel room, even cheap ones.

Tangling one hand in her silky tresses, he cradled her head as he kissed her deeper, all while he used his other hand to hold her tight against him.

She pulled back, looking temptingly aroused and breathless. She raised her gaze to his. "We can get into bed if you want to."

If he wanted to? Was she kidding? She couldn't seriously have any doubt. Not with the rigid length of his raging hard-on pressing into her stomach.

"Yeah, I want to." He lifted her easily and she squealed with surprise.

He carried her to the mattress and laid her on top of the covers. Since this time he had no intention of leaving, he sat in the chair by the bed and pulled off his boots. He let them drop, the heavy leather falling to the floor with two thuds before he stood.

She made a hell of a fine sight, leaning against the pillows, watching him move toward her. They'd been in this situation already once today. He still couldn't believe he'd had the strength to leave her then. He wasn't sure he would now.

"I've wanted you since Texas."

She smiled. "Really?"

"Yup." He planted one knee on the edge of the bed.

"Then why didn't you say anything?" she asked.

"I was stupid." He crawled onto the mattress.

He drew in a deep breath through his nose and let out a groan as he moved over her. Straddling her legs while kneeling, he ran his hands down her body, from her waist, over her hips, pausing at her thighs. "Man, I love these shorts."

A crinkle formed between her brows. "They're old and ratty."

Not ratty, as she called them, but they were old and soft, worn so thin he could see the outline of her perfectly through the fabric. All the parts he wanted to get his hands on were just beneath this cotton.

He held her hips in his hands, using his thumbs to trace small circles over the fabric covering her warm body.

"I like them, but if you don't, I'd be happy to take them off for you." He cocked one brow and watched her face.

"Okay." She breathed the answer, her voice full of need.

His mouth watering at the thought of what lay beneath, he didn't waste any time. Hooking his fingers beneath the stretched-out elastic waistband, he slid the shorts slowly down, over her hip bones and then lower.

She lifted her hips to give him the access he needed. His focus narrowed to one thing and one thing only—Phoenix and how he wanted to please her.

Tossing the shorts to the floor, he moved back and spread her legs wider. She drew in a sharp breath. Lowering his head, he got the reaction he'd been seeking when his mouth connected with her core.

He could do this all night if she'd let him. But he had a feeling they both had a few other activities in mind.

She drew in a staggering breath as he spread her with his thumbs and worked her with his tongue. Sliding two fingers inside her, he doubled his efforts as she raised her hips.

When she cried out the first time, he wondered if there was anyone in the neighboring room. That concern didn't make him ease up on her, though. In fact, the sound of her cries only intensified his motion.

By the time he felt her muscles convulse around his fingers, he couldn't care less how loud she was or who heard them.

She'd barely stopped coming when he was up and off the bed. Phoenix's eyes flew wide.

Breathless, she asked, "You're going?"

"Hell no." He reached down and began unbuckling his belt. He wasn't nearly done yet, but he paused with one hand on the button of his jeans. "Unless you want me to."

"No." She said it with such force he had to laugh.

"Good."

That would have been more than uncomfortable, driving home while he was harder than a sack of nickels. The denim containing him was torture. He felt sweet relief as he lowered the zipper of his fly.

She watched every move he made. He felt as if he was in some sort of strip show—a really bad one—as he shoved his jeans down his legs. The jeans caught on his socks. He kicked his feet free of the denim while reaching for the hem of his T-shirt.

With her eyes still on him, he pulled the shirt over his head and tossed it to the floor. That left him standing before her in nothing but slightly dingy white socks and navy blue briefs.

The socks had to go. He tried tugging them off while standing, hopping on one foot, and almost toppled over. He didn't miss the smile on Phoenix's lips as he sat—nearly fell—into the chair. He pulled the offending pieces of clothing off and tossed them.

Then there was nothing to prevent him from closing in on the bed, where he intended to show her that although he might have looked like a klutz getting undressed, he could be pretty damn smooth once he got horizontal.

Lying on his side on the bed next to her, he propped his head on one hand and rested the other on her stomach. She rested her hand on top of his and he felt the warmth of her palm against his skin.

She was still wearing her T-shirt. He'd dispense with that soon enough.

First he wanted—no, needed—to kiss her. He leaned low and brushed his lips against hers before sinking deeper into the kiss, thrusting his tongue against hers.

He couldn't kiss this woman without wanting more of her. He slid his hand up, pushing her shirt higher and feeling the silky smooth skin beneath it. He reached the plump flesh of her breast.

Brushing a thumb across her peaked nipple, he felt a shiver run through her.

That was before she started to do some exploring of her own. She moved her hand to the bare skin of his stomach and then slid beneath the elastic band of his underwear.

His breath caught in his throat when she made contact with the tip of his hard length. She moved lower, stoking his already burning-hot desire. It had been too long since anyone but he had touched his cock.

He should have been very happy as she held him in her hand and stroked him, but he didn't want foreplay. He wanted her. All of her.

Groaning, he threw one leg over hers. He pulled his mouth away only long enough to wrestle her shirt over her head. He wanted them skin to skin. She must have shared his desire. She shoved at his briefs, pushing them down as far as she could reach.

Smiling, he decided that even as hot as it was to have her stripping him bare with her own hands, it would speed things along if he helped. He wiggled his legs out of the briefs and then there was nothing separating them.

He kissed her mouth before moving to tug her earlobe between his teeth. "Want you."

She hissed in a breath. "Want you, too."

That was all he needed to hear. In a move that was worthy of an Olympic gymnast, Justin managed to twist his torso and reach back with one arm to grab his jeans off the floor, all while his lower half stayed happily pressed against Phoenix.

Once the pants were on the bed with him, he felt inside the pocket, pulling out a condom.

Her brows rose as her eyes zeroed in on the small square packet he held between his fingers. "You carry those around, do you?"

Uh-oh.

Snarky questions such as that, at this stage of the game, were like a penalty flag on the field. It put an immediate stop to his forward momentum.

"No. Not usually. I put it in my pocket when you texted that I could come back over. Wishful thinking, I guess." He was scrambling to find a way to fix the mess he'd made, simply by being prepared. Then he noticed the corners of her lips tip up in a smile, confusing him more.

"Justin, relax. I'm only teasing you." She grabbed the packet from his hand and pushed him onto his back. He landed on the mattress with a bounce.

This woman was real good at keeping him on his toes. She continually surprised him. The changes and revelations were enough to give a man whiplash, but he couldn't be upset by that. Not with her straddling him, naked.

Justin wouldn't have been able to tear his gaze away from her even if he'd wanted to as Phoenix tore into the wrapper with her teeth.

She covered him with the latex sheath. When she lowered

herself over him, her warmth engulfing him slowly, completely, he threw his head back, pressing into the pillow.

Eyes closed, he basked in the sensation of being surrounded by her. He settled his hands on her hips as she set the pace. He could get into letting her be in control. He usually liked to be the one running the show, but letting her lead was damned nice. It almost made him forget what a stupid decision it was to do this with her.

Almost, but not quite.

As he opened his eyes and her gaze captured his, all the reasons they shouldn't be doing this fled. He couldn't think of a single one.

Chapter Twenty-Five

Justin was still breathless. His chest, slightly damp with sweat, rose and fell beneath Phoenix's cheek when he said, "I really hope you're not Bonnie's daughter."

Surprised by that comment, Phoenix lifted her head from where she rested it against him so she could see his face. "You do?"

"Yeah." Justin cringed. "That sounded really selfish and I'm sorry. But it's true."

"I'll forgive you, but only if you tell me why you feel like that."

"Besides how it would be more than a little awkward that I just had sex with the secret daughter of my boss's fiancé, you mean?"

She couldn't help but smile at his joking as she lay back down on his bare chest. "Yeah, besides that."

Justin lifted one shoulder beneath her head. "I'm afraid of what it will do to Bonnie and Rohn's relationship. He was alone and lonely for so long."

"Why?" she asked.

"He was married for a long time. Like fifteen, maybe

closer to twenty years, I think. But he hadn't even really dated anyone since his wife died of cancer five years ago."

"Wow. Five years is a long time. I mean for a man who was used to having a woman in his life for decades. Being alone for that long must have been hard."

"I know. And I understand his needing time to heal." Justin let out a breath. "Believe me, I understand, but it was more than that. It seemed as if he was like a . . . shadow during that time. I mean, he was there but not really. Like he was going through the motions but not really living. You know?"

"Yeah." It was easy to understand what Justin was talking about. He spoke with such emotion. Such empathy for the loss Rohn had experienced.

Justin was a surprise. She knew he ran deeper than he let on, but he liked to hide that part of himself. Hearing him talk about Rohn's loss, she felt as if she could see inside him. She saw at least hints of the parts he usually hid.

"But what the hell do I know?" He lifted one shoulder. "I only know it made me feel good to see that he came out of it. And I don't want to see him go back into the shadows again."

Phoenix's heart broke for the man, even if she had yet to meet him. Hearing Justin talk about him with such concern and conviction made it feel more personal, more pertinent to her. And if Bonnie turned out to be her mother, and she married Rohn, they'd be connected.

She could only imagine what it would feel like to lose someone she'd dedicated her whole life to. How her father would feel if he lost her mother. Though he wasn't the kind to gush romance, she knew he and her mother were tied together. They were partners for a lifetime and either one would feel the loss of the other keenly.

"But you said he's better now?" she asked, needing the reassurance that Rohn was okay.

"Oh, yeah. From almost the moment Bonnie came back to town. All of a sudden he's like a new person. He redecorated the house. For the first time in a long time he seems . . . happy. And now they're engaged and going out on dates. It's like he's a teenager again."

"That's great."

"Yeah, it is. But if she didn't want him to know about the baby, I mean about you, but he finds out, what then? That is if she's your mother at all, which she might not be." He drew in a deep breath and let it out. "Damn, this shit is confusing."

"*Pfft*. Tell me about it." Phoenix lifted up on one elbow so she could see him when she said, "But I can't leave without at least meeting her."

"I know. And I want you to meet her. I just hope it all works out for everyone when you do."

"So do I. Believe me, so do I." She blew out a breath. "As long as we've suddenly gotten so serious . . ."

He frowned. "Uh-oh. That doesn't sound good. What's up?"

She smacked his chest with one hand. "Don't look like that. I just wanted to say, I know this was a one-time thing, so I don't want you to worry, or get freaked out and avoid me."

"Nuh-uh. I wouldn't do that . . . I can't. You've got my truck." He grinned, earning him another smack.

"Don't kid. You're the only person I know in town and I have a feeling when I go to meet Bonnie, no matter how it works out, I'm going to need a friend. I don't want to think I've lost your friendship because of this one time."

He frowned deep. "I'm a little concerned."

"About this?"

"I really don't like how you keep repeating that *one-time* business. Because looking at that clock over there, I see that I've got time for at least one more time. Possibly two."

Phoenix rolled her eyes. "Can't you be serious for even a minute?"

He'd flipped her over onto her back before she knew what had happened. He hovered above her, his face close, his weight pressing her into the mattress.

"I'm gonna be there for you, Phoenix. I promise. I'm too invested in this to abandon you."

His words had her heart thundering. "You are?"

"Yeah. Rohn, Bonnie, you, me. Like it or not, we're all tied together now. That happened the moment I told you where to find Bonnie and agreed to drive you here. Your confiding your secret to me only sealed the deal."

"Oh." She did her best to hide her disappointment when she realized Justin wasn't invested in her, just in the mess of her life that she'd unfairly involved him in.

"Stop frowning." He focused on her forehead and brushed his thumb across what were no doubt some unattractive wrinkles. "And stop worrying."

"I'll try." Sex changed things. She knew that. But if he wasn't worried about it, she'd try not to be.

"Try harder." Smiling, he lowered his heard toward hers. "I'll help you."

He closed the final distance and pressed his mouth over hers. He kissed her thoroughly enough to take away some of the worry.

By the time he'd eased his hand down her body and between her legs, she couldn't remember what she'd been concerned about in the first place.

Chapter Twenty-Six

It had been a long time since Justin had woken up next to a woman. A very long time. So long, it took him a few seconds to figure out what that warm, soft body was doing pressed up against him in the dark.

He might have been confused at first, but he sure as hell wasn't unhappy about the situation. In fact, parts of him were very, very happy indeed. One part in particular was perfectly satisfied being pressed against Phoenix's backside.

Damn, he missed waking up like this.

He didn't bring girls back to his mother's place, and he'd been living with her since Jeremy's death.

On the road, the few times he let himself take an overnight trip with the boys to the rodeo, it would have been a bit awkward while sharing a room. Besides, he wasn't really into buckle bunnies. He was too old for the eighteen- and nineteen-year-olds who dressed up to scoop a cowboy.

But this, right here, was very nice.

Sex with a friend. He hadn't done that in—the more he thought about it, the more Justin realized he'd never done that.

He'd had girlfriends, but they'd been just that, girlfriends, not friends. But he and Phoenix had moved into the friend territory.

Friends with benefits, actually.

Very, very nice benefits, which he wouldn't mind partaking of some more now.

He nuzzled her hair as he drew her closer to him. They were so close together their heads were on one pillow. His arm was around her as his legs tucked in behind her bent knees.

They'd been spooning in their sleep. He'd never been a spooner in the past. But it seemed that even in his sleep he hadn't wanted to be too far from the warmth of Phoenix's body.

Actually, that shouldn't be a surprise. After two bouts of some damn good sex last night, it was no wonder he'd woken up raring to go and seeking out her warmth again.

He wondered what time it was. He should leave, go home and check on his mother.

Maybe checking his phone would be good enough.

Crap, being interested in a girl was turning him into a bad son. Probably one reason he'd avoided serious relationships these past couple of years.

But friends with benefits could be a different situation. At least while Phoenix was still around. If he could drag himself away from her long enough to check on Momma and get to work.

Not quite yet, though.

He compromised with himself. He'd check his phone and look at the time, and if it was as early as he thought it was, and if there were no messages from his mother, he'd start this day off right with a little help from his friend.

Grinning at his idea, he angled to reach back for the nightstand, trying not to disturb Phoenix in the process.

Swiping his hand blindly across the surface of the side

table, he finally felt his phone. He closed his fingers around it and pulled it to him. In the dark, he hit the button and the screen lit, making his little section of the room bright as day.

He cringed, hoping the light wouldn't wake Phoenix up as he checked for a text. The screen was blank.

He chose to take that as a good sign. No news was good news. He'd check in with his mother later, but for now, he needed something else more than he needed reassurance. He saw the clock readout. There would be time for one more taste of her. Smiling, he reached back and replaced the phone.

Ironically, he hadn't wanted to wake her with the glaring light from the cell, but he had no problem nudging her awake with the tip of his morning hard-on. Sometimes a man had to make a choice. Besides, he'd never mind being awoken for sex, no matter how late or how early it was.

He wrapped his arms around her and pulled her closer, smiling when he heard the soft, sleepy groan rumble through her and vibrate against him.

"What time is it?" she asked.

"Very. Early." He reinforced each word with a kiss against her ear.

"Then why are you awake?" There was a smile in her voice as she asked the question.

"I can't help it. A situation arose." He gave his hips a tiny thrust forward and felt the laugh vibrate through her. He grinned as he teased her further. "Circumstances beyond my control."

"Yes, I see." She snuggled more closely against him. "You're awfully chipper for the crack of dawn."

"Actually, the crack of dawn is still about an hour away. Which is very lucky, because when the sun comes up I'll have to leave and get to work."

"What the hell do you do for a living that you have to start right after dawn?"

He laughed. "Spoken like a true city girl. Ranching starts early, darlin'. There are animals to be fed and watered and turned out. Horses to be broke. Fences to check and repair. Hay to cut and haul and stack. There's equipment to maintain and fix when it breaks. We got fields to plow to prep for next season—"

Phoenix held up her hand. "All right. Okay. I get it."

He grinned. "Just answering a question, but if you're done talking, I got something else in mind to do."

"Oh, do you?"

"I do." He rolled her over. "At least I'm up for it, if you are."

She laughed. "I see you're *up* for it. Are you sure you have time?"

"Oh, yeah." He smiled, loving that she could take his joking and give it right back to him. But the time for talking was done. His ideas for this morning's predawn activities relied less on conversation and more on cardio. Phoenix was the best way he could think of to raise his heart rate.

It wasn't until they were sweaty and breathless a long while later that Justin had the opportunity to look at the time again.

"Shit. It's late." Justin flipped back the covers and swung his legs over the side of the mattress. Standing, he looked at the mess of clothing on the floor. He kicked his jeans to the side, trying to find his underwear and socks.

Phoenix watched from the bed. "I warned you we wouldn't have time."

"Oh, hush up. No one likes a know-it-all." He leaned down and pressed a quick kiss to her lips before he sat on the edge of the bed so he could pull his socks on. "So, you decide what you're gonna do?"

"Yeah. First I'm going to go to the office and tell hopefully a different desk clerk I'm keeping the room for another night."

He glanced back at her. "You are?"

"You think it's a mistake?"

"Hell no. I was just wondering."

"Well, the guy fixing my car said it's no problem to keep it there a few days until I can get a bus back to Arizona."

He nodded, happy she was thinking about alternate modes of transportation so he didn't have to worry about her driving a rental car all that distance alone. "A'ight. That's good."

"And I really don't want to rush this thing with Bonnie."

"What's your plan on that front?" He stood to pull on his underwear, not missing how Phoenix's eyes followed the move.

"I want to meet her. Today."

Bending to grab his jeans, Justin stopped in midmotion. "How you reckon you'll go about that?"

Her expression had him wary even before she said, "I was hoping you'd help me."

"Help you how?" Crap. He was already in this thing too deep. There was no getting out of it now.

"Maybe text me when Bonnie is alone. Without Rohn. So I can approach her without an audience. Unless you think that's a bad plan."

There didn't seem to be any good plan in this situation. Her idea was probably the least undesirable. At least if Bonnie was alone, and she wanted to keep her secret from Rohn, she'd have the option—the freedom—to do so.

"No. It's fine."

"So you'll text me?"

"I will." He tucked in the T-shirt he'd pulled on and buckled the belt on his jeans. "But now I really gotta git. Okay?"

"Yeah."

He leaned on the bed, close. "You sure you're gonna be okay here?"

"Yes."

"Okay." He had to hurry if he wanted to get home, then to work. Maybe he should take today off, as Rohn had suggested.

"Justin, stop worrying."

"I'm not."

"You are. I can see it." She ran a finger over his forehead. "Go. I'll be fine."

"A'ight." He pressed one hard kiss to her mouth before straightening. Grabbing his phone, which he put in his pocket, and his hat, which he shoved on his head, he glanced back at her. She looked all too tempting on the bed.

He moved to the door, regretting every step. "I'll text in a bit."

"Okay." She looked so serious he thought she was going to say something else, but all she said was, "'Bye."

"'Bye. Don't wreck my truck." He grinned as he unlocked and opened the door.

She smiled. "I'll try not to."

He closed the door behind him. Leaving her was harder than he'd thought and he was only going to work.

How the hell was he going to feel when she headed west? He didn't even want to think about that.

As he unlocked the door of Jeremy's truck, he told himself all these feelings must be caused by the sex. He'd gone too long without. Now that he'd had some again, it was messing up his head.

The certainty of her leaving made all these feelings damned inconvenient, if you asked him.

Chapter Twenty-Seven

Justin peeled into the driveway of the ranch, shooting gravel from beneath his tires as he went. It had already been a hell of a morning, and theoretically his workday was just beginning.

"Crap." He breathed the cuss beneath his breath. Both Tyler and Colton's trucks were already parked by the barn. He didn't need to be the first one there, but he'd hoped he wasn't going to be the last to arrive. He was late and he knew it. His one hope had been that one or another of his coworkers would be later.

But he had done Rohn a favor, driving all the way to Arizona, so he should get a pass from his boss. It was the other guys who were going to give him shit. He knew that with certainty, right down to his bones.

He'd just cut the engine of Jeremy's truck and swung down to the ground from the driver's seat when Tyler came out of the barn.

"Welcome back. And you're late."

"Yeah. And you were late two days last week. So?"

Tyler grinned. "What can I say? Janie made me late."

"Don't blame Janie." Justin knew Tyler, and there was no way Janie was responsible for his being late.

This was just Ty's way of rubbing it in his face that he had a woman in his life to make him late while Justin and Colton didn't.

For once, Justin had a female making *him* late and he couldn't say a word about it. He just had to stand there and take the razzing. Though memories of the night before took a bit of the sting out of it.

Colton came out of the barn. "Hey, you're back."

"Yup." Justin braced himself for more questions and comments from his other buddy.

"I wasn't sure you were home yet when you didn't get back to me last night."

Justin cringed. "Yeah, sorry. I was beat from the drive."

Not exactly a lie. The drive was a bitch, but he'd managed to overcome the exhaustion with a little help from Phoenix.

"We already took care of the morning feeding. You're welcome." Tyler scowled.

"Thanks." Justin rolled his eyes at Tyler's making a big deal out of throwing some feed and hay at the stock. He wasn't even that late. It was just that by the time he'd driven home from the hotel and spent a little time with his mother to make sure she was doing all right, he was later than usual. "And FYI, Rohn told me I could take the morning off if I wanted, and I said I'd come in anyway, so lay off."

Tyler made a point of looking up at the sun. "Looks to me like you did take the morning off."

Justin drew in a breath and held back his annoyance. The only person whose opinion he gave a damn about was Rohn, and as luck would have it, Justin spotted him coming out of the house.

The older man headed toward the group standing by the barn. "Hey, I see you made it in."

"Yeah. Sorry I'm a little late."

Rohn waved off Justin's concern. "I told you to take whatever time you needed."

"Thanks." Justin shot Tyler a look and then brought his attention back to Rohn. "We unloading the trailer?"

"That's the plan. I went over yesterday and took a look. It was all I could do to keep Bonnie and her momma from starting. They're chomping at the bit to pretty up that old house. I had to get creative to keep them from it last night."

"Oh, really? Whatcha do?" Tyler waggled his eyebrows suggestively.

Justin cocked a brow. He could come up with a few ideas of creative ways Rohn could occupy Bonnie, but not her momma, too.

"Not what you're thinking. I took them out to dinner and made sure we weren't done until it was too late to be unpacking anything."

"Aw, that's no fun." Tyler grinned, probably knowing he was annoying Rohn and enjoying every moment of it.

Rohn raised one graying brow. "Whatever. And I'll ask you to stop talking shit about Bonnie. She's my future wife, thank you."

Rohn's future wife. For the dozenth time in as many hours Justin hoped that if Bonnie had given up a baby for adoption twenty-five years ago, it wouldn't change things for her and Rohn.

"So, are we heading over to Bonnie's house or what?" Justin decided to move this little party to town.

The sooner they got the truck unloaded, the sooner Rohn and the guys would go back to the ranch, leaving Bonnie at the house so Phoenix could talk to her.

Colton turned to Justin. "You in some kind of hurry?"

"Hell no. If Rohn wants to pay us to hang around and shoot the shit, that's fine with me." Justin folded his arms and leaned back against the fence rail, settling in for the long haul.

As Justin had hoped, that kicked Rohn into action. He turned on a bootheel and headed for his truck, glancing over his shoulder as he walked. "Come on. Justin's right. Y'all got a full day of work ahead of you after you get that truck unloaded, so let's get going or you'll be here half the night finishing up."

"What? Hey." Tyler's brow furrowed.

"Hush up. You know he never sticks to the shit he threatens. He'll probably let us go early." Colton followed Rohn, Tyler scowling next to him as they walked.

Justin jogged to catch up to Rohn. "We taking one truck over?"

"We better take two. I might stay to help the girls and send you three back to work."

"Oh." Justin was going to have to play it by ear regarding Phoenix's plan. If Rohn stayed with Bonnie, she'd have to wait.

"Justin can ride over with me. Ty and Colt, you two can follow us over."

Colton nodded. "Got it. We'll meet you there."

Justin followed Rohn to the truck and climbed into the passenger seat. They were barely out of the driveway when Rohn turned to him. "So, that truck must've treated you okay on the trip because you're still driving it today."

Rohn was referring to Jeremy's truck. The one Justin had, before this trip, only driven once a month or so when he was feeling low and missing his brother. The man had noticed that Justin was using it now.

Justin nodded. "Yup. She ran just fine."

What else could he say? This wasn't the time or place to discuss how he was trying to get himself over the mental hurdle of what that truck represented to him. How, healthy or not, it had become some sort of shrine to his brother.

And Justin sure as hell couldn't get into the quagmire of the Phoenix and Bonnie saga, or why a strange woman he'd just met was currently driving his truck. Or how this mysterious woman, whom he was having sex with, could be Bonnie's love child.

Nope. Justin wasn't touching any of those topics with a ten-foot pole.

It wasn't a long drive from Rohn's ranch to Bonnie and her mother's place. It had been Bonnie's father's farm back when she was little, but he'd sold off most of the fields right before he died. All that was left was the house and some acreage.

The trailer was in the driveway, right where he'd left it parked the night before. Next to it was Bonnie's car.

He glanced over and saw Rohn smiling and wasn't sure why until he looked at the house and saw Bonnie standing in the front doorway. Just seeing the woman he loved put a smile on the man's face.

Bonnie was smiling, too, as she lifted her arm in a wave.

They were so happy. The perfect couple. And Justin was the keeper of a secret that could ruin all that.

He felt as if he was sitting on a bomb that could go off and blow Rohn and Bonnie apart.

Would it? Would Rohn dump Bonnie for keeping the pregnancy from him? Justin couldn't predict that.

It had all happened twenty-five years ago. Maybe it was such a long time, it didn't matter to Rohn. Maybe they'd already broken up before she got pregnant so he wouldn't care. Hell, maybe he was already dating Lila by the time Bonnie had Phoenix. And maybe Phoenix had the wrong Bonnie Martin altogether.

It was enough to make a man's head spin, which was the

perfect reason to stop thinking about it, so Justin said, "Let's go. I'm ready to get to work."

Rohn was already opening the driver's side door and stepping down onto the driveway as Bonnie walked toward the truck. They were like two magnets. Whenever they were near each other, they moved closer together.

He sighed, wondering what that felt like. He'd never been that in to a woman. At his age, it was probably strange he hadn't found the one yet. Then again, every generation lived longer and longer. How could he be expected to recognize the woman he'd still love at ninety years old when he was in his twenties?

What Bonnie and Rohn had found in their forties was more likely to be a relationship that would last. Justin didn't have to worry that he hadn't fallen head over heels for a woman. He had time. Years more before he settled down. And until then, his new friends-with-benefits thing with Phoenix made him pretty happy.

Everything except for the secret part. Hopefully that would be over soon and everything would all work out. Armed with that hope, he followed Rohn toward the house.

Bonnie was in Rohn's embrace by the time he reached them. She pulled away to say, "Justin, I can't thank you enough for going to get all our stuff."

"No problem at all. My pleasure." He waved away her thanks and glanced at the open doorway of the trailer. "You started unloading on your own."

"I saw that." Rohn shot Bonnie an unhappy glance. "Even though I told her to wait for us."

Colton pulled his truck up to the curb with Tyler in the passenger side.

Bonnie eyed the new arrivals. "And I told you that you didn't have to bring the whole crew over just to help us unload."

"Sure he did," Justin defended Rohn in a show of male

solidarity. "I might have stacked the light boxes on top, and I see you moved those already, but the rest is man's work. Some of those boxes are heavy, and the furniture is much too big for less than two or three men. No gentleman is going to let you struggle with that. My momma would tan my hide if she knew I let you even try."

Bonnie smiled. "Spoken like a true gentleman. Thank you, Justin."

Rohn frowned. "Hey, when I said you should let the men do it, you called me a chauvinist, not a gentleman."

"You said it like a chauvinist. Justin said it like a gentleman."

Rohn shook his head. "Take my advice, boy. Don't fall for a teacher. You'll never win an argument again. They'll talk their way around you every damn time."

Justin smiled. Phoenix was a teacher and yeah, she could talk her way out of pretty much anything. He'd already seen that. It was one of the traits he found as endearing as it was annoying. He could definitely commiserate with Rohn.

Bonnie smiled at Rohn. "Thank you, sweetie."

He rolled his eyes. "It wasn't a compliment."

"Sure it was." She patted his cheek. "Let me tell you which rooms we're going to want the furniture moved to."

"Yes, ma'am. Let me grab Ty and Colt so we all know where we're going. It'll save some steps and confusion."

"Good idea." She glanced at Rohn. "See. He's organized and a gentleman."

Rohn cocked a brow. "Do I need to be jealous of Justin? Because I have to say, I don't know if I can compete with a young buck like him."

"Sure you can, Rohn." Justin laughed. "Maybe not in all things, but in some things. Age and wisdom and all that."

Rohn lifted his brows. "Thanks, I think. Okay. Let's all take this planning tour of the house and get moving before

Bonnie here starts complimenting Tyler and Colton, too, and I start getting really jealous."

Justin couldn't help but smile as Bonnie stood on tiptoe and pressed a kiss to Rohn's lips before she turned and winked at Justin. "Gotta keep him on his toes."

He laughed, but in the back of his mind a certainty was beginning to form. Bonnie's laugh. Her smile. Her eyes. It was like looking at Phoenix but older. All he could think was *shit*. This woman had to be her mother.

He could only hope that would turn out to be a good thing.

Chapter Twenty-Eight

Phoenix must have paced across the narrow expanse of the room and back again dozens of times.

Waiting for something was never easy. Waiting for the text from Justin that would tell her the coast was clear for her to drive over to meet the woman who was possibly her mother was unbearable.

She'd entered the address of Bonnie Martin's house into her phone and had gone over the route she'd have to drive from the hotel so many times she'd memorized it.

That was probably a good thing. She was nervous enough about driving Justin's truck, on top of being worried about the encounter with Bonnie. At least she wouldn't have to think too much about directions.

But if Justin didn't call or text soon, she would surely lose her mind.

Phoenix's cell phone rang, startling her out of her stress pacing. She dove for the nightstand and let out the breath she'd been holding when she saw the name on the caller ID.

"Kim. Hey."

"Hey. What's wrong?"

"I'm just waiting for a call."

"And not mine, I'm assuming, judging by your tone."

"Sorry. I'm just a little out of sorts." Meeting your mother for the first time did that to a person, Phoenix supposed.

"Everything okay? When I didn't hear from you, I started to worry."

"No need to worry. I'm kind of in a holding pattern, but I think I'm going to get to meet her today."

"Your birth mother?" The excitement was evident in Kim's question.

"Yeah, or at least the Bonnie Martin who I think is my birth mother. Remember, that has yet to be proven."

"Yeah, I know." Kim sighed. "I hate that you're doing this all alone. I wish I was there with you."

"I know. It's okay. I understand." Besides, until a few hours ago, Justin had been there to keep her company.

He'd kept her mind—as well as other things—occupied. But since he'd left, the waiting had been really getting to her.

Kim was right. Phoenix could use a friend right about now. But at the same time, she was so distracted, it was difficult to even keep up her half of the conversation.

"So what's the plan? What are you waiting for? You got there yesterday, right? I figured you'd have met her by now."

"I'm trying to catch her alone. Just in case I'm a secret or it's not her. I don't want to accuse her of giving me up at birth in front of her friends and family only to find out she's the wrong Bonnie Martin."

"Yeah, that is a tough situation. But how are you going to know when she's alone? Oh my gosh, you're not staking out her house, are you? Dammit, I always wanted to go on a stakeout."

Phoenix laughed. "Don't worry. You're not missing any stakeout. I'm in the hotel room waiting. Justin's going to text me when the coast is clear."

"Justin, huh? And how is tall, dark, and cowboy?"

Phoenix rolled her eyes. "He's not dark. His hair is so light brown it's practically blond."

"That's all you have to say about him? To correct me on the color of his hair? How about some other information? Like how you and he worked out this plan together. How he has your cell phone number now so you can keep talking to him when you come home. How you're in a hotel room in a town where no one knows you, which is the perfect setting for some wild sex."

"You've been reading too many romance novels."

"And maybe you need to read some, too, if you let a hot guy drop you off and drive away."

"Who said I did?" Phoenix regretted it the moment she said it.

Kim reacted as expected, drawing in a huge breath and squealing. "Oh my God. You had sex with him? You tell me everything right now."

"No."

"No, you didn't have sex, or no, you won't tell me about it?"

Phoenix sighed. "No, I don't want to tell you."

"Oh my God. You tell me right now. I thought I was your best friend."

"It's just so not like me. Having sex with a man I've only known a couple of days. One I'm not even dating." She whispered the words, even though there was no one there who could hear her.

"So what? He's a nice guy. You probably spent more hours with him on that drive than you would have on half a dozen dates. I mean live a little. Once you get married and settle down there'll be no more partaking of the single-man buffet, you know."

Phoenix laughed. "I don't see anyone asking me to marry him anytime soon, so I don't think I have to worry."

"We'll see," Kim said, sounding smug. "Maybe Justin is that guy."

"Yeah, right." Phoenix's thoughts turned back to Justin, and his waking her up this morning in his creatively enticing way.

Truth be told, she'd be happy to turn in her all-you-can-eat man-buffet privileges to settle down with one guy. With him. But right now, she'd be happiest if he'd just text to tell her the coast was clear. After that she could think clearly about her future.

The phone pressed to her ear vibrated in her hand. She pulled it away to glance down at the readout. There was a new text. "Kim, I gotta go. He's texting. It could be about Bonnie."

"Let me know what's going on—"

"I will. 'Bye." She barely let Kim finish her sentence, let alone say good-bye back, before she'd disconnected the call and checked the text.

Not easy but I got Rohn away from the house. You don't have long. Go now!

Her mind reeling with questions, Phoenix grabbed her purse and headed out the door. How long did she have? Half an hour? Less? She should have already driven over and parked the truck somewhere nearby so she'd be closer. Now she had to waste time driving to Bonnie's house.

She did her best not to drive too fast. That was the last thing she needed, to put Justin's truck in a ditch because she wasn't being careful.

Even after memorizing the directions, the actual drive

looked much different from behind the wheel of Justin's big truck than it had on her cell-phone screen in the maps app.

She almost missed the road and had to flip on the directional signal and swing into the turn much too fast. Miraculously, she managed the maneuver without getting into an accident. It was only luck or good driving on the part of the guy in the car behind her that prevented a crash.

Heart pounding, she blew out a breath and slowed the truck now that she was off the highway and on the side road, the road that Bonnie's house was on.

It wasn't the near miss of the accident that had her pulse racing. It was how close she was to Bonnie's house. She watched the numbers on the mailboxes count down the brief moments remaining until she met the woman who could be her mother.

The excitement inside her warred with the guilt she felt because she already had a mother. The one who'd raised her. Who loved her. Who had no idea she'd even left California because Phoenix had been ducking phone calls and lying to her parents for days. She should have been upfront with them to begin with, but she'd known what they'd say.

The very practical people who'd raised her would have talked some sense into her. Reminded her that Bonnie Martin had wanted her identity to remain a secret and she should respect that. Pointed out how many Martins there were in the world and how low the chances of finding the right one were.

How in the world was she going to admit all this to her parents?

She couldn't deal with thinking about that. First, she had to get this meeting with Bonnie over with. Then she'd worry about her parents.

The Double L Ranch trailer parked in the driveway caught her eye first. She should be familiar with it after having been inside the truck that had towed it from Arizona to Oklahoma. After seeing that, she didn't really need to check the address but she did anyway, confirming that the street number on the mailbox matched the one Justin had given her.

This was the place. No doubt about it. Especially when a blonde woman ducked out of the doorway of the trailer and glanced in the direction of the street, where Phoenix realized she'd just stopped in the middle of the road. Good thing there was no traffic.

It was now or never. Feeling light-headed with nerves, Phoenix pulled forward and parked Justin's truck along the curb. She cut the engine, took a bracing breath, and opened the door.

In true Okie small-town fashion, Bonnie was already walking toward her, smiling. It had to be Bonnie. Phoenix recognized her from the photos she'd found online.

Bonnie shaded her eyes against the glare of the bright noonday sun as she wandered toward the end of the drive. "Hey. You lost? Can I help you find something?"

"Um, yeah. Actually, I'm looking for you. Are you Bonnie Martin?"

"I am."

Phoenix took the final few steps to close the distance between them. That put her in the shadow of the trailer. Bonnie stepped into the shade as well and lowered the hand shielding her eyes.

"I'm Phoenix Montagno." She watched for a reaction and realized she wouldn't get one from Bonnie.

The closed adoption had worked both ways. She wasn't meant to know Bonnie's name, just as Bonnie wasn't meant to know the name eventually given to Female Martin by the adoptive parents.

An older woman came out of the house. "Bonnie, do you know where the box cutter got to?"

Bonnie turned and shook her head. "No. Sorry, Mom."

Mom. If Bonnie was her mother, this woman was her grandmother. The older woman came closer and stopped dead at the sight of Phoenix.

Phoenix's gaze cut between the two women opposite her before she said to Bonnie, "I was hoping I could speak with you for a moment. In private."

Bonnie's mother pressed a hand to her chest, her eyes pinned to Phoenix's face. "Good Lord, Bonnie. She looks just like you at that age." Her words were spoken to Bonnie so softly they were barely audible, but Phoenix caught them.

Emotions clouded Bonnie's features as she reached back and grabbed her mother's hand and then said to Phoenix, "Whatever you wanted to say, you can say it in front of my mother."

Now that the opportunity had arisen, she didn't have the words she needed. Coming right out was probably the best way. It felt as if her heart was lodged in her throat as she said, "I'm looking for the Bonnie Martin who gave me up for adoption twenty-five years ago in Phoenix, Arizona. Was it you?"

Bonnie glanced at her mother before nodding. Her eyes glistened with tears. "How did you ever find me?"

"I know it was a closed adoption and you didn't want to be found."

"No. That's not true. I mean, at that time I needed it to be closed. But I've thought so much about you this year. I didn't know how to find you. And now you've found me." The tears spilled over onto Bonnie's cheeks.

Bonnie's mom was crying, too. "It's a miracle."

Phoenix wasn't raised by people who believed in miracles. Just cold hard facts. "Actually, it seems like more of a clerical error. I lost the amended birth certificate my parents got at the adoption. When I applied for a duplicate, they sent me a copy of the original by mistake. The one with your name on it."

Some overworked, probably underpaid clerk had made the mistake that had brought them together, but it didn't matter how they'd been reunited. The point was that they had been.

"That sounds like a miracle to me." Bonnie smiled through her tears. "Phoenix. I love what your parents named you."

"Thanks."

"Heck, if you're not going to ask, I will. Can I hug you?" Bonnie's mother stepped forward.

Phoenix laughed, her own tears making her vision fuzzy. "Sure."

While in the older woman's embrace, Phoenix heard her say, "I'm Tammy. I'm your grandmother."

"I don't have any living grandparents from my adopted parents."

"Well, you have a grandmother now." Tammy pulled back and reached for Bonnie. "Come and hug your daughter."

Bonnie nodded, her tears streaming freely now. "I'd love to."

Chapter Twenty-Nine

Justin glanced down and checked his cell phone. No new text from Phoenix.

In fact, nothing at all since he'd texted her that it was safe to go over to Bonnie's house. Not that it had been the optimum time, but he didn't see a better one coming.

It hadn't been easy, but he'd convinced Rohn that they should all grab lunch at the barbeque place before the guys headed over to the ranch to work and Rohn went back to help Bonnie and her mother at the house.

It was no problem to get Tyler and Colt to agree to sit down and eat some smoked brisket. But keeping Rohn from getting the order to go and bringing it back to Bonnie's had been a challenge.

Rohn checked his own phone where it lay on top of the picnic table next to the remains of his lunch. "I guess we should get going."

"Yup. I reckon we should, before all that food I ate makes me want to take a nap." Tyler reached across the table to gather up the garbage while Colton stood to toss his empty pop can in the recycling bin.

Justin panicked. How long had they been gone? Was it long enough for Phoenix to have talked to Bonnie?

He glanced up at Rohn, who was now standing. "Sit and relax for another minute, Rohn. You know once you get back to the house Bonnie is only going to put you to work."

"Yeah, I know, but I've been away too long already. Bonnie and her momma will be waiting for the lunch I promised to bring 'em. I said I'd be right back and that had to be over half an hour ago."

Justin cocked a brow. "The term *whipped* comes to mind, but a'ight. I understand."

Tyler and Colton chuckled as Rohn leveled his gaze on Justin, who was still seated, hoping everyone else would give in and do the same. "No, you don't understand. But you will one day. Now if you're done eating, I gotta get back, and you three have work to do at the ranch."

He'd convinced Rohn to take them all to the restaurant in the ranch truck because it had the extended cab, figuring he'd have more control over Rohn's movements if the man couldn't go anywhere without the rest of them. But apparently, he couldn't stall any longer. Or maybe he could.

"A'ight." Justin stood. "Let me just hit the head here before we go."

Rohn frowned. "You can't wait until we get back to Bonnie's?"

He pressed a hand to his gut. "You really don't want me using Bonnie's bathroom, Rohn. I'll be right back."

Rohn cringed. "A'ight. Just get done and be quick."

"Sure thing, boss." Justin grabbed his cell off the table and headed for the restroom. He didn't have long, but long enough to text Phoenix a warning that they were on their way back.

Phoenix had no idea how many lies Justin had told in the name of her secret. He only hoped it wasn't going to be a secret for much longer. The situation was starting to wear on him.

He texted her that they were on their way back and shoved the phone in his pocket, heading out to the truck before Rohn got annoyed and left him there. He could only hope he'd given her enough time.

"You ready?" Rohn leaned against the truck, arms folded.

"Yup." Justin strode to the passenger side door and swung it open. He glanced over the hood at his boss. "Come on. What you waiting on?"

Rohn rolled his eyes at Justin. The best way to keep Rohn distracted was to annoy him. Tyler had demonstrated that often enough. Justin was happy to see it worked just as well for him.

Hiding his pleasure, he waited for Tyler and Colton to climb into the backseat before he slid into the passenger seat.

The barbecue joint wasn't far from Bonnie's house, but it felt like an eternity today as Justin waited for the house to come into sight. Justin saw immediately that the truck he'd loaned Phoenix was parked on the side of the road.

She was still there. And there was no way anyone was going to miss her connection to Justin. He shot a look at Rohn next to him.

Rohn looked at the truck and frowned. "How'd your truck get here? Is your momma driving it?"

Crap. "Uh, no. Momma has her own car."

Colton leaned forward from the back. "Then how did your truck get here while you were with us?"

"I, uh, loaned it to someone."

"You what?" Tyler grabbed the back of Justin's seat and leaned forward, joining Colton in the inquisition. "I asked you to borrow it last year when I was waiting for that part and my truck was out of commission and you said no."

"I know."

"What the hell, Justin?" Tyler's frown was deep.

"I'm sorry. I wasn't comfortable with driving Jeremy's truck."

"I'm thinking it's more your lack of mile-long legs and C-cup boobs, Tyler." Colton's stare was pinned on Phoenix, who stood in the driveway with Bonnie and Tammy.

All three women looked toward the truck as Rohn pulled it slowly into the driveway. Rohn threw the truck in Park and cut the engine before he turned to Justin. "Who's the girl?"

"She's the one I told you about. The one who was looking for Bonnie at the house in Arizona."

"The one I thought might be a student of hers?"

"Yeah."

Rohn glanced back toward the driveway, taking a closer look this time. He reached blindly for the door, his eyes never leaving the women as he stepped down.

Justin scrambled to get his own door open. He ran around the truck and looked on as Rohn gazed at Phoenix, and his eyes widened. Rohn and Bonnie made eye contact. There was a question clear in his expression. Bonnie nodded, tears streaming down her face.

Justin let out a cuss under his breath. Things were coming to a head and fast.

Tyler and Colton didn't take long to join him. "What the hell is going on? Why is Bonnie crying?" Colt asked.

"And who's the girl driving your truck?" Tyler added, still obsessed with the stupid truck and totally missing the point.

Rohn braced one hand on the hood and the other on his hip as he blew out a big breath. Finally, he straightened and said, "She's my daughter."

Phoenix was Rohn's daughter? Suddenly, it all started to click. Bonnie and Rohn had dated right before she left for Arizona for college. She'd given up the baby in Arizona.

The thoughts spiraled fast through Justin's head at the revelation. He'd spent the night getting sweaty with his boss's daughter. *Shit.*

Tyler frowned. "Wait. She's your *what?*"

"Whoa." Colton blew out a big breath. "Holy shit."

Rohn didn't seem to hear Tyler's question or Colton's exclamation. Instead, he strode to Bonnie and drew her into his arms. At least Rohn didn't seem unhappy about it. Or angry. Just shocked.

That was understandable. Justin was pretty shocked himself.

Phoenix glanced in Justin's direction. He saw the tears in her eyes and mouthed, "You okay?"

Smiling and crying at the same time, she bit her lip and nodded.

Relieved, Justin sagged against the truck. It had already been a hell of a day and it was only noon.

"I'm still confused." Tyler folded his arms and turned to face Justin. "You wanna explain to me how Rohn suddenly has a daughter and what you're doing with her?"

"Nope. Not really."

Colton pressed his lips together and moved from staring at the reunion in the driveway to Tyler and Justin's standoff. "Do I need to go pick up a twelve-pack of cold ones for this?"

Justin could only think that a little alcohol right about now couldn't hurt. But instead, he said, "Maybe we should give them some privacy and go back to the ranch."

He didn't want to leave, but he wasn't sure he wanted to be there either.

"Seriously?" Colton opened his eyes wide.

"Yeah. It's none of our business."

"I hate to say it, but I think I agree." Tyler shook his head. "Look at Rohn. Now he's crying right along with the women. I really don't think he's gonna want us here for this."

"Okay. Let's go." Colton fished his keys out of his pocket. "We telling him we're leaving?"

Justin watched Rohn wipe his eyes as he hugged Phoenix. "No. He'll figure it out."

If he noticed they'd left at all.

Chapter Thirty

In the whirlwind of the family reunion in the driveway, Phoenix hadn't gotten to talk to Justin. He'd left, she assumed to go back to work at the ranch because he'd been with two other guys at the time.

She didn't know, but she wished he was there with her now. There was so much to tell. So much had happened in so short a time.

Bonnie was her mother and Rohn was her father. She'd never expected that twist. To have them both there was overwhelming and amazing at the same time.

Though she didn't know the events that had led to her birth or her adoption, her existence wasn't a secret anymore. Justin had been worried that her being there would break up Rohn and Bonnie's relationship. She'd worried that herself, once he'd mentioned it.

Thank goodness it hadn't. In fact, the news seemed to make Rohn and Bonnie incredibly happy. She was pretty happy herself.

After the teary scene in the driveway, they'd all gone inside. The house was in shambles, but it didn't matter as Tammy, Rohn, Bonnie, and Phoenix sat at the kitchen table.

They'd tried to talk, but it turned out there was just a lot of crying—the joyful kind.

It was going to take everybody a bit of time to get over the surprise and process it all. Phoenix had had a week to get used to the idea that she'd found her birth mother, but Bonnie and Rohn had been blindsided.

They wanted her to stay at the ranch, but she'd already paid for the hotel room for the second night. Besides, she needed a bit of space to get her thoughts together. And of course the privacy would be nice should Justin come over again.

They wanted her to stay for longer, but that was impossible. Besides the fact that she was still avoiding telling her parents where she was, school was starting shortly. And she still had to get back to Arizona to retrieve her car from the service station. Short of flying to Phoenix, which would cost a small fortune on such short notice, that trip wasn't going to be fast even by train or bus.

Then she still had to drive to California—not to mention decide how she was going to tell her parents she'd searched for and found her birth mother and father. She'd feel better doing that sooner rather than later. Lying didn't sit well with her.

They'd all finally agreed she would go to the ranch for dinner with Rohn, Bonnie, and Tammy that evening. First, she wanted to go back to the hotel, shower, and change. A nap would be good, too, because she hadn't gotten all that much sleep the night before.

Memories of why that was had her thinking of Justin. He'd be wondering what was happening, she was sure. She picked up the phone and punched in his number.

He answered on the second ring. "Hello."

"Hi. It's me." She was still so overwhelmed by everything, it was nice to hear his now familiar voice.

"What's going on?" he asked.

Phoenix let out a breathy laugh. "A lot."

"I can imagine. Did everything go okay?"

"Yes. Rohn's my father."

"Yeah, so I heard. He seemed shocked, but pretty happy about it when I left. Things good in that area?"

She knew what he was asking. Was Bonnie and Rohn's relationship going to survive this revelation? She was pretty confident when she said, "I think things are pretty great. We spent like an hour sitting together, just catching up. When I left them, they were all hugs and smiles."

The sight of Bonnie and Rohn holding hands at the kitchen table had warmed Phoenix's heart.

Her adopted parents loved each other, but they weren't the type to show their affection. Maybe they had been years ago, when they'd been dating. She didn't know.

She had to remember that Rohn and Bonnie were newly engaged. That could explain the public displays of affection and why they were both practically bubbling over with love for each other.

It made her think things she shouldn't—like how it would be to have that kind of relationship herself with Justin, who lived across the country from her.

Though maybe her dating a man in Oklahoma wasn't such a stretch after all. Not now that it appeared as if Bonnie and Rohn wanted to be a part of her life, and she theirs.

She pictured herself visiting them a lot—and seeing Justin.

"So they invited me over to the ranch later for dinner." It was a hint, but she wasn't sure he'd pick up on it.

"That's great."

"Will you be there?"

"I'm actually driving home right now. Rohn called to tell

us we could leave early because we helped Bonnie with the truck."

"Oh."

"Phoenix, from what I saw today, you'll be fine without me at dinner." He must have heard the disappointment in her voice.

"I'd be better with you there."

He laughed. "Well, thanks. I'm honored you think so. I gotta get home and check on my mother. Spend some time with her."

She wasn't sure what to think of how dedicated he was to his mother. It was kind of sweet—a guy who loved his mother so much and spent so much time checking in on her.

On the other hand, it seemed kind of excessive. To the point that he couldn't do anything until he checked in on her.

The last thing she would have thought of Justin—so tough and manly—was that he'd be a momma's boy, but the evidence was there.

"Can I call you later, after dinner?" she asked.

"Of course you can. I wanna know how things go. Hell, I'm dying to know what was said today. He—uh—mention me?"

Realization began to creep up on Phoenix. "Oh, I get it. You're worried my new daddy is going to guess you and I spent last night together."

"Maybe. A little bit. So, did he?"

"They did want to know how I got to Oklahoma from Arizona. I told them you were a gentleman and offered me a ride. I did *not* tell them that if you were late for work this morning, it was partly my fault."

He let out a snort. "Thank you for that. I appreciate it."

"Anytime." She smiled. She'd love to make him late for work again tomorrow, too. "So, maybe I'll see you later?"

"Maybe." His hesitation, however slight, didn't do anything for her ego. Neither did his lack of commitment.

"Oh, okay. I'll let you know how dinner with the birth family goes."

"Please do."

"All right. Talk later."

"Okay. 'Bye." Justin disconnected the call and Phoenix was left confused.

She didn't have much time left in town. She probably should leave tomorrow, though she hated to go so soon. She'd have to leave the following day at the latest.

Maybe Justin didn't realize how short their time was. How soon she'd have to go back to California. If that was the case, she'd have to be sure to tell him.

Telling Justin she was leaving would be easy. It was telling her parents about this whole spur-of-the-moment Oklahoma trip and the reason for it that would be the hard part.

She supposed she'd have plenty of time to think of what to say on her way back. For now, she had to call Kim.

Maybe Kim could help her brainstorm the best way to confess. She'd already passed one huge hurdle—approaching Bonnie—and that had gone better than she ever could have imagined. Kim would want to know about it.

Picking up the cell phone again, she dialed Kim. So much for that nap. That had been a pipe dream. Phoenix was much too wound up to sleep anyway. She'd never felt so exhilarated in her life—worried about all that lay ahead, but exhilarated nonetheless.

Her life had just gotten a whole lot more complicated, but it was a wonderful feeling.

Chapter Thirty-One

"You're really a teacher?" Bonnie asked the question with amazement, leaning forward in her spot on the leather sofa next to Rohn in the living room.

It was a surprisingly nice room.

Phoenix felt bad even thinking that to herself, but she'd expected something totally different inside the house on a cattle ranch in Oklahoma.

What exactly she'd expected she didn't know. It hadn't been this beautiful room with a large flat-screen television hanging on the wall and a combination of modern leather furniture and weathered wooden antique tables.

The room was a mix of many things, giving it character, just like its owners.

Phoenix nodded in response to Bonnie's question about her job. "I am."

"What grade?" she asked.

"First."

"I taught fifth in Arizona, but now I'm teaching sixth. Huge difference one year makes. I never thought it would, but it has."

Phoenix nodded. "I can imagine. Lots of hormones flying around at that age. My friend Kim teaches third grade, and she swears even at that age the students are worlds different from those in first."

Rohn watched the conversation between mother and daughter, smiling.

Phoenix looked enough like Bonnie that both Rohn and Tammy had seen the resemblance immediately. But now that she knew he was her father, Phoenix had started to see traits of Rohn in herself, too. The way his smile was just a little bit crooked, like hers. Her height, too. Phoenix assumed she'd gotten that from Rohn because she was a few inches taller than Bonnie.

Bonnie reached out and grabbed his hand, squeezing it. She looked almost like a teenager when she gazed at Rohn and smiled. "I'm sorry. We must be boring you with all this school talk."

"Nope. Not one bit. You two could talk about anything and I'd be happy simply being in the same room."

There was one subject they hadn't covered, and it was one she wanted to bring up. While Tammy was in the kitchen putting away the last of dinner, Phoenix decided to brave the topic. "Can I ask you both something?"

"Of course." Bonnie nodded. "Anything."

"I was just wondering how . . . why . . ." Phoenix couldn't seem to get the words right.

Just the idea of asking how Bonnie could have given her up was enough to make her throat tight.

"Why did I give you up?" Bonnie supplied the words Phoenix hadn't been able to get out.

"Yes. You don't have to answer if you don't want to."

"It's okay. You deserve an answer." Bonnie glanced at Rohn and then back to Phoenix. "Rohn and I were both young. Both about to leave for our first year of college. You were an accident."

Phoenix nodded. It was as she'd suspected. "I understand."

"No, you don't. None of that would have mattered if things had been different at home. I was just so afraid." She cleared her throat as Rohn wrapped an arm around her.

Phoenix waited until Bonnie finally continued. "My father was a hard man. I don't want to speak badly about the dead, especially about the man who was your grandfather, but he could get . . . violent. When he found out I was pregnant, he beat me and threatened to kill the boy who'd done it. Rohn and I had been seeing each other secretly, so he didn't know who the father was, and I didn't tell him."

Bonnie drew in a shaky breath while Rohn looked as if he felt every emotion right along with her.

Holding up one hand, Phoenix said, "You don't have to go on."

"I'm okay." Bonnie swallowed hard and started again. "I was planning to leave for Phoenix for college shortly anyway. When my father went crazy, my mother put me on a bus the next day. I stayed with her mother in Arizona, your great-grandmother. I had the baby—had you—and then gave you up."

Phoenix sat quietly, digesting all she'd learned. It was a lot to absorb.

"I want you to know that Rohn didn't know I was pregnant. I couldn't risk my father finding out he was the one. I was afraid of what he'd do to him. And I knew he would have given up college and his scholarship to support me and the baby. I didn't want him to do that for me."

Bonnie shook her head sadly as Rohn leaned in and kissed her cheek. "I loved you. I wanted to marry you even when we were eighteen. We would have figured something out."

"I know that now. But I believed I was making the right decision back then."

"You had good reasons for what you did, and I don't know what I would have done in your place." Phoenix felt the need to soothe Bonnie's guilt. "And you don't have to feel bad because I had a really good life."

She realized that made it sound as if her life were over, which was far from the truth. It was as if a whole new world had opened up for her. Another family. Another state to call home, at least part-time. A new man . . .

Phoenix dragged her thoughts away from Justin and back to her birth parents. "My mother and father—uh, I mean the people who adopted me—"

Bonnie smiled. "Phoenix, you can call them your mother and father. That's exactly what they are."

"Okay. Anyway, they really are amazing people."

"Tell us about them. What are they like?" Rohn asked.

"Well, my father is a very hard worker. It's expensive to live in California and our house is in a really nice neighborhood, so I guess he has to work hard. They're kind of traditional, so Dad worked and Mom stayed home to raise me. They value education, so I always had to keep up my grades. And they paid for me to go to college."

What she didn't tell them was how she'd never seen herself in either one of her parents. Not her father's workaholic nature nor her mother's happy-homemaker mold.

Strange that though she'd never seen a cow up close before today's tour of the ranch, she could see herself in these people.

Even the quick tour they'd given her of the house had shown her how like them she was. How the paperwork in Rohn's office was as messy and unorganized as hers was at home. How Bonnie seemed to favor a casual pitcher full of wildflowers, like Phoenix did, rather than the formal arrangement of roses her mother always had on the dining table when company was coming over.

"How did your parents feel about you coming to Oklahoma?" Rohn's question had Phoenix cringing.

"I didn't tell them. In fact, I kind of snuck away. They don't even know I left California."

Bonnie drew in a sharp breath. "Phoenix, you came all this way and didn't tell your parents?"

"Um, yeah."

Bonnie opened her eyes wider. "What if something had happened to you?"

"My friend knew where I was." Phoenix realized there were now two more people in her life to reprimand her when she did something stupid. That was one side issue with having two sets of parents that she hadn't anticipated.

Rohn raised one thick brow. "You really should have told them."

They might not have been her parents for long, but Rohn and Bonnie sure had stepped into the role easily enough.

"I know. I'm sorry."

"How are you planning to get back to California?" Bonnie asked.

"I thought maybe I'd take the bus to Arizona so I can pick up my car. From there it isn't too long a drive home to California."

Rohn drew his brows low. "You said you left your car in Arizona?"

"Yes. It kept overheating—" Phoenix saw Rohn react to that, his eyes going wide. She rushed to finish. "It's fine. I took it to a shop and they fixed it."

"You sure it's fixed?" Rohn looked ready to call the shop himself.

"Yes. Justin talked to the mechanic on the phone. And they explained to me what was wrong and what they did to repair it, and Justin told me the price they quoted me was good."

Finally, Rohn looked moderately satisfied. "A'ight. Tyler's the one who has the most experience with car trouble, but Justin's pretty good with engines. He should know what he's talking about."

Thank goodness Rohn thought so or Phoenix imagined Rohn would have been on the phone personally grilling the service station mechanic.

"Oh, Justin definitely does." She made sure to agree with Rohn enthusiastically. "And he was kind enough to let me use his truck while I'm in town."

"So I saw. That *was* nice of him. Surprising, though. He don't usually let anyone borrow his truck." Rohn eyed Phoenix.

Would Rohn guess that there was more going on between her and Justin than just their being road trip buddies? She tried to make light of the loan and shrugged. "Maybe because he's got two trucks, he figured he could spare one for a couple of days."

Rohn cocked a brow. "Maybe, but still, you can take one of the ranch trucks to use for the rest of the time while you're here and give Justin his vehicle back."

"When are you leaving?" Bonnie came to the rescue by changing the subject and Phoenix couldn't have been more grateful.

As for when she'd be leaving, she had waffled before, but she was pretty sure now that she had to get home sooner rather than later.

Her guilt over lying to her parents had grown steadily as the night went on. That had made the decision for her. "I'm going to check the bus schedule, but I think I should probably leave tomorrow."

Bonnie frowned. "I hate that you have to leave so soon. You just got here."

"I know, but school's starting soon, and as you know, the staff reports a couple of days before the students start class. I promise I'll come back for a visit the next break we have."

"I hope you do. And next time you're staying here with us. Not in some hotel. I insist."

"Okay." Phoenix smiled at Rohn's insistence, while loving the idea of staying at the ranch with Rohn and Bonnie. Of course, that would make it more difficult to spend time alone with Justin.

They'd just have to figure something out. Hopefully, they'd have tonight together. They could talk about it then, *after* they did other things.

Tammy—Phoenix's very own grandmother as of a few hours ago—came through the doorway. "Ready for dessert? I've got my caramel apple sour cream cake on the dining room table."

"Yum." Rohn couldn't have stood any faster. "I'm ready."

"I know you are." Laughing, Bonnie stood, too, though more slowly than her fiancé had. "And you should have called, Mom. I would have helped you."

Tammy waved off Bonnie. "You had more important things to be doing, like getting to know Phoenix."

The older woman's smile was infectious. It had snuck inside and warmed Phoenix's heart the first time she saw it that afternoon.

Phoenix returned the smile now as she said, "I do have something I need to confess."

"What's that, sweetie?" Tammy asked.

"I can't bake. I mean I'm terrible. Like seriously bad. I could probably poison someone with my homemade cake." It was the craziest thing, because her mother was the best cook and a wonderful baker. She'd tried to teach Phoenix, but it just hadn't stuck.

Tammy shrugged. "Then we'll have to start you on something simple and go from there. No one can mess up a pie."

Phoenix raised one brow. "You might be surprised."

Bonnie leaned close as they all moved toward the dining room across the hall. "The good news is that after being a bachelor for the past five years, Rohn will eat pretty much anything and enjoy it, so don't worry."

Phoenix smiled. She loved her new family.

That thought brought to the surface the guilt she felt regarding her old family. She needed to get home to clean up her mess. Then maybe she'd be able to fully enjoy this amazing time in her life, surrounded by all the people who loved her, both old parents and new. And, with any luck, maybe even one hot cowboy.

Chapter Thirty-Two

Hey. You awake?

The text came through as Justin was watching television with his mother.

It was from Phoenix. He glanced at the time. It was only a little after eight, but he supposed it was a fair question. They'd both missed out on some sleep the night before.

As it was, he had his boots off and his feet kicked up on the coffee table. Settled in as he was against the sofa cushions, he wasn't far from dozing off. If the plot of the show he was watching didn't pick up, it would surely put him to sleep soon.

Yes. Dinner over?

He punched in his reply and hit Send.

Yes. At the hotel again. Want to come over?

Her question had him glancing at his mother. The answer was hell yes. He wanted to go to Phoenix's hotel, but he didn't want to leave his mother alone again.

He hesitated long enough with the phone in his hand, unsure of how to respond, that his mother noticed.

She glanced over. "Everything okay?"

"Oh, yeah. Just a friend asking if I wanted to come over."

"So go."

"I left you to go out last night . . ."

"And I was very happy watching my shows without you. Justin, go."

Damn, it was tempting to believe her. He really wanted to. "You sure?"

She widened her eyes, reinforcing the point. "Yes."

"Okay. But I won't be out late."

"Whatever you want to do."

"A'ight. Thanks, Mom." Justin only took long enough to text that he'd be right over before he reached for his boots. After pulling them on, he jumped up from the sofa and shoved the cell in his pocket. Leaning down, he dropped a quick kiss on his mother's cheek. "See you later."

"Okay. Have fun."

"I will." He had no doubt of that. As long as he wasn't pulled over for speeding while trying to get to Phoenix faster.

Justin made it to the hotel without incident and pulled into the lot, but what he found sucked the fun out of his safe arrival. There was a Double L Ranch truck he would have recognized as Rohn's even without the name and address painted on the door. One glance told him that his own truck wasn't in the lot.

What the hell? He strode to the door and knocked hard.

When she opened it, he didn't even give her a chance to say hello before he asked, "Where's my truck?"

Despite his worry about the current state and location of the vehicle he'd loaned her, he still had to admit she looked adorable as she planted both hands on her hips.

Eyes narrowed, she glared up at him. "Your truck is fine. It's at the ranch, where Rohn told me to leave it when he gave me his truck, so you can take it home with you tomorrow. And hello to you, too."

Letting out a breath of relief coupled with shame, Justin dropped his chin to his chest. "I'm sorry. It was just a surprise. I wasn't expecting it."

She put on a pretty pout. "I might be able to forgive you. Think you're persuasive enough to make me forget that you assumed I wrecked your truck?"

"Yeah, I think I might be able to manage it." He smiled while backing her up as he moved into the room.

Pushing the door shut with one hand, he left the outside world and all its concerns behind him. He hoisted her up. She wrapped her arms and legs around him. Kissing her, he closed the final distance to the bed. They tumbled to the mattress as one.

"Don't you want to hear about dinner?"

"Sure." He did, but he wanted her naked, too. Of course there was nothing that said they couldn't do both at the same time. He reached for the button on the waist of her jeans. "Tell me all about it."

"Tammy and Bonnie and Rohn are so great. And can you believe that Rohn is my birth father?"

That put a halt to Justin's motion, just as he was about to push her jeans down over the curves of her hips.

"Yeah, that was a bit of a shock today. Y'all talk about that?" Justin stopped stripping her long enough to wait for the answer.

"A little, but not too much. They were eighteen. Both of them were on their way to start college. Rohn had a scholarship. Her father didn't approve, I guess, so she gave me up." Phoenix shrugged, but he didn't buy her nonchalance.

"You okay?" He knew her whole life would have been different if Bonnie had decided to keep her baby.

"Yeah, I'm fine. I don't blame Bonnie for the choice she made." She looked lost in thought for a second before she tore herself out of it. A sly look crossed her face. "I thought you were supposed to be distracting me."

"You're the one who wanted to talk about dinner before I got to the distracting."

"I know. Sorry. I'm done now. You have to make me forget I'm leaving tomorrow."

"Tomorrow?" Now *he* was distracted, and not in a good way, like he'd planned to distract her.

"I really have to get home. I'm still lying to my parents about where I am."

His eyes widened. "Phoenix—"

"I know. I've already been reprimanded once for that today. That's why I have to go home."

"You could call them." *And stay here.* He left the rest of his thought unspoken.

"I think this is something I should tell them in person."

"Okay. I guess I can appreciate that." Even if he didn't like how little time they had left together.

With that in mind, he decided the moment for talking was over. They could discuss all she wanted later, but now he had other plans.

He glanced down at her below him. The bulb of the light on the wall cast a soft glow over her features as she gazed up at him.

"God, you're beautiful."

Justin watched her react to the statement. A crinkle formed between her brows and she pressed her lips together until he feared she was getting ready to cry. All over one little compliment.

He hadn't meant it as flattery. It was simply something

he felt, so he'd said it, without thought, but if she got so few compliments that one could almost bring her to tears, he might have to make a point of saying nice things to her more often.

Except that as of tomorrow, anything he said would have to be by long distance. He cupped her face with his palm and leaned low to press his lips to hers.

If she really did have to leave tomorrow, he'd make sure she felt special tonight.

Lying over her, he braced his weight on his elbows and plunged his hands into her hair. With her head cradled in his palms, he leaned low and kissed her gently.

Her lips, so warm and soft, yielded to his kiss.

There were times when a man just wanted to get to business. There were other instances when a man might want to prolong things. Justin was torn between the two.

Phoenix would be gone soon, so he should savor every moment. On the other hand, the temptation to possess her completely grew with every moment. Her kisses were an event in themselves, but they were also a prelude to so much more.

Lying on her, tasting her sweet mouth, hearing her sigh, was amazing, but it wasn't going to be enough. There was no fighting that fact. He already felt the near painful pressure behind the zipper of his jeans.

The promise of what was to come won out. He wanted her naked. Wanted them skin to skin with nothing between them.

Intent on finishing the job he'd started before he'd gotten distracted by conversation and then her kisses, he gripped the waist of her jeans with both hands and worked them down her legs.

He tossed her pants onto the floor. The rest of her clothes

and his joined them there shortly, but only after he'd grabbed the condom from his pocket first.

Her gaze held his and he fought back the regret that this time tomorrow she'd be gone. She was there now and that was all that mattered. He kept that in mind as he plunged inside her.

When she came around him, he couldn't think about anything at all. He only felt.

Chapter Thirty-Three

Justin arrived home at just about eleven o'clock. He'd hated to do it, but he'd had to drag himself away from Phoenix's bed. He'd promised his mother he'd be home early, and last time he was with Phoenix, he'd ended up staying until morning.

As he walked into the back door, he was glad he was home. All the lights in the house were on. His mother was never one to leave lights burning for no reason. Their bills were too high and money too tight for that.

For her to have the whole house lit up this late at night, something must be wrong.

"Momma?" Justin walked through the kitchen, half-hoping to find her cooking.

She wasn't there. He moved on to the living room. The television was on, but she wasn't there. He went toward her bedroom.

The door was ajar. He pushed it open, holding his breath, but she wasn't in bed. Her bathroom door was open and the room dark. She wasn't in there either.

Frowning, he moved back out into the hallway. Where could she be? Her car was in the driveway, so she hadn't driven anywhere.

"Mom?"

Maybe his aunt had picked her up and they'd gone out together. He'd love to think that she would actually go out on the spur of the moment just because someone asked, but he knew better than that.

Besides, if she had gone out, she would have texted or left him a note. And even if she had left a few lights on so the house wouldn't be dark when she got home, she would have shut the television off.

Starting to panic, he was about to pull out his phone and call her cell when he heard a noise. The sound came from the direction of Jeremy's room.

Frowning, he moved down the hall and slowly pushed open the door.

She sat on the floor in front of the dresser with the drawers pulled open and half of the contents spilled out. She had one of Jeremy's Army T-shirts pressed to her face as she rocked back and forth.

"Mom." He had trouble getting the one word out. The scene was so heartbreaking.

"Momma. What are you doing?" He kept his voice low and steady in an attempt to hide how upset he was at finding her like this.

This was worse than usual. She wasn't hiding in her room or wanting to be alone. This was the behavior she'd displayed in the days just after they were told Jeremy was killed in action.

Something had set her off and he hadn't been here to prevent it. He'd been buried deep inside Phoenix without a care in the world while his mother was alone having a breakdown. The guilt was like a knife to his heart.

She'd been fine when he'd left. For days now she'd been good. It had been wishful thinking on his part that they were on the road back to normalcy.

He knew he shouldn't be shocked. It wouldn't be the first time she'd had a couple of good days before crashing. But this seemed worse than just another pendulum swing from good to bad.

"He loved this T-shirt." She didn't look at him as she spoke but kept facing the pile of clothes. "He wore it all the time. Everywhere."

"Yeah, I remember." He moved farther into the room.

What had been the trigger this time? He knew it could be anything. A soldier in a television commercial could remind her of Jeremy.

So could any number of things, completely unrelated.

Maybe this was just a reaction to the upcoming anniversary of his death and he didn't need to panic that she was in a full-blown relapse.

Sighing, Justin kneeled down next to her. "I also remember he had like half a dozen of them, so even if they were in the wash, he still had one to wear."

She nodded but didn't comment.

He drew in a breath. "Mom, are you sure this is healthy? Maybe it's time we took all of this stuff—"

Her head whipped around as she glared at him. "No!"

"But—"

"Everyone made me get rid of your father's things. I don't even have one damn shirt left of his. I won't let you do it again." Judging by the panic in her voice, she was nearing hysteria.

"Okay, Mom. We won't touch Jeremy's room."

Justin had been a teenager when his father had passed. Even at that young age, he'd realized well how his aunt had taken control of the chaos.

She'd come to the house two weeks after the funeral and insisted she was doing them all a favor by cleaning all of his father's stuff out. She said it was the healthiest thing to do.

There'd been piles of clothes to donate to the church and another pile of things to toss.

His father had been a pack rat when it came to anything he might be able to use in the future, even if it was broken. So there were trash bins filled with broken tools or parts of things that didn't go with anything else. Instruction manuals for old appliances they no longer owned. Empty boxes and jars he thought he might find useful one day for something.

There had been things to pass on to relatives and friends, too. Jeremy had gotten their father's .22 rifle. Justin had gotten the shotgun. Neither of them wanted or needed the golf clubs, so they'd given those to one of the neighbors.

His father's tools still remained in the garage where they'd both used them, Jeremy during the times he had been home and was working on his truck or helping make repairs around the house.

Of course the family photos were still in the albums, but he supposed that wasn't the same as his father's favorite flannel shirt. Or the T-shirt he wore every time OSU played a game.

They had kind of bowled her over after his father died. His aunt, his parents' friends, even the people from church, had pretty much taken over.

There had been a steady stream of cooked meals delivered. The neighbors had even cut their grass for a month. And his aunt had orchestrated Justin and Jeremy in the cleanout of his dad's things. She'd been like a general going into battle.

Aunt Phoebe had a firm plan, no questions asked, all while his mother sat by in a shocked daze.

They'd all thought they'd done his mother a favor by telling her they'd handle everything. That there was no need for her to help. To just take care of herself.

He saw now that maybe they hadn't done her any favors.

No wonder she had dug her heels in so deep every time anyone even suggested cleaning out Jeremy's room or getting rid of any of his stuff. But leaving his brother's things where they were was one thing. Sitting on the floor crying and rocking while surrounded by his T-shirts was another.

And Justin had gone and left her alone with his aunt for company, once again thinking he was doing the right thing. She was probably the last person he should have left with his mother. With her presence probably came lots of memories from times that weren't so good.

Had his aunt said something about Jeremy's stuff while she'd been here? Even if she hadn't, just the memory of that last great purge of her treasures might have been enough to set his mother off.

The amazing part was that it had taken this long for her to end up on the floor because of it.

Sometimes it was easiest just to go along with her. Justin knew that by now. Besides, how could he fault her for wanting to surround herself with Jeremy's things when he'd pretty much done the same thing with his truck?

Justin drove his brother's vehicle because he felt closer to him in it. How could he not understand his mother wanting to cling to some T-shirts that held so many memories for her? He couldn't even bring himself to change the damn radio station in the truck or throw away an old tin of chewing tobacco.

He sat next to her and picked up a navy blue shirt. "I remember when he bought this one. He thought it was so clever."

It was one of those cheap shirts you could buy that had a dumb saying on it. *Save Water, Drink Beer*. It was pretty goofy, but Jeremy had loved it.

She nodded but didn't speak, the Army shirt still in her hands.

"Mom, maybe it's time you start seeing someone."

His mother shook her head.

Justin continued, "Not a doctor. Just like a therapist or a counselor. Someone to talk to."

Clutching the shirt to her chest, she said, "I know you think I'm crazy."

"I don't think you're crazy. But I'm not sure this is healthy. Mom, you have to start to live again."

"I know it's not fair that you're the only one working." She finally looked at him. "We have your father's life insurance and his pension, but I should be out, earning something to help."

"We're okay for now."

She had been working as a cashier full-time at a store nearby when Jeremy died. She'd asked for time off and just never went back.

With what Justin earned at the ranch, they weren't starving. They could pay the bills.

Of course it also meant he'd never be able to move out. He couldn't afford a place of his own as well as the upkeep on this house.

Just one more reason he wasn't in a relationship. Why he shouldn't have even thought about spending the night with his boss's daughter. He couldn't give Phoenix the kind of commitment she deserved and it was wrong to be with her knowing that.

One problem at a time.

He pocketed that guilt and turned his attention back to the issue at hand. "What if we didn't get rid of anything? We could just pack the clothes into bins. Those nice big plastic lidded ones that keep the moisture and dust out. We could stick them upstairs in the attic—"

"No." She was rocking again, shaking her head, and Justin knew it was pointless to keep pushing.

"Okay." Sighing, he hoisted his tired body off the floor and stood.

He didn't bother telling her that he was going to the kitchen to put the kettle on for hot water so he could make her some herbal tea, just as he didn't ask if she wanted any. She'd only tell him no. He'd make it, and maybe a plate of food anyway, and hope she'd pick at it, just as he always did.

Two years was a long time to live like this. He'd survived so far. He could do it for a little bit longer.

Chapter Thirty-Four

Phoenix pulled into the drive of Rohn's ranch, taking it nice and slow. She wasn't quite used to driving a truck—and a big powerful one with a backseat in it—nor was she used to driving on gravel. There weren't gravel roads and driveways where she lived.

It was all pretty crazy. Three days in Oklahoma and she'd somehow gone from a big truck to an even bigger one. After having only driven a VW Bug for the past few years that was quite a change, but she didn't mind. She was starting to feel like she belonged here—just as it was time to leave.

She recognized both of Justin's vehicles parked over by the barn. The one she'd left there the night before, as well as the one they'd driven from Arizona. He was definitely here.

Even though she knew they shouldn't indulge in public displays of affection in front of Rohn and Bonnie, knowing he was so close made her heartbeat quicken.

They'd have to steal a kiss behind the barn.

Smiling, she decided she liked that idea. She could definitely get into this ranch life. Maybe even try out a roll in the hay. Even though she was leaving that day, she knew she'd be back. That thought made her happy.

With visions of farm girls and cowboys dancing in her

head, she steered Rohn's truck toward the barn. Rohn, Bonnie, and Tammy had promised to drive her to the bus station, so she would park next to Justin.

Even with the seat pulled all the way up, Phoenix had to sit up totally straight and lean forward over the steering wheel to see the nose of the truck. She wanted to pull up close to the fence so the bed wasn't sticking way out, but she still left plenty of room to make sure she didn't bump the rails. The last thing she wanted to do was wreck both Rohn's truck and his fence in one move.

She accomplished the feat and grabbed the gear shift, struggling to move it into Park. It seemed the bigger the truck, the bigger all the parts.

Smiling at the thought of seeing Justin soon, she cut the engine and wrestled out the key. She left it in the cup holder, where it had been when she'd gotten in the day before.

There was no crime around here, she supposed. She hadn't grown up in a sleepy small town surrounded by acres of nothing. She wasn't used to parking and then walking away from the vehicle, leaving the doors open and the key inside. It was kind of nice but something that would definitely take some getting used to.

Her suitcase was on the floor by the passenger seat. She hadn't been able to figure out how to get the tailgate on the truck bed down. Besides, she had an irrational fear that her bag might somehow fly out with the wind if it was outside in the back.

It was still early in the day. Bonnie had invited her to come over for breakfast this morning. She'd considered it until she found out it was served at seven a.m. Apparently, that was when the ranch hands arrived. Seven Central Time was a bit early for her. She was still getting acclimated after leaving California's Pacific Time zone.

If she started dating Justin seriously, they'd have to work

out a schedule of communications so he wasn't calling her at the crack of dawn and she didn't wake him after bedtime.

Just the thought of Justin had her walking faster toward the barn in hopes that he'd be in there. Where else would he be?

She glanced around her at the acres of sprawling land and outbuildings.

Okay, maybe there were a few other places he could be working, but the barn was closest, so she might as well just take a peek inside.

She opened the door slowly and peered through the crack. She didn't know if there was an animal loose in there that might charge at her.

With no loose bulls or horses in sight, she opened the door a bit farther.

"Can I help you?"

She jumped at the man's voice.

Turning, she waited until her eyes adjusted to the difference in light so she could see two cowboys standing to one side. A wheelbarrow full of buckets filled with some sort of food stood between them.

They were like models from a hot-guys-of-Oklahoma calendar. They were every bit as cowboy as Justin was, right down to the hats, jeans, and boots, not to mention the bulging muscles visible through their tight T-shirts.

Damn, if she'd known these were the kind of men they grew in Oklahoma, she would have come here long ago. She needed to bring Kim here. In fact, they should probably cancel their Aruba plans and switch their midwinter break vacation to Oklahoma.

"Um, hi."

"Hey there." The lighter-haired guy tipped his hat to her.

"I'm, uh, looking for Justin."

"Are you now?" The dark-haired one grinned wide.

"Phoenix." Justin's voice came from the back of the barn.

She looked up and saw him striding forward, but it was a big barn and he still had a long way to go, which gave the dark-haired cowboy time to take a step forward and extend his hand. "I'm Tyler."

"Tyler." Phoenix shook his hand as the other one came closer.

"And I'm Colton."

"Colton." She let him grasp her hand, too, realizing these were the two guys she'd seen briefly at Bonnie's house yesterday with Rohn and Justin.

By then Justin was there, eyeing his two coworkers before facing her. "What are you doing here?"

"I had to drop off the truck, and then Bonnie and Rohn are driving me to catch the bus. I thought I told you that last night."

"Last night?" Tyler raised a brow and leveled a gaze on Justin.

"Well, now, isn't that interesting?" Colton crossed his arms over his chest and leaned back against the stall, as if settling in for a show.

Justin took a step forward, effectively putting himself between Phoenix and the two other cowboys. He reached out to lay his hand on her shoulder, turning her and basically marching her out the door of the barn.

"Let's find Rohn and Bonnie."

When they were outside and clear of the two guys hovering in the doorway, Phoenix glanced up at Justin. "You're keeping me away from your friends."

"No, I'm trying to keep my friends away from you. There's a difference."

"Why?"

"Well, first off, they'll do nothing but tease you and me, so it's best if you don't get to know them. Second, I don't want them knowing my business, and I sure as heck don't want them mouthing off to Rohn—your father—that I was with you last night. Do you?"

"No. Not really."

They might be new to her, but Rohn and Bonnie were still technically her mother and father. She hadn't been raised in the kind of household where things such as sex were discussed openly between parents and children. She didn't think she wanted to start doing it now.

They neared the house and Justin paused. He tipped his head toward the door she knew led to the kitchen.

"As far as I know, they're all in the house. At least they were when I got here this morning and stopped in the kitchen to grab a cup of coffee." He sounded weary.

"Okay. I'll find them. Thanks." Looking closer, she noticed the dark shadows beneath his eyes.

He hadn't been at her room that late last night. He must not have slept well, or else he had to be at work really early.

"A'ight." He nodded and turned, as if to go.

"Wait. Justin." Phoenix took a step forward.

He turned back. "Yeah?"

"We're probably going to be leaving shortly. This might be the last time I see you."

He drew in a deep breath. "Sorry. I'm just tired and I got morning chores to finish."

"I understand. I just thought we should say good-bye now. While no one else is around." She hoped he understood that when she said *say good-bye*, she really meant she wanted a kiss. Or at least one final hug. After two nights together, she'd thought he'd want the same.

Maybe his hesitation was because of where they were. He was at work. She knew she wouldn't be hugging and kissing him good-bye if they'd been in the hallway of the school where she worked. But this seemed to be about the most casual working environment you could get.

Finally, he pulled her into a hug and squeezed her tight. "Please text and let me know when you get your car and how it's running. And then when you get home safe to California. Okay?"

She felt disappointment when he released her too soon. "Okay. I will."

His gaze remained on her face for a few seconds before he nodded. "A'ight. Have a safe trip."

"Thanks."

He hesitated and she waited, for more words, a kiss, one more hug . . . for anything. But nothing came. Justin turned and strode away. She watched as he went back to the barn and to his morning chores, leaving Phoenix standing in shocked silence.

What the hell?

Had she done something to turn him away from her? Was it because she'd slipped and let his friends know they'd seen each other last night? The doubts and questions swirled through her mind as her stomach clenched with a sick feeling.

"Hey, you're here."

At the sound of Rohn's voice, she turned. "Hi. Yeah."

"Come on in. There's coffee in the pot and muffins Tammy made on the counter. Grab yourself some, if you want. We have a few minutes before we have to leave. I'll run upstairs and tell Bonnie you're here."

"Okay. Thanks." Good thing Rohn was doing most of the talking because after that strange, almost cold good-bye from Justin, Phoenix was in no condition to make small talk.

Chapter Thirty-Five

"You're seriously not going to tell us anything about you and this babe?"

Justin set his jaw and ignored Colton's question, staunchly concentrating on scooping the manure out of the stall bedding instead.

It was the same question Colton had been asking in one form or another for the past few hours, ever since Phoenix had showed up at the ranch.

Tyler knocked his hat back. "I don't know why you're surprised, Colt. You know Justin never tells us shit."

"That's about everyday stuff. But this is pretty huge."

"God almighty, just quit." Justin shook his head. "It's not huge. It's nothing. She's nobody."

He knew the last part of his statement was a lie. Phoenix was much more than a nobody. Sadly, the other part was accurate—nothing was exactly what he could have with her.

He was certain of that after what had happened last night, when he'd been in her bed instead of home where he belonged, taking care of his mother. He had to leave his mother to come to work—they needed the income—but he didn't need to have a relationship distracting him. He could live without women.

Hell, if all those monks and priests could do it, so could he.

"Nothing? You come home from Arizona with this hot girl—"

"Who's allowed to drive his truck when I'm not. Don't forget that part," Tyler added.

Colton continued, "Right. Driving your truck *and* she's Rohn's long-lost daughter nobody even knew existed. You call that nothing?"

Justin refused to look at them as he kept his head down, focused on the stall bedding, and said, "Nothing that's any of your business."

Colton let out a snort. "Well, hey, at least I know why you were ignoring my texts the past two nights."

"Uh-huh. And I know how come she gets to drive his truck and I don't. He's not getting sweaty nights with me. Apparently, that's part of the loan deal."

"If you two can't shut the hell up, I'm leaving." He was in enough of a crap mood already without his two supposed friends messing with him.

"Seriously, dude, you probably should get outta here." Colton nodded. "Who knows how Rohn's gonna react when he figures out you're banging his only daughter."

Tyler snorted. "No shit. Then again, maybe she's not his only daughter. We didn't know about this one. There could be more."

Colton's brows rose. "You think? Wow, I hadn't thought of that. That would be pretty cool. If they all look like Phoenix, I wouldn't mind having a go."

Justin let out a cuss that would have had his mother washing out his mouth with soap in the old days and turned. If he didn't get away from these two, he'd end up taking a swing at one of them.

Leaning his pitchfork against the wall of the barn, he pushed open the door and headed outside. He wasn't sure where he was going, just that he had to get the hell away from them.

He headed for the house.

The kitchen was empty when he pushed through the back door and went down the hallway toward the bathroom. Bonnie and Rohn hadn't yet returned from taking Phoenix to the bus station.

That was a good thing. It gave him some much needed time alone as he flipped on the water in the sink and splashed a handful over his face. He repeated the action before turning off the faucet and reaching for a towel.

Straightening, he wiped his face and looked at his reflection in the mirror. Not even thirty yet, but he felt like he was an old man. Beaten down and tired. Sleepless nights and worry had combined to do that to him.

Hell, life had done that to him and he'd let it. How could he fight it? He couldn't.

He couldn't have done anything to prevent his father's heart attack or Jeremy's IED, just as he hadn't done anything to cause them either. But here he was, still suffering the pain of both, alongside his mother.

Death didn't play favorites or play fair.

Life dropping Phoenix in his lap at a time when he couldn't even think of being with her wasn't fair either. And just like everything else, there was nothing he could do to fix that.

He sighed and turned for the door, flipping the light switch off as he walked through.

Justin heard the back door slam. He came into the kitchen and found the new parents looking a little sad.

"Hey. Just using the bathroom." Justin hooked a thumb toward the hallway, probably unnecessarily.

He and the guys were allowed to come into the house

whenever they wanted to grab something to eat or drink in the kitchen or to use the bathroom. He just felt funny being there while they'd been out. Kind of like he'd been creeping around alone while they weren't looking. Then again, he was probably being irrational due to lack of sleep and guilt over Phoenix.

Rohn frowned and lifted one shoulder. "A'ight."

"So, uh, Phoenix get off to Arizona okay?"

"Yeah." Bonnie pressed a hand to her chest and glanced at Rohn.

"Aw, jeez. Don't talk about it." He pulled Bonnie to him and said over her head, "She cried all the way from the bus station until we dropped her momma off at the house to finish unpacking."

Justin could understand how Bonnie felt. He missed Phoenix, too. Or he would if he let himself.

That was the difference between him and Bonnie. Where Bonnie had the leisure to let herself miss Phoenix, Justin didn't. He had his mother to worry about, so he was going to fight missing Phoenix with everything he had.

"Got it. Sorry. I'm gonna get back to work."

He was almost free of the emotions suffocating him when Rohn said, "Hang on."

"Yeah?"

"Can you ask the guys to come on in?"

"Um, sure. What's up?"

Rohn's request felt kind of like getting called to the principal's office in school and not knowing why.

"I'll tell you all together."

"A'ight."

Cringing as thoughts of what this could be about spiraled through his head, Justin strode across the yard and into the barn.

Colton glanced up when the barn door swung open. "Look who's back."

Tyler raised a brow when he saw Justin. "Just as we're done cleaning stalls."

"Rohn wants us all inside." He turned to go back out before Tyler pissed him off.

"For what?" Tyler asked.

Justin paused and glanced back. "I don't know. Some sort of meeting."

"About what?" Colton repeated Tyler's question almost exactly, but he needn't have because Justin still didn't have an answer.

"I don't know." He did leave this time.

Tyler and Colton knew the way to the house just fine on their own. He didn't have to walk with them and endure more razzing or inane questions.

Back in the kitchen, Justin saw that Rohn was alone. He glanced up when Justin came through the back door.

"They're right behind me." He tipped his head toward the two cowboys he could hear stomping their boots on the mat outside the door.

"A'ight." Rohn nodded and pulled out a chair from under the table.

"Bonnie better now?" Justin asked.

"Yeah. She looked like she was going to start bawling again so I suggested she get on the phone and call Phoenix."

Justin supposed the phone was the next best thing to being there. In fact, he would call or text Phoenix himself, *if* they were going to have that kind of relationship. The kind where he and she talked all the time while they were apart, and did so much more when they were together . . . but they couldn't have that.

At this point in his life, he couldn't have any kind of

relationship at all. Just work and home. That would be his existence and he'd learn to be okay with it.

The overwhelming presence of Tyler and Colton encroached upon Justin's thoughts as they moved into the room and began questioning Rohn regarding the impromptu meeting.

"If you sit down, I'll tell you." Rohn frowned up at the pair. When they'd finally settled in chairs and stopped chattering, he said, "Now, I know you've all seen Phoenix—"

Tyler threw his hands in the air. "About time we talked about her."

Lifting a brow, Rohn waited. When Tyler didn't interrupt again, he continued, "You're probably curious, so rather than have y'all speculating, I'm going to answer your questions now, and then I don't want to hear another word about her."

Rohn glanced around the group. Amazingly, Tyler and Colton both kept their mouths shut.

So did Justin. He was too involved in this to make any comments.

The whole thing had been risky. He'd taken a huge chance, trusting a complete stranger. Driving her all the way from Arizona. Delivering Rohn and Bonnie to her on a silver platter.

It had all worked out, but he was very aware that it could have gone another way. She could have been a wacko who'd lied to him about everything with the intention of hurting or taking advantage of his friends.

He pushed that pointless thought aside. She hadn't been bad, and he'd helped unite a family. And all it would cost him was a few days of missing her. He figured that was about how long it would take for him to get her out of his mind.

Wasn't that how these things worked? He'd only been with her for three days, so he'd get over her in that time, maybe less.

At least Justin hoped so, as Rohn launched into his explanation. "Phoenix is my daughter, and Bonnie is her mother. We were very young when she was born, so she was adopted and raised by a couple in California. Now that she's an adult she's going to be part of our lives. Any questions?"

Justin noticed there were a few gaping holes in Rohn's explanation. But he wasn't about to ask.

Apparently, neither were Tyler or Colton. Both kept quiet.

"All right, then." Rohn planted his palms on the table and pushed up from his seat. "Back to work. I want to try bucking those new broncs today to see how they do."

That was it, then, back to normal . . . or what was Justin's new normal.

Work. Home. No Phoenix in his life. That was his life now, what he'd have to learn to accept.

He stood up too and felt the cell in his pocket vibrate. As Tyler and Colton headed out the door and Rohn turned toward the hallway, probably to go check on Bonnie, Justin pulled the phone out of his pocket.

It was a text from Phoenix.

On the bus. Not as fun as road trip with you. Wish you were here.

So did he, but he couldn't say that. In fact, it was better if he didn't respond at all. Yeah, it would hurt her now, but in the long run they'd both be better off. He shoved the phone back into his pocket and headed for the door.

Chapter Thirty-Six

Phoenix wrestled her bag out of her car and dropped it onto the ground. She slammed the trunk and turned toward the welcome sight of her apartment building.

Home sweet home. Finally. It had been a long trip, made even longer by the fact that Justin had all but ignored her the whole way home.

She'd texted him half a dozen times and so far had only gotten one response. If it hadn't been for that one reply, she would have assumed the texts weren't going through and probably would have called by now.

But that single-word response told her volumes. He was getting her texts. He just didn't want to talk to her.

Good.

That was it. That was all she'd gotten from him. One word after she'd texted that she'd arrived in Phoenix, had gotten her car back and it seemed to be running fine.

No response to all the texts she'd sent from the bus. Nothing after the text telling him she was getting on the road back to California. Now, about five hours later, she held the cell in her hand and contemplated what to do next.

She'd promised back in Oklahoma, when he'd already been acting odd as they'd said good-bye, that she'd let him know when she was home. She'd keep her word and typed in two words.

Home safe.

Hitting Send, she refused to wait to see what, if anything, came back. She shoved the phone in her jeans and reached for the handle on her suitcase . . . and felt the cell vibrate.

Crap. She had to look. She wasn't the type to be able to wait and never had been. Phoenix had been the kid who woke before dawn to tear into the gifts under the Christmas tree before her parents were awake. She was no different now.

That the response had come back so fast had to be good, right?

As she dropped the handle of the bag, her hope grew.

Maybe there was a good reason he'd been so unresponsive yesterday. Maybe, while she'd been bored on the bus and texting him, he'd just been really busy at work all day, and then so tired he went to bed early that night.

She pulled out the phone and read the text. It was a single letter this time.

K

Just when she thought it couldn't get worse than his last one-word reply, she realized she'd been wrong. That one letter was like a slap in the face.

Maybe he was driving. Texting while driving was dangerous, but he might have risked it. That could be why he could only type one letter, because he had to get his eyes back on the road and his hands on the wheel.

And maybe pigs would start to fly.

She sighed. She always did this. Made excuses, kept hoping even when she probably shouldn't . . .

But she'd believed Bonnie was her birth mother and that had worked out.

Drawing in a bracing breath, Phoenix decided she'd reach out one more time. She couldn't let that one letter be the final communication, so she typed up what could be her last text to Justin.

Thank you for everything you did for me this week. The ride. Your truck. Bonnie's address. I couldn't have found her and Rohn without you. I appreciate it and you.

She hit Send.

There. Now the ball was in his court. He could do with it what he chose, but at least she knew she'd reached out and left things the way she wanted them.

Refusing to wait around for the reply that might not come, she shoved the phone into her pocket one more time and grabbed her suitcase.

It had been a very long day and night on the bus, followed by the drive from Arizona to California. Thank goodness Kim had talked her through a substantial part of that time. Together, they had worked out how to tackle the next problem facing her—telling her parents.

Kim had said that because Phoenix's parents loved her and always would, they'd be happy that she was happy.

Phoenix hoped Kim was right.

Getting dumped by Justin was one thing, but Phoenix

couldn't handle having her parents angry with her, too. That would be more than she could bear, and all just as a new school year was about to begin.

She sure had some shitty timing when it came to making major life decisions such as seeking out her long-lost birth parents and getting involved in a new—and failed—relationship.

Her apartment looked just as she'd left it. Homey but messy, it was a very welcome sight.

After hotel living for days, and then a night spent in a bus seat, she would appreciate sleeping in her own bed. But before she could indulge in even a much-needed nap, she had to call her parents. She had ditched another phone call from her mother while she'd been on the bus yesterday, figuring it was better to let her mother assume she was busy than to lie about where she was again.

Besides, how could she have explained all the background sounds that could have tipped her mother off? The people. The road noise. A giant bus filled with travelers wasn't exactly a controlled environment.

Unpacking could wait. So could laundry. This phone call couldn't.

Dumping her bags inside the door, Phoenix pulled her phone out of her pocket. She reprimanded herself for noticing there was no reply from Justin and dialed her parents' house number before she let herself obsess over it as she walked to the sofa.

Falling heavily onto the cushions, Phoenix wished she could pull out a pint of ice cream, put on a chick flick, and forget about the world. At least for a little while.

Sadly, that wasn't in the cards. She had something else to do.

"Hello?"

"Hi, Mom."

"Hi. I tried calling you yesterday."

"Yeah, I saw the missed call. Sorry." Phoenix left the apology without explanation. No more making up bogus excuses. "I need to talk to you and Daddy about something."

Her mother hesitated. "Okay. Phoenix, are you all right?"

"Everything's fine. I just want to talk to you both together in person. Can I come over this afternoon after he gets home from work?"

"Sure. Come over for dinner. I'm making fajitas."

This conversation was going to be hard, but at least she'd be well fed. "Sounds good. I'll see you later. I love you."

"I love you, too." There was another pause. "Phoenix, are you sure you're okay?"

"Yeah, I'm good. 'Bye, Mom."

Phoenix disconnected the call and drew in a huge breath. There were still a few hours before she had to go to her parents' house. She should take a nap. She hadn't gotten the best rest dozing in her seat on the bus last night. And the drive alone had been enough to wear her out.

But there was a restlessness inside her. She knew she'd never be able to nap, so she scrolled through the numbers on her phone and dialed Kim.

When her friend answered, Phoenix said, "Any chance you're free?"

"Yup. I'm free as a bird until that calendar page flips and we have to report for the start of classes. Ugh, I just depressed myself thinking about it."

"Can you come over so we can be depressed together?"

"Sure. Are you okay?"

Phoenix let out a breath as she felt the full force of everything weighing heavily on her mind. "No."

"All righty. Then I'll pick up a bottle of wine on my way."

She wasn't sure she should be drinking before this conversation with her parents. And between the lack of sleep and the depressing fact that Justin had pretty much blown her off for no apparent reason, she was already feeling close to tears without alcohol.

In spite of all that, Phoenix said, "That sounds good. Thanks."

Chapter Thirty-Seven

"Dang it, it's colder than a witch's tit out there." Colton came into the kitchen accompanied by a gust of cold wind.

From his seat at the kitchen table, Justin cocked a brow at Colton's colorful metaphor. He waited for him to close the door before saying, "It's December. What the hell did you expect?"

Colton screwed up his face unhappily and reached for a coffee mug in the cabinet. "Doesn't mean I have to like it."

The door opened again and Tyler pushed through. "God, I really hate shoveling snow and now I have to do it at four different places."

Tyler took off his hat and knocked the snow from it before planting it back on his head. "I hope there's coffee."

Justin nodded. "Yup. I put on a fresh pot when I got here. And Bonnie put out the leftover Christmas cookies for us."

That got Colton's attention. Mug in hand, he came over to the table and eyed the open tin. "Any of the ones with the jam in the middle left?"

"No. I ate the last one of those." Justin laughed at Colton's scowl. "Sorry. You should have gotten here earlier."

"How the hell early did you get here that you had time to make coffee and eat all the good cookies?"

Justin shrugged. "About twenty minutes ago, I guess."

Because his life for the past few months had consisted of nothing more than going to work and then going home, with an hour or so a day spent in the garage lifting weights to try to keep some semblance of sanity, it wasn't like he had any reason to be late.

"You trying to make us look bad?" Tyler asked.

"You don't need me for that." Justin grinned at his own little joke. His life was so uneventful, it didn't take all that much to amuse him nowadays.

Colton grabbed a peanut butter and chocolate cookie from the tin and glanced at Tyler. "Why are you shoveling snow at four houses?"

"I had to clear the drive over at Janie's. Then I ran home and did my parents' driveway. While I was there I saw the neighbor's place wasn't done. The old man's still using a walker after that stroke he had, so I did the driveway and the walk and wheelchair ramp for them. And now we're going to have to shovel here."

"Tough being a saint, huh?" Justin hid his smirk behind his coffee mug as Tyler shot him an unhappy glance. He didn't feel too bad teasing Tyler. Their area rarely got as much snow as they'd gotten from the last storm so it wasn't like Tyler had to suffer often.

"Yeah, yeah. Shut up."

"At least you get paid for shoveling here at Rohn's. That eases the pain a bit, no?" Colton asked between bites of cookie.

Tyler scowled. "A little."

The sound of footsteps on the stairs alerted them to someone's approach. Judging by the heavy step and boots, Justin wasn't at all surprised when Rohn came through the kitchen doorway. What was a surprise was how exhausted he looked.

"You just waking up?" Colton asked, eyeing Rohn.

"Yeah." Rohn rubbed a hand over his face.

"What's up? Bonnie keep you up late last night?" Tyler waggled his brows, but by the look of Rohn, tired and cranky, Justin figured they'd all better be on their best behavior.

Rohn raised a brow at Tyler as he moved toward the coffeemaker. "Yes, she had me up late, but not in the perverted way you're insinuating, boy. She decided we needed to shampoo all the upstairs carpets before Phoenix's visit. If they were gonna dry in time, she figured it had to happen last night."

Colton looked from Rohn to Tyler. "Between Tyler having to shovel extra snow for his girl and you having to play janitor for yours, you're making me glad I'm single. Right, Justin?"

The sound of Colton saying his name caught Justin's attention, which had previously been completely focused on Phoenix and the impending visit Rohn had mentioned. He knew she'd planned on visiting, but he hadn't realized it would be so soon.

Justin looked at Colton but had no idea what he'd been asking him.

Figuring if it was important he'd ask again, Justin ignored Colton and turned his attention to Rohn. "When is Phoenix coming?"

"Tomorrow. We're picking her up from the airport, which is another reason I was up half the night. Bonnie's obsessing over the weather and worried about flights."

"She staying here?" Justin asked, trying to sound casual but feeling anything but.

He might not have seen her in close to four months, but that didn't mean he hadn't thought about her, or the decision he made to ease his way out of her life. He hadn't done such a great job. He hadn't texted or called, but he also couldn't bring himself to delete her number. He still had it saved in the contacts list on his phone.

It twisted his heart just a tiny bit every time he had to scroll past her name to get to a number he needed.

"Of course she's staying here," Rohn said.

Justin's head was spinning. If she was here, he'd definitely run into her. How would he act? How would she?

Unaware of Justin's turmoil, Rohn continued, "Bonnie wouldn't have it any other way. We've got the guest room. Tammy has room at her house, too, but we want to keep Phoenix close. She can only stay for the week, and then she has to get back. School starts up again the Monday after New Year's."

"Rohn?" Bonnie's voice came from the direction of the staircase.

"Yes, dear?" he called back as the rest of them sat by, smirking at his compliance.

"Can you come up and help me with the mattress in the guest room?"

"What in the world are you doing with the mattress?" he called back.

"Flipping it over. They say you're supposed to do it every couple of months."

"Even when there's no one sleeping on it?" He sighed and stood anyway. "I'll be right back."

Colton smiled. "Oh, I'm sure she'll find something else for you to do."

Rohn leveled a stare at Colton. "Most like. And in that case, you can work on clearing the snow from the driveway and all the paths."

"See? You had to make a smart-ass comment and now we're shoveling paths." Tyler scowled at Colton.

"We would have been shoveling anyway and you know it." Colton's eyes moved from Tyler to Justin. "But let's talk about what's really important here."

"What's that?" Tyler asked.

"Rohn and Bonnie's daughter coming for a visit." Colton's focus stayed pinned on Justin.

"And?" Justin asked, feeling the weight of Colton's stare.

"You tell us." Tyler raised a brow. "You two been talking?"

"No." For better or worse, Justin spoke the absolute truth.

"So does that mean I'm free to take a shot at her?" Colton asked.

Justin frowned at Colton. "No."

He grinned and glanced at Tyler. "Yup, you were right. He still likes her."

Tyler grinned. "Yup. He sure does."

These two had been talking about him and Phoenix behind his back? They both needed to get a life and leave his alone.

"Aw, jeez." Justin stood and carried his mug to the sink. "I'll be outside making up the feed buckets."

A man couldn't even enjoy his coffee in peace. Unfortunately, Justin had a feeling there'd be no more peace for him until after Phoenix flew back to California.

Chapter Thirty-Eight

"Your flight leaves in two hours. Are you at the airport yet?" Phoenix's mother asked.

"I'm on the way. Kim's driving me."

"Are you close? There could be traffic."

"We're close. Don't worry."

Kim cocked a brow and shot Phoenix a glance over that fib.

The reality was they weren't all that close because she hadn't been ready when Kim had arrived to pick her up. Consequently, Kim was driving like a bat out of hell to get her there in time, none of which Phoenix was going to tell her mother.

"Your father is reminding me that you have to be there at least an hour in advance if you're checking a bag."

"I'm carrying on only so we'll be okay." Phoenix rolled her eyes as she saw Kim smirking in the driver's seat.

"All right. Did you put all your travel-size carry-on liquids in a clear plastic bag so you can get through security?"

Phoenix cringed and stifled a curse. She rarely flew anywhere, so she'd forgotten all about that TSA rule. "Yes, Mom. I got it." She'd have to figure something out when she got there.

"All right. It sounds like you're all set. Call us when you get there."

"I will."

"Oh, wait. Did you remember the photo album I made for Bonnie and Rohn?"

Phoenix smiled. "I did."

That very important item she had remembered. That her adoptive parents had so readily accepted her birth parents into all of their lives—after the initial shock had worn off of course—was amazing and wonderful and made this odd situation so much easier.

Her mother had taken the best pictures they had from her childhood and had them reproduced in an album as a gift for Rohn and Bonnie. The first time she'd seen the album, custom printed and bound, Phoenix had broken into tears. Hell, even thinking about it now had her getting misty.

"Okay, well then I'll let you go. Text when you're through security."

She cringed one more time. Because they weren't near the airport yet, that would be a while. "I will. 'Bye. Love you."

"Love you, too."

Phoenix disconnected the phone as Kim shot her a glance. "If you miss this plane, I'm not taking the heat from your parents. You're going to have to confess you weren't packed yet."

She scowled at the friend who was supposed to be on her side. "I was packed. I just hadn't quite finished yet. And we're going to make it in plenty of time. We're fine. There's no need to be there two hours ahead of time for a domestic flight, no matter what my father says."

"Fine. Let's move on to more pertinent topics, such as are you going to see your hot cowboy while you're there?"

Phoenix had a feeling there was no avoiding that as long as Justin still worked for Rohn and she was staying at the ranch. Unless she hid in her room and was completely antisocial, they were bound to run into each other at least once or twice, even if she hadn't heard from him in months.

She sighed. "I suppose so."

"You guys could rekindle things while you're there. Who knows what could happen."

His last text had been the unforgettable *K* in response to her telling him she'd made it home safely.

For whatever reason, he'd ended things. Maybe it had been something she'd done. She couldn't forget the look on his face as his friends teased him after she'd slipped and let out the fact that they'd been together the night before she left. But if she didn't mean more to him than a little teasing, if he wasn't man enough to stand up for them with his friends, then he wasn't worth her time.

The problem was, that didn't seem like the Justin she knew, and her instincts were rarely so off about a person.

"Can we please not talk about Justin?" It was too depressing to think about. She just wanted to be excited about seeing Rohn and Bonnie again.

"All right. Whatever you say. What would you like to talk about?"

Phoenix remembered her other problem. "You don't happen to have a quart-size clear plastic bag in the car, do you?"

The expression on Kim's face at the random ridiculousness of the question was so priceless, Phoenix couldn't help but burst out laughing.

Chapter Thirty-Nine

"They're back from the airport." Tyler glanced toward the driveway and then back to Justin. "You know what that means, don't you?"

Yeah, he knew exactly what that meant. It was only a matter of time before he ran into the woman he'd slept with but hadn't contacted in four months. And she happened to be his boss's daughter.

Justin kept all that to himself. Looking down and focusing on his task, he shook his head. "Nope."

"It means Phoenix is here."

"And?" Justin struck the ice in the water tub with the metal edge of the shovel.

"Don't you want to go say hello?" Tyler's question was definitely not as innocent as it sounded. That was made obvious by his smart-ass grin and the way he waggled his eyebrows up and down suggestively.

Justin took another stab at the ice before he turned to Tyler. "No. I want to get this ice broken up so Rohn doesn't get pissed that the bull ain't got no water to drink. If you're not gonna help, you can at least stop bothering me while I do it."

"Jeez. I seriously hope you get some this week while she's here. Maybe you'll be in a better mood."

Justin closed his eyes and counted to ten, trying his best to control his temper before he took a poke at Tyler instead of the ice. Ty should know better than to provoke a man wielding a shovel.

The ice was as broken up as it was going to get. Justin shot Tyler a look that he hoped expressed his feelings before he turned to head back down the hill.

There was no way to avoid seeing the truck parked by the house, or the happy family piling out of it. Bonnie and Tammy were on either side of Phoenix, leading her into the house, while Rohn pulled some pieces of luggage out of the back.

A happy homecoming.

With the wreaths still decorating the doors and windows of the house and the snow blanketing the ground, it was like a scene playing out in some Christmas commercial.

He ran his gloved hand beneath his nose. It was running from the cold. So were his eyes, watering from the brisk, biting breeze. If he was going to run into Phoenix while she was visiting, he sure as hell didn't want it to be now, while he looked like this.

Pulling the brim of his hat lower, he angled his head against the wind and headed for the barn.

That should be one place he could warm up without any risk of running into Rohn's guest from sunny California. He was pretty sure Bonnie wouldn't be taking her daughter to visit the barn, especially because it was empty. They had the horses turned out for the day while they cleaned the stalls.

In this weather, and after not seeing her for months, Bonnie and Phoenix should have plenty of catching up to do inside the nice warm house.

Visions of the kitchen, toasty warm and smelling of

fresh-brewed coffee, nearly had him saying *screw it*. He was almost willing to risk seeing her again just so he could head inside to defrost. Though after the way he'd left things with Phoenix, it was very possible his reception from her would be as frosty as the December air.

He had to stay firm. He'd had to do what he'd done to cut things off with her.

His sacrifice had been totally worth it, in his opinion.

Sure, he did nothing but go from work to home, with the occasional quick stop off at the store to pick up food or supplies. No, he hadn't gone out or done anything else fun for months. But the results were visible.

His mother hadn't had a bad day in at least two months. They'd even gotten through the holidays unscathed, and that had always been a tricky time in past years. He had nothing else to attribute it to besides his being present and focused on her.

If he wasn't at work, he was with his mother, mentally and physically. His one concession to maintaining his own sanity was the nightly hour of solitude he allowed himself to lift weights. Even then, it was only one hour, and he was right there in the garage, just steps from his mother should she need him.

Seeing her living a normal life, eating and sleeping and even smiling more often, had been well worth it. Even if he did have to endure watching her favorite television shows.

Things weren't completely back to normal. She hadn't gone back to work yet. They were still living off his earnings and the money in the savings account from his father's life insurance. But her going back to work would come with time. And if that time never came and he never had the freedom to move out, then he'd just have to figure out a way to deal with the situation.

Justin was working on mucking out the first stall when the barn door opened and Colton burst in.

"Hey. Rohn says to take a break and come on in and warm up. He's got a fresh pot of coffee on and Bonnie made cake."

Damn, warming up and having homemade cake and a nice scalding hot cup of fresh coffee sounded good. Almost good enough to make him forget about his plan to avoid Phoenix.

Almost, but not quite. "Thanks, but I'm not hungry."

Colton shrugged. "So then don't eat. Just come in and warm up for a bit."

"Nah. Thanks, but I think I'm just gonna stay here and get this done. You go on."

"What's wrong with you?" Colton frowned.

"What do you care what I do?"

"I don't except that you're acting weird. Is it Phoenix? You two have a fight?"

"Colton, I swear—" He gritted the words out through a clenched jaw.

"Fine. Stay out here and freeze. See if I care." Scowling, Colton turned and went out through the door he'd come in through.

He'd hear more about it later, he was sure. These guys didn't have enough to occupy their minds to keep them out of his life, but for now at least he'd have a few minutes' peace.

He'd just gotten the first stall stripped of soiled wood shavings when the door opened again. He blew out a breath. He'd been hoping for a longer reprieve, but apparently, he wasn't going to get it.

He walked out of the stall and into the aisle and found Rohn standing there, watching him.

"You wanna take a break and come in?"

"Nah. I'm good."

Rohn pursed his lips together and nodded slowly. Crossing his arms, he leaned against the wall and waited.

Justin wondered what the hell was going on. Not quite sure what to do, he stood, torn between going to work on the next stall and asking Rohn what the hell was up with him.

While he decided, he pulled off his gloves and blew on his frozen fingers to warm them, then pulled the gloves back on.

Rohn watched, his brow cocked. "Why don't you tell me what's going on between you and my daughter?"

Now that he knew what was on Rohn's mind, he kind of wished he didn't. Luckily, he could tell Rohn the truth on that. "Nothing's going on with Phoenix. I haven't spoken to her since she went back to California."

He nodded. "A'ight. Then I guess whatever's keeping you out here in the cold and away from Bonnie's cake just to avoid Phoenix must have happened before she went back to California. Am I right?"

Justin drew in a breath. "I didn't know who she was when we first met. Then, once I knew she was your daughter, it was too late. We'd already . . . become involved."

"Boy, she's twenty-five years old. She can make her own decisions, and I'm under no illusions that she's still a virgin at that age. Damn, even thinking that word in relation to my own daughter creeps me out, but anyway . . . Whatever happened between you two happened. That isn't the issue. The issue is what happened afterward. So you're telling me you were with her and then just never talked to her again?"

It sounded worse when Rohn said it, but it was the truth, so Justin nodded. "Yeah."

"You think that was the proper thing to do?" Rohn asked.
"No."

"Then why'd you do it?"

"I figured I had no choice." Justin shrugged.

Realization dawned on Rohn's features. His eyes widened.
"Because she's mine? Is that why you dumped her? You
didn't think I'd approve of you being with my daughter?"

"Well, the thought had crossed my mind." It hadn't been
the main reason, but Justin would be lying if he didn't admit
to being a little afraid of what Rohn would think about him
screwing around with his daughter.

"Son, of all the guys I've had working for me over the
years, you're probably the only one I'd approve of dating my
daughter. You work hard. You got your head on straight
when it comes to money and family. I've never known you
to be a partier or a player. Tyler, back in the day, before
Janie, or Colton—if either of them were with Phoenix, I'd
worry. But not you."

"Thank you. That means a lot to me actually." Justin had
to tell him the truth. Rohn was the closest thing he had to
a father figure in his life since his dad had died. Besides,
he'd already come this far with his confession. "It's more
than that."

"Then talk to me. What else is bothering you?"

"It's Momma. She needs me. I can't be distracted with a
relationship. Not one with a girl nearby, and not with a girl
halfway across the country. Momma needs one hundred
percent from me right now. I've tried dividing my attention.
It didn't work out well." Justin shook his head as he remembered coming home from being with Phoenix and finding
his mother in such a horrible state. "I know it's not fair to
Phoenix, but I think it's best if I just avoid seeing her."

"Does she know the situation with your ma?"

Justin shook his head.

"Maybe you should tell her."

Justin lifted one shoulder. "What good would it do? It doesn't change anything. I can't be with Phoenix the way I'd want to if things were different."

"But you would want to be with her if things were different?"

"It's useless to even think about—"

"Just answer the question, son."

They'd been in a truck together for two straight days and hadn't wanted to kill each other. They'd talked. They'd laughed. In bed, they'd fit together like hand and glove.

He pushed that thought aside and answered Rohn's question. "Yeah, I'd want to be with her. Who wouldn't? I mean, she's great."

"Then tell her everything you told me."

"Why? I made the break months ago. I'm sure she's moved on."

"I don't know. All I know is, the second we drove onto the property and she spotted your truck, she started asking round-about questions about the ranch that always seemed to lead back to the subject of you. She hasn't stopped looking at the kitchen door since we got home. If you really think you two can't be together, she at least deserves to know why."

"You're right." He wouldn't let himself hope they could be together because they couldn't, but she did deserve an explanation. It was only fair to her.

"So, you ready to come inside?" Rohn waited, but Justin hesitated.

Trying to act friendly and social and pretend it wasn't ripping him apart to see her was too much for him to handle.

He'd talk to Phoenix alone. He'd confess everything about his messed-up family life, but not in front of everyone. His coworkers and her family.

His decision made, Justin shook his head. "I don't think

I'll come in right now. If Tyler or Colt make any smart-ass comments, I can't promise I won't slug them."

"Just don't let me see you doing it and that's fine with me." Rohn shrugged.

He laughed. "Thanks, I'll keep that in mind, but I'd rather stay out here and work."

"Should I send Phoenix out with a cup of coffee for you?"

"Nah. I'm good. Thanks."

He didn't need any cake and coffee. Seeing Phoenix, whenever that happened, was going to be bittersweet enough.

And if they were alone in the barn, she'd expect them to have a serious talk. He wasn't sure he was ready to have that talk with her yet. He needed a little time to wrap his head around what he was going to say.

Justin continued, "Besides, she's not used to this weather. Keep her inside where it's warm."

Rohn eyed him for a moment, then finally nodded. "A'ight."

Chapter Forty

Phoenix glanced up when the kitchen door opened, but Rohn was alone.

"Justin doesn't want to come inside?" Bonnie asked.

Rohn shook his head and looked around the group. "More coffee for anyone?"

That was it, then. Justin wanted to avoid her so badly he was hiding in the barn. No surprise. That sounded exactly like the actions of a man whose final text had read *K*.

"More hot tea, sweetie?" Tammy asked.

She forced a smile, hoping it didn't look as fake as it felt. "No, thank you. I'm good."

"Phoenix, I hate to ask you this, but would you mind running this out to the barn and giving it to Justin for me?" Rohn held a stainless-steel coffee cup with a lid in his hand.

"I can take—" Colton's offer was cut short as he glared at Tyler. "Ow. You kicked me."

Tyler raised a brow. "Did I? Sorry. I'll actually take more of that coffee. Colton here, too, if there's any left." Tyler pushed his mug forward.

"Sure thing." Rohn set the to-go mug on the table in front of her and turned to reach for the coffeepot on the counter. "Phoenix, run that outside while it's still hot."

Apparently, there was a reason Rohn wanted her to go to the barn, and it seemed that Tyler was in on it. And though Bonnie and Tammy weren't pushing her out the door like Rohn, they were watching the exchange with interest, while Colton continued to frown over the whole thing.

There was only one thing to do. She stood and reached for the cup. "Okay. Be back in a minute."

Rohn shot her a glance. "No rush. You take your time."

"Okay." She'd be seeing Justin whether he wanted her there or not. She only hoped he wouldn't be upset.

"Put on your jacket. It's cold out there," Bonnie called after her.

Phoenix smiled at how much she sounded like a true mother. "I will."

Rohn let out a snort. "Her jacket won't help. It's too light, and she doesn't even have gloves. Put on Bonnie's coat instead."

"Good idea. It's hanging right inside the door. My gloves are in the pockets."

Rolling her eyes, Phoenix put the coffee down on the wide wooden windowsill and reached for the coat. She didn't know what they were all so worried about. She wouldn't be outside long enough to get chilled. It was more than obvious that Justin didn't want to talk to her or he would have come inside.

Her bringing him coffee wouldn't change that. It would only make things more awkward when she intruded upon his hiding place, so she wasn't going to hang around.

As she slipped her arms inside the heavy winter coat, she decided she'd drop off the coffee, apologize for bothering him, and leave. She'd be back indoors before Tyler and Colton's refills had cooled. Then she'd have to figure out what Rohn's motivation was for throwing her at Justin.

That was a mystery she'd have to wait to solve. She left the warmth of the kitchen and felt the cold outdoor air against her face. It felt good, invigorating, making her skin tingle. They didn't get snow or cold like this in her part of California. It was nice.

The ranch was beautiful. It was like stepping into another time. Another era. She could easily see herself spending Christmas break in Oklahoma every year. Summer breaks, too, when the fields were green and the stock dotted the landscape.

But all the natural beauty along the way didn't change what was waiting for her in the barn. She reached the door and swallowed hard, remembering the last time she'd set foot in this building. She had gone there to say good-bye to Justin.

Just the memory had her tea and cake churning in her gut as she reached for the latch and pulled the door open.

The barn was warmer than outside, especially once she pulled and latched the door shut behind her, blocking the wind.

The bulbs burning above her provided a warm glow, but she didn't see Justin. It didn't take long to figure out where he was, though. She saw a pitchfork full of manure fly through the air and land in a wheelbarrow resting in front of a stall. The first was followed by another.

She must be crazy—it was nothing more than animal crap—but she smiled at the charm of the quintessential ranch scene.

It could be the city girl in her, but life seemed simpler here. Love, however, not so much. That was just as complicated and confusing. And painful.

She felt the full force of that pain when she peeked around the doorway of the stall, making sure to stay clear of the path of the manure.

Justin was faced away from her, using the tines of a

pitchfork to scoop the small round lumps of manure out of the wood shavings on the floor of the stall.

He turned. She knew Justin saw her just as he was about to let one more pile fly toward the wheelbarrow. He stopped the motion in time, his eyes widening.

"Phoenix."

"Hey. Rohn asked me to bring you this." She held up the coffee cup.

"Oh." He stepped forward and dropped the manure into the wheelbarrow before leaning the pitchfork against the wall. He reached out and took the cup. "Thanks."

"You're welcome." Four months since they'd last spoken and their first conversation was over a cartful of horseshit about coffee.

"How was your flight?"

"Good. A whole lot shorter than the drive was last time so, yeah, good."

Justin put the cup down on the ledge of the stall and sighed. "I owe you an explanation."

"No. Seriously, you—"

"Phoenix. Let me talk, please."

"Okay." She rolled her lips in, sealing her mouth shut before she lost control and interrupted him again.

"I was a dick about us. I know that." The honesty of his confession caught her off guard.

"Well, they say admitting you have a problem is the first step." She watched him lift one brow at her cocky comment. She backed down. The man was trying to apologize. She should at least let him. She could be bitchy about the extreme lateness of the apology later on the phone with Kim. "Sorry. Go on."

"I want you to know why I acted the way I did." He paused. When she didn't jump in again, he continued.

"About two years ago, my brother was killed by a roadside bomb in Afghanistan."

Her intake of breath was involuntary. "Oh my God, Justin. I'm so sorry."

"Thanks." He nodded. "Anyway, it was a shock to all of us, but my mother took it hard. She got severely depressed. My father died about ten years ago and after Jeremy . . . well, that left only her and me, so I moved back home."

Phoenix swallowed hard as she grasped for the first time why Justin had been so concerned about his mother. Always checking in at home. Worrying if she didn't answer.

"I thought . . . hell, I wanted to think that I could have a normal life and still be there for her. I tried. With you. But that last night I was with you in the hotel, I got home and found her . . . let's just say it was pretty bad." He shook his head and drew in a shaky breath. "That's when I realized I couldn't have it all. I couldn't have you and be a good son. I'm sorry."

"You should have told me."

"I know that now."

She took a step closer to him and touched his arm. "I would have understood. I do understand."

"I'm glad." He glanced down and covered her bare fingers with his gloved hand. "You should be wearing gloves."

"So I've been told." There were supposedly gloves in the pockets of the coat, but as Justin lifted her hand in both of his and brought it to his mouth to blow warm air against her cold skin, she decided she'd much rather have him heat her hands.

Her mind spun with all the information he'd dumped on her. Missing pieces fell into place and a picture formed.

"The reason you have two trucks. Was one of them your brother's?"

He nodded.

"The one we drove from Arizona." The truck she wasn't allowed to drive.

"Yeah."

Another realization hit Phoenix. "And the radio station?" The one he'd freaked out about when she'd tried to change it.

He smiled sadly. "Was the one he listened to before he left for that last deployment. I can't bring myself to change it. I know it's not healthy. I'm not doing much better than my mother at dealing with it, I guess."

"It takes time. And maybe if you let people help you . . . Let me help you." She brought her other bare hand out of the coat pocket and up to join his hands. He held them both in his, close to his chest. They were standing toe to toe when she asked, "How is your mother doing now? Any better?"

Justin nodded. "Yeah. I only leave her to come here, and I try to cut out as early as I can in the afternoon. It seems having me home more is helping."

So he went to work and then went home and had no social life. The jealous part of Phoenix was happy there weren't other females in his life. That he hadn't been dating, or even going out, by the sound of it. The practical side of her knew that was no kind of life for a guy his age.

"But is it helping you?" she asked.

"Knowing she's doing better? Yeah, it does help. I'm not saying I don't think about how things could be different." He squeezed her fingers and then released his hold on her hands. "But this is how they have to be."

He reached for the coffee mug as the chill of his reality crept through her more than the cold air ever had.

"So, how long are you here for?"

Apparently the confessional portion of the discussion was over and they'd moved on to small talk.

"I'm flying back after New Year's. School starts that

Monday." She shoved her hands deep into the pockets of Bonnie's coat.

Putting on the gloves she felt inside wouldn't help defrost the cold hard truth that, even if he did have a good reason for it, Justin couldn't be with her. Apparently, not even for a little fling during the week she was here. Except for that one little lapse when he'd held her hands, he was staunchly keeping his hands off her and on the coffee.

He nodded. "Bonnie and Rohn are real happy you're here. Tammy, too."

"Yeah. I'm happy I got to visit."

"Hey, how'd things go with your parents? You told them everything, right?"

"I did. They were really great actually. Of course they weren't at all happy I'd traveled all that way alone."

"You weren't totally alone. You had me for one leg of the trip." He cocked a brow.

"Yeah, like that would have helped. Telling them I got into a truck with a man I didn't know. And then shared a hotel room with him in Texas." She lifted one brow.

He grinned. "Touché. But I'm glad they were okay with you finding Bonnie and Rohn."

"Oh, yeah. In fact, I'm hoping they'll come out here for a visit next summer when I'm here. So they can all meet and get to know one another."

"You'll be here this summer?"

His interest in her spending time here had her hopes rising. She nodded. "Yup. That's the plan."

Having two sets of parents, and splitting holidays and school breaks between them, was a little bit like being the child of divorced parents but without the divorce.

Phoenix had plenty of parental figures in her life. It was the boyfriend department in which she was lacking. As she watched Justin nod and look politely interested in the news that she'd be in Oklahoma all summer, she had to think there wasn't much hope of that changing anytime soon.

"Well, that'll be real nice for everyone, I'm sure." He'd shut down again. She watched as he pulled up the invisible walls around him.

At least this time she knew she wasn't the reason. It wasn't something she'd done or said.

She wished that knowledge made it easier to see him, want him, but not be able to be with him. It didn't.

"I better get back to the stalls. Thanks again for bringing out the coffee." He reached for the pitchfork.

"You're welcome." She'd obviously been dismissed.

The cold creeping into her heart surpassed the chill of the barn as she turned and left.

Chapter Forty-One

Justin walked through the kitchen door, ass dragging. Even when they did finish with chores early in the afternoon, the sun set so damn early in December it was getting dark by the time he got home.

It was no wonder people got depressed in the wintertime.

Seeing Phoenix today, touching her even briefly, talking as he explained why things had to be the way they were between them, hadn't cheered him. All it had done was make him feel more keenly the gaping hole in his life. The spot that she would fill so nicely.

That wasn't in the cards right now. He sighed and tossed his truck keys onto the counter. "I'm home."

His mother walked into the kitchen, smiling. "Hi. I have dinner in the oven."

"You do?" He frowned and glanced toward the stove. Now that she mentioned it, he detected the aroma of cooking beef that his cold and stuffy nose had previously missed. "Meat loaf?"

"Yup. Ground beef was on special today."

"You went out?"

"Of course. The store doesn't deliver chopped meat to your door, silly."

Now that he thought about it, they hadn't run out of any staples recently. Not milk or eggs or bread. She must have been running out to the store during the day while he'd been at work.

How had he not noticed that?

Probably because he'd been so busy wallowing in his own misery, feeling like a martyr for devoting his life to his mother, he hadn't noticed that she was making strides all on her own.

He glanced around the kitchen. It was spotless. There wasn't a bowl in the sink, or even a crumb on the counter, even though she'd made the meat loaf.

"I only put that in a little while ago, so it's got at least an hour in the oven. Why don't you go do your weight lifting now? That way you can work out and shower and it will be ready when you are."

"Um, okay." He was too flabbergasted by this change in his mother to argue. He pulled off his jacket and headed out to the garage.

Sitting on the weight bench, he grabbed the barbell and started to review the past few weeks in his mind. Maybe he hadn't noticed the small changes in her because, just like every year since Jeremy's death, they hadn't decorated the house for the holiday. No tree. No wreaths. No baking of cookies.

But now that he thought about it, there had been other subtle changes he'd missed.

A few times this month, he'd walked into the living room to find her watching holiday movies, when this time last year she would have changed the channel.

He hadn't taken out the vacuum in weeks, but the carpets

were clean. He'd assumed they just hadn't gotten dirty, but undoubtedly his mother had vacuumed when he'd been at work.

Counting the reps for his workout was a lost cause. His mind was whirling with thoughts. He put the bar back in the brace and got up from the bench. He headed to the kitchen. His mother was setting the table with plates for dinner.

She turned when he came into the room. "You done already?"

He looked at her more closely. Her hair looked shorter. And not as if she'd taken the scissors to it herself either, but like she'd gone to have it done.

"Um, I just wanted to grab a bottle of water." He didn't want to bombard her with questions or make a big deal about the small signs that she was improving.

She smiled. "In the fridge."

"Thanks." He opened the door and took note of everything inside. Oranges. Lettuce. Nothing he'd bought. Acting as casual as he could, he closed the door and turned toward her. "So, what else did you do today? Besides food shop and make meat loaf?"

"Well, I went to the church and helped set up the chairs for the group meeting there. Then I stayed and helped clear out all the poinsettias because they're starting to drop their leaves."

"Oh, that was nice of you." He nodded as his mind spun.

There were only two types of meetings he knew about that took place at his church in the middle of the week. Those were the grief group that he'd been trying to get his mother to go to for years and the alcohol group.

Because it was a big deal if his mother had a glass of wine with his aunt over dinner, he figured she'd been at the grief support group today.

"How come you never go out with your friends after work anymore?"

Her question surprised him. "I'd rather come home and be with you."

She cocked a brow in his direction. "You'd rather be here with me watching television than going out and having fun with the guys? Or with a girl?"

Justin shrugged.

"Sweetie, I know you want to be here so I'm not alone, but you need to have friends your own age."

"I do. I see Tyler and Colton all day long at the ranch."

"And what about girls? At your age you should be out dating."

This was ironic. He'd given up going out and dating for his mother, and now it was his mother who was lecturing him for not going out and dating.

"Isn't there anyone you're interested in?" she asked.

Justin's mind turned to Phoenix. "There is one."

"Really? Then why aren't you taking her out?"

God, how he wished he could believe his mother would really be okay if he did start to live his own life again. But they'd been down this road before, when he'd thought she was on the mend, only to come home and find her sobbing in Jeremy's room.

He shrugged. "I don't know."

"Justin, I think you should call this girl and ask her out. Or text, because that's what you kids like to do nowadays, even though I think it's way harder than just picking up the phone."

"Okay. I'll think about it." He shook his head at her ongoing argument about text messaging versus calling and moved on to find out more info. "You know, you and I could go out to a movie if you wanted to."

It might take baby steps to get her back to normal, but he was more than willing to take them with her.

"You're not ashamed to be seen with your mother?" she asked.

"Of course not."

She smiled. "Okay, we can see a movie, but not tonight. It's the two-hour season finale of my show."

"Two hours. Great." He knew by now what shows were on which nights and he knew exactly which one she was talking about.

God, how he hated that show, and as hard as he tried to hide it, his mother was aware of his feelings. She even joked with him about it, but good son that he was, he watched it with her every damn week.

She must have heard his lack of enthusiasm. She laughed. "Tonight might be a good night to call that girl."

"You're right. It might be." He didn't argue the point.

He was about to head back out to the garage to finish his workout and mull over this strange and enlightening conversation when he noticed her biting her lip, as if she had more to say. He leaned against the counter, cracked open his water, and took a sip.

Finally, she said, "The church secretary offered me a job today."

He almost choked on the water. "Really? Doing what?"

"Answering phones. Helping like I did today to set up for meetings and services. Putting together the weekly newsletter. Just part-time."

A job, even part-time, seemed like a huge step. Would having responsibilities and someplace to go every day help her? Or would the pressure be too much and send her back into the darkness to hide? He didn't know. He wasn't sure she did either.

He tried not to react as he asked, "So what did you tell her?"

"That I had to talk to you first."

He raised a brow. The decision was hers to make. Not his. "Well, I think you should do whatever makes you happy. Do you want to take it?"

"I think I do. I've been going over to help out for a few hours a week since Thanksgiving. I enjoy being there and seeing the people. This would be basically the same thing except I'd get paid for it."

"Then I think you should say yes. It sounds like they appreciate all your help." He reached out and hugged his mother as his hope grew. He didn't want to get excited, but the hint of a light at the end of the very long dark tunnel they'd been in was hard to ignore.

"I think I will." She hugged him back and then pulled away. "Now go finish your workout."

"Okay."

Outside, he put down his water and sat on the bench one more time. The workout couldn't be further from his mind. He had a lot to think about.

Chapter Forty-Two

The text came through after dinner. Phoenix was lying on the sofa, so stuffed from the meal she couldn't imagine moving, even to go up to bed, when she felt the phone in her pocket vibrate.

Figuring it was Kim, she wrestled the cell out of her jeans. Her eyes widened when she read the message.

It's Justin. Is it ok if I come over to talk?

He didn't have to identify himself. Crazy girl that she was, she'd kept his number saved in her contacts list all these months, just in case.

There had been more than a time or two she'd been tempted to use it over the past months, usually when a glass of wine with Kim prompted her to give him a piece of her mind.

Now that she knew why he'd acted as he had, it turned out it was a good thing she'd controlled that impulse.

She was still staring at the phone, deciding what to do, when Rohn stood, stretching as he did. "Well, it's been a long day. I think I'm gonna hit the hay."

"I'll come up, too." Bonnie stood as well, smiling at

Phoenix. "I was so excited about you getting here, I barely slept all night."

"All night? You hardly slept all week." Rohn grinned, wrapping his arm around Bonnie. "Good night, darlin'."

"Good night."

"I know you're on California time, so feel free to stay up as late as you want." Bonnie broke away from Rohn's grasp long enough to lean down and hug her. "I'm so glad you're here."

Phoenix smiled. "Me too. Good night."

Tammy had already gone home to her house after dessert, so once Rohn and Bonnie went upstairs, she'd be alone downstairs. And if she texted Justin back and told him to come over, she'd be alone with Justin.

Heart racing, she punched in the text.

Come on over. Kitchen door unlocked. Don't knock. Parents sleeping.

His reply came back fast, as she'd hoped it would.

Be right there.

Something had changed. Maybe it was their conversation. She didn't know, but he wanted to see her and that was good enough. She stood. She had things to do before he arrived.

She'd barely had time to settle back onto the sofa in the living room to wait for him before she heard the truck in the drive.

Justin was good as his word. He'd driven over in the short time it had taken her to make sure the kitchen door was indeed unlocked as promised and then run to the bathroom to check how she looked in the mirror.

She smiled as she made her way down the hallway and into the kitchen. She reached the room in time to see him creeping through the back door. A six-foot-tall man in cowboy boots trying to tiptoe was a comical sight.

"Hi." She kept her voice down as she greeted him.

He glanced up. "Hey."

She was happy he'd kept his voice low, too. She didn't want to disturb Rohn and Bonnie, or wake the old deaf hound dog Cooter, who'd long ago crawled into his bed in the pantry in the back of the kitchen to go to sleep.

Phoenix told herself she was being nice not wanting to wake anyone, but in reality she wanted time with Justin without an audience. There was no risk of his coworkers walking in on them, but she didn't want her new mom and dad around right now either. It had to be just him and her. Maybe then he'd let down those walls.

Justin eased the door closed and wiped his feet on the rug in front of it. She waited, wondering what had inspired him to come out in the dark cold night to talk.

Their gazes collided as he pulled off his gloves and tossed them onto the counter. His eyes narrowed as he strode forward and grabbed her shoulders with both hands.

"Phoenix." That was all he said before his mouth closed over hers.

She sank into his kiss, wrapping her arms around him, winter coat and all. His embrace felt familiar. Like coming home. His lips cleared away all the doubts she'd felt for months. His tongue claimed her, letting her know she was his, which was exactly what she wanted to be.

When he broke the kiss, he leaned his forehead against hers and sighed. "Sorry. I couldn't help myself."

"That's quite all right. I'm very glad you came over to talk. I like this kind of talking. In fact, let's go into the living room where we can get comfortable and *talk* some more."

He laughed. "I really did want to talk to you."

"All right. We'll get to that. Later." She reached up and pressed a kiss to his lips.

"You trying to distract me?" He tightened his hold around her.

"Maybe." Kissing seemed safer than talking when there was a very real possibility she might not like what he had to say. "Besides, you started it."

"I know. I'm a weak man. I've thought of nothing but kissing you since I saw you in the barn today."

"You should have kissed me in the barn, then."

"I shouldn't even be kissing you now."

Phoenix didn't like the sound of that. She drew in a breath and decided it was time to face whatever was to come. "Want to take off your coat and sit down? Or aren't you staying that long?"

"I think I can stay for a little." He reached for the buttons on his coat.

She took a step back and let him divest himself of his winter jacket, watching as he hung it on the back of a kitchen chair.

When he was done, she led the way to the living room. It was warm and cozy, lit only by one table lamp and the flicker of the television with the volume turned low. Perching on the edge of the sofa, she waited as he sat next to her.

"Phoenix . . ."

She held her breath, waiting for what, she didn't know. It wasn't as if he could dump her because they weren't in any sense of the word a couple. She should have just kept kissing him in the kitchen.

Whatever he was trying to say obviously wasn't coming easy. She reached out and took both of his hands in hers and just held them, not saying anything. Just being there for him.

He stared down at their joined hands. "I can't make any promises."

"Okay." She didn't remember asking for any promises, but she didn't bring that up.

Justin finally raised his eyes to meet hers. "It might not work out."

Still confused about what he was getting at, she sat quiet and waited.

He continued, "But I'd like to give it a try."

Phoenix waited for more. Some clue that he was really saying what she hoped he was saying, that he wanted to give them a try.

Finally, she couldn't wait anymore and said, "Give *us* a try?"

"Yeah." He drew in a breath. "I'm sorry. I'm no good at this."

He was good enough. He might not have all the right words, but the meaning behind them set her heart pounding. "I'd like to give us a try, too."

Justin pulled her closer. He wrapped one beefy arm around her neck, pressing her face into the flannel covering his rock hard chest as he buried his face in her hair. She felt his already broad torso expand as he drew in a deep breath.

With her face crushed against the brick wall of his chest, she managed to mumble, "Have you been working out?"

His laugh vibrated beneath her cheek. "Yeah. I was bored . . . and frustrated."

"I like it." She pulled back to look up at him, though she didn't take her hands off his muscles because she was enjoying the feel of him. "When I'm bored and frustrated I eat, as you can tell by the increased size of my ass."

"I like it." He smiled and moved his hands down to rest on the swell of her hips.

"That's good, because I'm not going to lose any weight

the way you people eat around here." Her gaze dropped to his lips, so close, so tempting. Dragging her focus up to his eyes, she saw a need there equal to her own.

She swung one thigh over his. Facing him, she straddled his lap, intent on getting as close to this man as she could while still fully clothed.

His eyes widened. "Phoenix, we can't do this here."

His cupping her ass with both palms as he spoke told her the opposite of his words.

"Sure we can." She leaned in, cradling his face in her hands as she moved closer.

"What if Rohn comes downstairs?"

"You can't tell me you never fooled around with a girl while her parents were in the house." She didn't like thinking of Justin with any female other than her, but she wasn't insane enough to think he'd lived like a monk until he met her.

"If I did, it was because I was a kid and we had nowhere else to go."

She raised a brow. "Well, short of sneaking out to get a hotel room, neither do we."

He sighed. "That's sad but true."

Having won the argument, she grinned. "We'll just have to be quiet. It'll be even more exciting."

"Oh, it'll be exciting all right. Especially when Rohn pulls a shotgun on me for taking advantage of his daughter under his roof."

"His daughter wants to be taken advantage of. Trust me. Besides, you'll be kissing me in front of Rohn shortly."

"Oh, really? And why is that?" Justin asked.

"He and Bonnie are throwing a New Year's Eve party and I fully expect a kiss at midnight, so prepare yourself."

He grinned. "Okay. I will."

"Good." She leaned low and pressed her lips to his, cutting off any further discussion.

His hand in her hair as he angled his mouth over hers told her the debate was over for now.

Phoenix had been away from Justin for too many months to be satisfied with just kissing. She leaned back and reached down to the waistband of her pants.

Justin reached out to stop her. "I don't think you should do that."

If he really thought they were going to do nothing but make out on the sofa like two teenage virgins, he was so mistaken.

"I think you're wrong." She pushed his hands away.

He smiled and shook his head. "Points for being persistent, but no."

Phoenix rolled her eyes. "Fine."

There was more than one way to skin a cat. She leaned in again, pressing as close to him as she could get while she kissed him. The right pressure in the right region while she straddled him soon had Justin groaning.

Still joined at the lips, she reached for the button on his jeans rather than her own this time. He didn't stop her. When she slipped her hand inside and connected with his hard length, he hissed in a breath.

It was easy to get distracted by the warm hard man beneath her, but Phoenix had a goal. Feeling her victory over his protests was close, she moved off him, until she was kneeling on the floor between his legs.

He was breathing hard, his eyes heavily lidded with desire, as he watched her push the waist of his underwear down and free his erection. He swallowed hard. "Phoenix, we shouldn't—"

Justin never finished the sentence as she slid his cock between her lips. All she heard was his deep intake of breath, followed by his moan. She felt his fingers tangle in her hair, putting pressure against her scalp. The sound of the television and the creaking of the leather sofa slipped further into the background as his breathing sped up along with the motion of her mouth and hands.

Phoenix felt him tense before she tasted his release.

Still panting, he pulled her back up onto the sofa.

When he reached to unfasten the button on her jeans, she figured he was done fighting her. She was more than glad of that.

Chapter Forty-Three

Rohn opened the back door at Justin's knock. His gaze traveled from Justin to his mother, standing next to him. "Hey. Happy New Year. Come on in. I'm glad you could make it. Both of you."

Justin was glad, too, as he guided his mother inside. "Thanks for inviting us."

Bonnie turned from the counter where she'd been transferring tiny hot dogs from a baking tray to a platter.

Smiling, she moved toward Justin's mother. "Hi, I'm Bonnie. It's so nice to meet you."

His mother smiled and handed Bonnie a covered plate. "I know you told Justin not to bring anything, but I made my bread pudding with caramel sauce. I thought you can't go wrong with a sweet."

"Oh my gosh. No, you can't. That sounds amazing. I can't wait to try it. Come on in. Take your things off. We're putting the coats in Rohn's office. Justin, you know where that is." Bonnie put the bread pudding on the counter and turned to Justin.

"That's where I go to get my paychecks, so I surely do know where that room is." He eyed Phoenix, hovering in the doorway. He motioned her closer while guiding his mother forward. "Momma, this is Phoenix."

His mother's eyes widened. "It's so nice to meet you finally. Justin has told me so much about you."

Looking nervous, Phoenix reached out to shake his mother's hand. "Nice to meet you, too."

It was crazy she'd be nervous. Of course his mother would love her. What was there not to love? He couldn't imagine a thing. Then again, he was pretty biased when it came to Phoenix.

His mother smiled at Phoenix's extended hand. "We're huggers around here." She enveloped Phoenix in a hug that looked like it surprised her, but she accepted the gesture.

Finally, his mother released Phoenix, and Justin had the opportunity to lean down and give her a peck on the cheek when what he really wanted to do was get her alone. "Happy New Year."

"Happy New Year." Her color high in her cheeks, Phoenix smiled at him.

Rohn appeared next to them. He paid particular attention to Justin's mother when he asked, "What can I get you to drink?"

"Um, I don't know. It's been so long since I've gone out to any sort of cocktail party, I'm not sure what to have."

Rohn laughed. "Well, I'm usually a beer man myself, but Bonnie is making me pretend I'm fancy for the holiday. Come with me to the bar and I'll show you what we have. Bonnie went a little crazy and we have stuff even I've never heard of, and I can tell you I've been drinking for quite a few years. Have you ever heard of a Kir Royale?"

His mother raised a brow. "I can't say I have. It sounds fancy, though."

"Oh, believe me, it is." Rohn grinned. "We had to break out the champagne glasses from the china cabinet and everything. Come on. I'll make you one. She had me watch some video on the Internet so I could do it."

With his mother safely basking in the warmth of Rohn's charm, Justin smiled at Phoenix. "I gotta drop our coats in the office. Wanna help me?"

"You need my help to carry two coats?" she asked as she followed him to the room down the hall.

Tossing the coats on top of Rohn's chair, he reeled her in with one arm. "No, but I needed this."

He kissed her hard and deep, groaning before he could bring himself to break away. "Mmm. I missed those kisses today."

"Sorry. I had to help Bonnie shop for the party. Then we were busy cooking and cleaning. I didn't have time to sneak out to the barn to make out with you while nobody was looking."

"Just make sure it doesn't happen again. I only have you for a few more days before you fly away."

"Shh. No talking about my leaving. Remember?"

"I remember. But can I say your summer break can't get here soon enough in my opinion?"

"Actually, I've been talking to Kim. I think I have her almost convinced that midwinter break in Oklahoma will be even more fun than the trip we'd planned to Aruba."

He raised a brow. "Have you now? When is this break of yours?"

"Mid-February."

"February in Oklahoma versus Aruba. Hmm, is your friend Kim a little touched in the head?" Justin joked, but the possibility he'd be seeing Phoenix again next month rather than next summer was very good news.

Phoenix smiled. "No. But I've been talking up the cowboy population of Oklahoma so much, she's intrigued. In fact, if

I could promise her a little cowboy action, I think it might be a done deal."

"Well, if that's all you need, I have no problem offering up Colton for the cause."

"Will Colton have a problem?"

"Your friend Kim is a female, right?"

"Yes, of course."

"Then, yeah. That's about Colton's only criteria for a date, so we're good."

"You're bad." She slapped at his arm.

"No, but I'd like to be bad." He eyed the door. "How long do you think we have before someone comes looking for us?"

"Not long enough." She ran her hands up his chest, making him wish they were skin on skin rather than in party clothes. "I'm glad your mother came."

That subject sobered Justin fast enough. "Me too."

His mother's decision to attend was incredible and shocking and wonderful all at the same time. When Rohn and Bonnie had decided to have a New Year's Eve party and invited Justin and his mother, he'd been astonished when she said yes.

He still couldn't shake the feeling that he was waiting for the other shoe to drop, but so far, she'd continued to improve. She was working at the church. She seemed to be enjoying cooking again.

For the past week, he'd gone home every night after work to eat dinner with his mother, but afterward she encouraged him to go out and spend time with Phoenix while she was at the ranch.

For the first time in a long time, he was tempted to let himself think about tomorrow. To plan for the future, even if their definite plans only extended as far as summer break.

But he let himself fantasize sometimes. Let his mind wander while he was mucking the stalls or scrubbing water buckets. He drifted to a time when maybe Phoenix might consider a change. Might start working in Oklahoma and visiting California on her breaks, instead of the other way around.

She had her adopted parents and her job and her best friend tying her to California. But she had Rohn and Bonnie and Tammy here for inspiration. And him. At least he'd like to think seeing more of him might be a small motivating factor.

Things were so new. He was still getting used to his mother getting back to her life. And he was still walking around in a haze from the times he and Phoenix acted like teenagers having sex on her parents' sofa while Bonnie and Rohn slept upstairs. But damn, if things stayed as good as they were right now between them, he could picture himself doing something to make her want to stick around Oklahoma.

Something more permanent. Something he'd never considered seriously before. He ran a thumb over her bare ring finger as the thought had his heart thundering.

All in good time.

Right now, he intended to enjoy having a girlfriend for the first time in a very long time. He wanted to sport Phoenix around, looking incredible in a clingy black dress and boots. He fully intended to make Colton jealous. To shut Tyler up after hearing him brag all last year how he had a girl of his own when neither of them did.

And he was definitely going to enjoy kissing her at midnight.

"Ready to go back out?" he asked.

"Ready." She nodded.

"Good." Justin was suddenly anxious to get the party started. It felt like the first night of the start of what was going to be a pretty great new year.

Did you miss the first of the Midnight Cowboys novels?

Read on for an excerpt from

Midnight Ride,

available now in paperback or eBook.

There were times when a man should stick around and fight, and there were times when it was wiser to cut and run. It was clear to Tyler this was the latter.

Shoving the woman he'd been kissing just moments before out of the way, he clamped his hat lower on his head and took off at a sprint as her bruiser of a fiancé followed him.

Cowboy boots weren't meant for running, but Tyler managed it. He sure had incentive. Avoiding being pummeled into the ground by a jealous fiancé served as fine inspiration. He knew the truck was unlocked, but he didn't have the keys to start the engine. Colton had those with him inside the bar. He wasn't about to lock himself inside a truck he couldn't flee in, not with an angry lunatic hot on his tail, so he kept running.

The terrain worked in his favor, as did the darkness, as Tyler crashed into the woods off the side of the parking lot. Branches whacked into him as he dodged between them. He twisted an ankle when one foot landed on a rock, but he kept going, limping in a half run. A pine bough caught him across the face, blinding him as he squeezed the injured eye tight and the tears began to flow. Still, he forged ahead. His life depended on it.

The woods broke into a clearing and he realized he was behind the lumberyard right off the main road in town.

Tyler slowed to a fast walk when he hit the concrete and glanced around him. He needed to get somewhere safe and tend to his eye, which hurt like hell and was still tearing up. He needed to zip his jeans and refasten the belt buckle the girl had undone, all while she'd kept to herself the one important detail that the fiancé she was mad at was just inside, working the door of the bar. He also needed to make sure his cell phone hadn't fallen out of the back pocket of his jeans so he could call Colton to come rescue him. But before any of that, he had to make sure the man in hot pursuit hadn't followed this far.

A crash in the woods behind him, followed by a loud cuss, told him the lunatic hadn't given up yet. Damn, but this guy was persistent.

Tyler took off running again, though at this point it was more of a fast hobble. He had to hide. A pickup truck parked in the lot in front of him provided his only hope. He should just take the truck and drive away. It wouldn't be stealing. He'd only be borrowing it. He could bring it back as soon as life and limb were no longer in jeopardy, but he didn't know if the owner had left the key inside and he couldn't waste precious seconds checking.

Maybe it was dark enough that if he lay flat and still in the back, he might not be seen. But if the guy looked close enough and saw him hiding, he'd be a sitting duck. It was a chance he was going to have to take.

Running out of time, he sprinted to the back of the truck, planted both hands on the tailgate, and vaulted into the bed. When he landed inside, Tyler knew his luck was holding. There was a big green tarp in the bottom of the truck bed.

He flipped it over himself and held his breath, trying to move as little as possible. While he waited to be discovered or not, he figured praying couldn't hurt. Silently, he vowed that if he got out of this night unscathed, he'd never make out with a stranger in a bar again.

As his heart pounded, he heard heavy footsteps in the lot, and then a few more loud cusses and what sounded like a bear—or a really big man—crashing back through the trees. Seconds ticked by in silence, and the crazed fiancé didn't come back to whip the tarp off him and beat him to a pulp.

Against all odds, he might just be safe. Out of the woods, literally. In light of that, Tyler decided to add a small amendment to his deal with God. It would probably be all right to hook up with girls he met in bars. However, he would be sure to ask them if they had a boyfriend or any kind of significant other *before* he kissed them and let them unbuckle his pants.

Satisfied that was a promise he could live with, and hopeful that the guy had given up the chase, Tyler was about to take a peek to see if the coast was clear when he heard footsteps heading toward the truck.

It sounded like two people walking. They hadn't come from the direction of the woods but rather from the building. He was most likely safe from being maimed by his pursuer, but he definitely wasn't in any position to be socializing with anyone. His jeans still hung wide open, his eye remained squeezed shut, and he was hiding under a tarp in a stranger's truck bed.

It wasn't as if he could pop up and say *hey*, but he also couldn't stay hidden. If the owner of the truck drove away, who knew where he could end up?

Tyler was weighing his limited options when he heard a female voice say, "Hang on. Let me move this and then you can slide it right inside."

He lay helpless while the tarp was whipped to the side, exposing him to the beam of the parking-lot light. At the sight of him, the woman screamed and jumped back.

Truth be told, he nearly screamed, too. He scrambled to sit up before he realized he might not want to be sitting up. He still wasn't positive where the scorned fiancé had gone.

"Hey, Tyler." There was amusement in the male voice that came from his left.

Still partially blinded, Tyler turned his head to the side to see a guy he'd gone to high school with standing next to the truck and grinning as he balanced a fence post on his shoulder.

Hell of a time for a high school reunion. Not having much choice, Tyler tipped his head in greeting. "Hey, Jed."

"You know him?" the woman asked.

"I do." Jed grinned wider. "Don't worry. He's harmless."

She let out a breath and held her hand to her chest. A fall of dark hair brushed her shoulders as her gaze swung from Jed to Tyler. "You scared the hell out of me. What were you doing under there?"

"Um, it's a long story." Sitting up, Tyler glanced at the woods and decided to take his chances with the crazed bouncer rather than look like more of a fool by continuing to lie in this woman's truck bed. He pulled himself upright and then went to work fastening the open fly of his jeans.

"Oh, don't worry, Ty. We have the time to hear your explanation. I'm sure it will be worth it." Jed grinned. He hadn't missed the fact that Tyler's pants were hanging open enough to show his underwear.

Neither had the woman. Tyler saw her bite her lip to control a smile as she averted her eyes. Didn't it figure? A beautiful woman who drove the crew-cab, extended-bed, dual rear wheel pickup truck he'd always wanted, and he looked like a complete ass in front of her.

Cursing his belt as buckling it with his shaky hands confounded him, Tyler finally got his clothes put back together. He jumped out of the truck and turned toward Jed. "Let me help you with that."

He reached for the fence post, but Jed took a step back. "Oh, no. You don't get out of telling us what's going on that easily."

Tyler shook his head. "Ain't nothing to tell. Just a simple misunderstanding is all." Grabbing the post off Jeb's shoulder, he guided it into the back of the pickup and angled it so it wouldn't stick out too far past the tailgate. "There. I don't think you need a warning flag on the end of it. It's in there pretty good."

Glancing over, he saw both the woman and Jed watching him and felt the need to keep talking. He turned to the woman. "Where you going with that? You need some help unloading it when you get there?"

Jed laughed. "You need a ride home, don't you?"

"No." Tyler frowned. "Besides, my truck's at Rohn's place anyway. Not at home. And I can call Colton for a ride if I need one." *If* the bruiser hadn't gone back to the bar and taken his anger out on Tyler's friend because he couldn't find him.

"You talking about Rohn Lerner's ranch?" the woman asked.

"Yup." He nodded. "I work there. You know him?" Sometimes this town was too damn small for his liking.

"Yeah, I do. Hop in." She tipped her head toward the truck. "I can drive you. It's on my way."

"You sure? You don't have to. I can—"

"Get in. It's fine." She dismissed Tyler's concern and turned to Jed. "Thanks for carrying that for me."

"No problem, ma'am." Donning another smart-ass grin, Jed turned to Tyler. "See you around."

"Yup." Though Tyler hoped that wouldn't be for a long while. He kept the thought to himself and reached for the passenger door handle.

The woman climbed into the driver's seat, and he realized he didn't even know her name. "I'm Tyler Jenkins."

"Janie." She glanced at him as she started the engine and threw the truck into gear.

"I do apologize again for the whole truck thing."

She laughed as she pulled out onto the main road. "Don't worry about it. This is the most excitement I've had in a long time, even if I did come in at the tail end of your mysterious adventure."

"I swear, I'm usually not getting into trouble—"

"Aren't you?" She raised a brow as her gaze cut sideways. "I somehow have difficulty believing that. I think your friend back at the store might, too."

His cheeks heated at being caught in the lie. Tyler let his chin drop before forcing his gaze up to meet hers. "You're right. I guess . . . sometimes . . . I can get myself into situations that maybe I shouldn't."

Her smile reached all the way to her eyes before she focused back on turning off the main drag and onto the side road leading to the ranch. "You do have a way with words. I bet that talented tongue of yours gets you out of many of those situations."

His mind went to bad places at her mention of his tongue. He glanced at her left hand where it gripped the steering wheel and thought what a shame it was she wore a wedding ring.

He dragged his attention back to the road. "That's the turn, right up there. Rohn's place is the next driveway."

A smile bowed her lips. "I know. That's my drive we just passed. We're neighbors."

Tyler frowned as the pieces fell into place. "You're Tom Smithwick's widow?"

"Yeah, I guess I am." She let out a short, breathy laugh. "Widow. I think that's the first time I've heard someone call me that."

His eyes opened wide as he realized how badly he'd screwed up. Her husband hadn't been gone for that long. The grief was probably still fresh. "I'm so sorry. I didn't mean anything by it."

"No, it's okay. Really. I mean, I'm sure they're all saying it behind my back. And it's perfectly true. That's exactly what I am. It's just strange hearing it, you know? It's even stranger saying it." She drew in a breath. "I'm a widow. At thirty-five."

He scrambled to make up for putting his foot in his mouth. "You don't look thirty-five." She didn't look like what he'd always imagined a widow would either.

"Thanks." She treated him to a small, sad smile as she pulled up to where his truck was parked in Rohn's drive.

"So, what are you doing with that fence post in the back?" He hooked a thumb behind him.

"A tree took down part of my fence. Broke the upright. I'm going to see if I can replace it tomorrow."

He figured she'd have to dig the broken post out to sink the new one. "Alone?"

"Yeah. I let our hands go after Tom died and I sold the bulk of the stock."

"Do you need some help?" Digging post holes was no job for a woman.

She shook her head. "No, really. You don't have to—"

"I know I don't have to. I want to." He shrugged. "Besides, it's the least I can do to pay you back."

"Pay me back for what? The ride? I told you, I was driving by here anyway."

"The ride." He laughed. "And the hideout."

She smiled. "You still haven't told me why you needed to hide out."

The last thing on earth Tyler wanted was for this woman to know the embarrassing truth about what had happened tonight. He looked bad enough already, he was sure. "How about this . . . I don't tell you, and I help you fix that fence instead?"

One brow cocked up before she nodded her head. "All right. Curious as I am, I'll take that deal."

She extended her hand. He took it and shook. "Good. I'll come over first thing in the morning."

As he felt the firm grip of Janie's hand, so tiny compared to his larger one, Tyler had to think he'd made a pretty damn good deal for himself. Not only did he get to save face, he also got to see her again tomorrow.

"I'll be there. And thank you for the help." A smile tipped up the corner of her mouth. He couldn't stop his gaze from dropping to her cupid's bow lips.

"You're welcome."

The pleasure would be all his.

Books by Bestselling Author
Fern Michaels

___The Jury	0-8217-7878-1	$6.99US/$9.99CAN
___Sweet Revenge	0-8217-7879-X	$6.99US/$9.99CAN
___Lethal Justice	0-8217-7880-3	$6.99US/$9.99CAN
___Free Fall	0-8217-7881-1	$6.99US/$9.99CAN
___Fool Me Once	0-8217-8071-9	$7.99US/$10.99CAN
___Vegas Rich	0-8217-8112-X	$7.99US/$10.99CAN
___Hide and Seek	1-4201-0184-6	$6.99US/$9.99CAN
___Hokus Pokus	1-4201-0185-4	$6.99US/$9.99CAN
___Fast Track	1-4201-0186-2	$6.99US/$9.99CAN
___Collateral Damage	1-4201-0187-0	$6.99US/$9.99CAN
___Final Justice	1-4201-0188-9	$6.99US/$9.99CAN
___Up Close and Personal	0-8217-7956-7	$7.99US/$9.99CAN
___Under the Radar	1-4201-0683-X	$6.99US/$9.99CAN
___Razor Sharp	1-4201-0684-8	$7.99US/$10.99CAN
___Yesterday	1-4201-1494-8	$5.99US/$6.99CAN
___Vanishing Act	1-4201-0685-6	$7.99US/$10.99CAN
___Sara's Song	1-4201-1493-X	$5.99US/$6.99CAN
___Deadly Deals	1-4201-0686-4	$7.99US/$10.99CAN
___Game Over	1-4201-0687-2	$7.99US/$10.99CAN
___Sins of Omission	1-4201-1153-1	$7.99US/$10.99CAN
___Sins of the Flesh	1-4201-1154-X	$7.99US/$10.99CAN
___Cross Roads	1-4201-1192-2	$7.99US/$10.99CAN

Available Wherever Books Are Sold!
Check out our website at **www.kensingtonbooks.com**